Pocket Full of Posies

A Snowberry Novel

Rebecca Rennick

Copyright © 2025 by Rennick Rennick

ISBN: 979-8-218-60307-6

All rights reserved.

No part of this book may be reproduced or transmitted in any form or by any means, electronic or mechanical, including mechanical photocopying, recording, or by any information storage and retrieval system, without permission in writing.

This book is a work of fiction and any resemblance to persons, living or dead, or places, events or locales is purely coincidental. The characters are productions of the author's imagination and used fictionally.

Cover by BloodWrit
Map by Pinapali
Formatting by Rebecca Rennick

For all the good girls who love themselves a naughty boy.

Daisy's Flower Index

Daisy - Happiness
Sunflower - Contentment, calm
Carnation - Curiosity
Peony - Embarrassment
Sweet Pea - Bashfulness
Iris - Anxiety
Geranium - Excitement, humor
Gardenia - Innocence
Hydrangea - Optimism
Black Dahlia - Fear, pain
Plumeria - Love
Jasmine - Sexual Arousal

Chapter 1
Daisy

Sunshine is my favorite thing. The way it warms your skin, brightens the world, and feeds every living thing on the planet nutrients they need to survive. Like right now, it's streaming in through the kitchen window heating my cheek where I sit at the dining table eating breakfast; a bowl of home-grown oatmeal with freshly picked apple slices from the tree off the back porch, raisins I dried myself in my dehydrator, ground cinnamon from my sacred Cinnamomum verum tree, and honey from the human woman who raises bees and collects their honey to sell in town.

I like my meals organic and fresh, what can I say?

It's Tuesday morning, and Tuesdays are slow days. Not many people come to the nursery on a Tuesday morning. Not the most important day to buy flowers I suppose. Even though we open later than usual, I still get up early and go through my standard morning routine. After I finish breakfast, I'll check on the gardens, make sure everything is doing well, and get rid of any creeping weeds in the soil. Then I'll go for a walk to check on Delphi in the forest surrounding our small plot of land. After that I have bouquets and centerpieces to work on for a wedding later this week.

It's the perfect time of year for weddings, just prior to the cold, snowy season—even though there are still plenty of weddings then as well—and on the cusp of the turning of leaves. The trees outside are just starting to change colors and the autumn equinox isn't far off. That one day when daytime and nighttime are perfectly equal before the nights grow long and the sun grows dim.

I love all the seasons, but winter is my least favorite. The clouds block out the warmth from the sun and the cold withers the plants into hibernation until spring. Plus, I have to wear shoes. I *hate* wearing shoes, but my feet can't handle walking through twelve-inch-deep snow. I know, I've tried and almost gave myself frostbite. Until that first flake of snow falls those galoshes are staying packed in the back of my closet.

My toes need to feel the ground beneath them. I need that connection to the earth, always have. It used to drive my mother crazy every time I would throw off my shoes and return home from school barefoot. Apparently, it's not normal for humans to walk around barefoot all the time. Among nymphs it's completely normal, although most have just acclimated to human behaviors to better blend and fit in. I, however, don't blend in very well. Being a half-breed, my glamour is too hard to maintain for more than a handful of minutes, my magic weaker.

Sage joins me when I'm halfway through my breakfast, making one of his own. He sits down across from me and begins eating. Sage is my older brother, by many years. He's a full-blooded earth nymph, having a nymph mother as opposed to my human one. He's never held it against me, or my mother, who is still married to our father- which is where I got my earth nymph half.

He's been the best big brother anyone could ask for. Sage and his mate/husband Tobias, moved into the house from the apartment they rented in town when mom and dad left to go on their world botany tour. I was eighteen and didn't *need* anyone to look after me, but it's been nice having them here these past five years. I'm not the most social person and if it weren't for them, I'd never know what was going on in town, or have anyone to talk to beyond Delphi and the flowers. People get sent to padded rooms if caught talking to flowers by a human, something that's normal among non-humans. So, I'll admit it's been beneficial having others in the house with me.

"Where's Tobias?" I ask Sage.

"Went to the Ugly Mug to open up," he answers around a mouthful of food.

I nod and spoon another bite of oatmeal into my mouth. Tobias is a fairy and works at the local coffee shop. He also happens to be a genius savant when it comes to coffee artistry. Able to sense what a person needs in their coffee order and gives it to them. If you're feeling anxious, he gives you something decaffeinated and calming. Feeling nostalgic? He'll know exactly what your all-time favorite coffee drink is and will make it just how you like it.

Tobias and my brother mated years ago before I was born. He's always been like a second brother to me. I love him as much as I do Sage. Normally Sage, Tobias, and I spend mornings together eating breakfast and going over what needs to be done for the day. It's nice, simple, and familiar. Some mornings it's just me and Sage, and I like our one on ones and quiet companionship. We don't need to speak to convey words, especially when sound and hearing are so important to nymphs. It enables us to hear truths, lies and emotions in another...usually.

"Sunflowers again, Daisy?" Sage looks up at me from behind his half-raised spoon, eyeing the sunflowers growing in my hair.

I shrug and stir the last remaining bits of my breakfast.

"I'd really love to see a different bloom some days. Maybe daisies, geraniums or even a sweet pea or two."

Sometimes I hate that the flowers that grow in my hair give away my emotional state. I especially hate it when Sage calls me out on it, since he knows the meaning for most of the blooms that sprout. If anyone else knew me well enough, no non-human would have to rely on their abilities to sense my emotions. They're right there on my head for anyone to see.

Sage says there are other earth nymphs that have a similar attribute, but I've never seen one. At least not one who can't control them. I think it has to do with my human side. Humans are wildly emotional, and I think my human half mixing with my nymph half causes them to grow of their own accord. I've tried controlling them to hide my emotions to no avail. Other nymphs don't have that problem. Their magic is full and complete.

Shaking away the thoughts that have plagued me since I was old enough to realize I was different from the rest of the nymphs, I refocus on my brother sitting across from me, giving me his concerned face. Another downfall to my weak magic is I can't hear emotions as clearly as a full nymph, so I've learned to read body language like a boring non-magical human. His current expression, mixed with the low calming tones of his voice, conveys brotherly concern.

"It's still early. Maybe they'll change as the day progresses.

Pocket Full of Posies

You never know what a Tuesday can bring. It's the most important day of the week. Didn't you know?" I try to ease his frown with my unpracticed humor. It works a little. The edges of his lips pulling up and smoothing out.

"You know what I mean Daisy. You spend too much time alone in the gardens."

"I'm not alone. I have you, and Tobias and Delphi. What more do I need? You know I'm no good at talking to people. The plants understand me."

My tail twitches anxiously and I pull it inside my denim overalls, wrapping it around my waist to comfort myself and sooth the uneasiness these conversations always bring. A habit I picked up because of my inability to glamour it on a regular basis to hide it from the humans and callous non-humans.

"People can understand you too. But first you have to talk to them, make friends. Maybe even partake in town events like the autumn equinox coming up."

Sage has been trying to get me to attend equinox and solstice celebrations for years, but I've never gone. Being in large groups of people—especially full-blooded non-humans—makes me uncomfortable. All the eyes watching me, judging me for my humanness, and everything I am lacking compared to them.

Granted, I know there are many non-humans who have no prejudice against half-breeds like myself at all, but there are those who do. Especially some that come to Snowberry to celebrate the changing of the seasons. I'm just more comfortable staying home and celebrating on my own. Well, with Delphi, she always stays with me.

"You know how I feel about attending the celebration, Sage. I just don't fit in. Never did."

"You don't have to fit in. I love that you don't. I just want you to make more connections with non-plant life than just me and Tobias. We won't be here forever."

My brows pull into a frown. What the hell does that mean? As a nymph mated to a fairy, Sage will live much longer than I will. He should be around a good long while. Obviously not forever, but centuries for sure. He's not even two centuries old yet. I expect him to be here for many more.

Sage notices my apprehension and his gold eyes soften. The rising sun, bathing his sage green skin in golden rays, the reason his mother named him Sage. I've never met his mother. He only knew her for a short time as a child. Apparently, she's even more of a free spirit than we are. Sage's mom and our dad weren't married or mated, just a passing relationship that resulted in pregnancy. Sage traveled when he was old enough, but moved to Snowberry when I was born, wanting to be close to family.

We don't have any other siblings. It's just the two of us and we've always been close. The thought of him not being here sours my stomach.

"You need to get out more, Daiz. Talk to people. You could start by attending the equinox celebration. There'll be plenty of others there your age. Nymphs, fairies and mix breeds. You don't have to worry about not fitting in. Just..." Sage sighs and reaches across the table to grip my hand in his. The green color of his skin against my tan, an ever-present reminder of our biological differences. "I just want you to be happy. To find someone who makes you happy. Whether that be a male or a female, a friend or a lover. Just someone else to make a connection with that isn't me or Tobias."

He has a valid point, but just thinking about *socializing* makes my skin crawl. I know he means well, and I don't completely disagree with him.

"I have a friend. Calliope from the bakery. She's my friend."

"She's also a human who has no idea what you really are," he argues. "Not that I don't love Calliope, she's a great girl and I'm happy she's your friend, but you need more than a local human who thinks your markings are tattoos."

The green swirling vines on my arms curl in tighter on themselves in response. When they started appearing, growing and moving, I had to start wearing long sleeves to school since I couldn't conceal them with a glamour. The schools in town are mixed with humans and non-humans and when we're toddlers we don't have to glamour our natural nature since toddlers can't talk and don't know the difference. But as we get older all non-humans are supposed to glamour when in mixed company. I couldn't, so long sleeves and pants it was. At least until I was old enough to pass them off as tattoos. Since I never got close to anyone enough for them to know any different, no one questioned them when I started wearing shorts and tank tops.

I exhale a heavy breath through my nose and consider Sage's words. Gripping his hand back, I give him a weak smile.

"I'll think about it. No promises though. And you can't try to use Tobias and his magic coffee making skills to persuade me."

"No promises," Sage chuckles, releasing my hand and leaning back in the dining chair. "Tobias loves you just as much as I do and what he does with his magic coffee making skills is up to him."

"No fair. You know I can't resist him or his coffee."

He lifts his hands in defense, his smile growing as the heaviness from our conversation lifts to good natured sibling squabble.

"Not my problem. You'll have to take it up with him."

"I thought big brothers were supposed to protect their

little sisters? Not sacrifice them to save their own skin."

We finish our breakfasts, and I head out to speak to the flowers.

Chapter 2
Daisy

My morning inspection of the gardens is short and uneventful. The gardens are quiet, the flowers not having much to say today. The butterflies in the greenhouse are awake and active, fluttering about and enjoying the last of the warm days. Inside the greenhouse is always kept warm but butterflies like the sunshine, just like me, and soon that'll be little to nonexistent.

Once I ensure the plants and butterflies are doing well, I use my menial magic to help a few stubborn flowers finish blooming. I head in the direction of the tree line to the forest that doubles as the property line to our land.

The land to the east belongs to the town, the north to the Evans's family who bought up much of the land before the town even existed, and to the west a few acres belong to the Kingsley's, one of the nymph families that keeps land here for holidays and seasonal celebrations. They don't live here full time, only visiting and using their mansion and property as a vacation home.

The Kingsley's are one of those families that have a lot of money and properties, traveling the world with homes in numerous states and countries. I've seen them from a distance, know who they are, just like anyone else in town. They're powerful and high ranking among the nymph and non-human community. Whereas I am considered to be the bottom of that totem pole, insignificant and unworthy of their time and association.

Entering the woods I stay to the north, making my way to where Delphi's nest lies deeper into the Evans's land. The land may belong to Hunter and his family but it's open to all non-humans to allow us a space to be ourselves and not worry about the outside world. I made Delphi's nest for her using what little magic I possess, twisting branches and leaves to form a hanging egg shaped nest house. With every change of the season, I check on its structure and solidity ensuring it is structurally sound and ready to withstand the weather to come.

Uncurling my tail from around my waist I let it fall and hang down the leg of my overall shorts. Here in the woods there's no one to see it or mock its short length and thin frame. As tails go, it's pretty pathetic, looking more like a mouse tail. It was surprising I had one at all, considering earth nymphs typically don't have animal characteristics. I think it's because humans have tail bones that somewhere in their evolution was a tail. Thus, mixing magic with recessive human genetics you get me and my strange little tail.

Mine just had to be the lamest of all the tails ever known, but it's mine all the same. Despite its slender shape, lack of fur and color matching my skin tone, I still love it. Even my green vine markings swirl around the end tipping it in green.

Pocket Full of Posies

I've only been walking for a few minutes when a blue and white furry blur leaps from a branch overhead and aims straight for my head.

Delphi, the energetic, loving, and playful sprite, lands right on top of my head, her fluffy body practically smothering me. With tiny, clawed hands reminiscent of a racoon's, she reaches out and grips at my hair and flowers, chittering a sound that's a mix of a fox's high pitch yips, a squirrel's clicking twitters, and a cat's purr. The sound is uniquely hers. I have no idea what she's saying but I've known her long enough to guess.

"Well hello to you too. Did you miss me?"

More chitters, this time louder and more animated.

"I missed you too. Where have you been running off to lately? Storing treasures and food for the winter?"

Delphi tends to have a bit of a thieving problem. Snagging small objects from unattended purses, backpacks, and strollers, storing them in the hollow of the tree her nest hangs from.

She chitters more quietly, sounding guilty. I can tell that much with my nymph hearing. Her blue and white striped body finally releases my head, and she plops into my arms.

When I first found her, I was ten years old, and Delphi was about the size of a kitten. She was lost in the forest and I had no idea what she was until I brought her home and Tobias explained she was an adolescent sprite. Sprites are creatures of pure magic, usually small and animalistic, living in the wild away from modern civilization. Peaceful and mischievous by nature but also extremely loyal and protective. If threatened they can defend themselves, viciously if needed. One should never cross a sprite. Their magic is more powerful than even a fairy's, which is unfortunately why elves like to use them for immoral purposes.

Now, nearly thirteen years later, she's more the size of a

small dog, weighing around twenty pounds. The general shape of her body something akin to a red panda. Covered in soft, thick white fur with rich blue horizontal stripes lining her body ringing all the way down her short fluffy tail, ending in a puff of the color that gave her her name.

Delphi is short for Delphinium, a small bloom flower a lovely shade of bright sapphire with veins and tips of lavender. A flower that symbolizes positivity, a sense of cheerfulness and optimism. She doesn't have the lavender coloring but it's still well suited for my sweet friend.

Her cute little ears twitch on her head as she looks up at me with round pitch-black eyes, trying to give me her most innocent and sweet expression. I don't believe it for one minute. Sprites are mischievous by nature and Delphi is no exception. She just happens to like my company and rummaging around town, unlike the rest of her sprite brethren, who remain hidden deeper in the woods only interacting with non-humans they deem unthreatening, and usually during celebrations held within the forest.

"Come on then. Let's see what you've *found* this time."

Delphi perks up and crawls onto my shoulder, wrapping her tail around my neck and holding onto my hair with one tiny hand.

As we walk, I talk with Delphi as I always do. She's the only one I feel I can open up to who won't judge me.

"Sage asked me to go to the equinox celebration again. He seems more adamant about it this time for some reason. I told him I'd think about it just to ease his fretting. I probably won't go, but maybe I'll give it a little extra thought before I say no this time."

I shrug the shoulder not occupied by Delphi, who has quieted to listen. I'd like to think she understands me even if I can't understand her.

"Do you think I should go? I know a few times you've snuck off to it yourself. Don't deny it."

Delphi lets out a high pitch rolling chirp I interpret as an indignant; *So?* I laugh and continue walking through the cooling forest. The green leaves are already shifting to yellow which will soon be orange and red, then none at all.

"It's okay, I don't care if you go. You should go if you enjoy it. I just don't know if I'd enjoy it."

Clicks and chirps come in rapid succession from Delphi on my shoulder, and I'm guessing she's listing all the reasons I should go and why I would enjoy it, if her jubilant and excited tone is any indication.

"Of course, *you'd* enjoy it. You're the most adorable sprite there is. I'm sure everyone who meets you, loves you. But not everyone feels the same about me. I'm half human, and half-breed hybrids are frowned upon in certain circles. I'm also too awkward and socially inept. I wouldn't know what to say. Every time I open my mouth all I can manage to talk about without sounding like an imbecile, is plants."

More chittering and now hand gesturing.

"Yes, I know most earth nymphs like to talk about plants but there are others that attend that aren't earth nymphs. What am I supposed to talk to them about?"

Groaning, I let out a large exhale. I should probably talk about this with someone who speaks English. At least then maybe the supportive pep talk might sink in and push me to step out of my bubble, like Sage wants.

"I knew you and Sage would agree. It seems I'm the only one who thinks this is a bad idea."

Delphi pets my head like a comforting mama, and I can't help but smirk at the gesture. I remain quiet the rest of the way to her nest. My thoughts boomerang from outright refusal, to attending the equinox, to a curious desire to experience the celebration. If only to know why everyone looks forward to them all year round.

Not once have I ever gone to a celebration. At least not that I can remember. After the failed attempt that was public schooling, I never wanted to go to parties or large gatherings. It was safer to just stay home and remain on the outside of society, only interacting when required at the nursery.

Not long ago, Sage had forced me to work the main entrance to the greenhouse and assist customers. It was torture, forcing me to smile and chat with everyone who entered, offering to help walk them through picking flowers. It was extremely uncomfortable until I met Lottie, a human from out of town. At least we all thought she was human. Now she's mated to our mayor and alpha shifter. According to Tobias's gossip, she's part siren. A recessive gene from her ancestor allowed her to have a mate bond with a non-human and even possess a few magical abilities.

We still don't know what this means for the future but it's sounding like half-breeds, like myself, will be even less prominent. If humans have recessive genetic links to non-humans allowing them to form mate bonds, it could mean full blooded non-human children. No more half humans lacking the ability to glamour or use their natural magic. I'll be even more of an outcast than I already am.

As a half-breed I am intrinsically able to form a mate bond since one of my parents is a non-human. If I were to mate with a non-human male my human genetics would still make our children partially human, not by much but enough that it could affect them to be different. Enough that in a world of dwindling non-humans and pure bloods it would persuade males to think twice before mating a half-breed.

I don't know what makes these new humans with recessive genes more able to have full blooded non-human children than me, but it's all too new to know anything. I can only go by what I know, and how it's been for thousands of years. I can't expect some miracle gene to appear in me like it has for Lottie. She could be a single mutation that may never occur again.

It doesn't matter how many times my parents and Sage tell me there's nothing wrong with me and anyone would be lucky to be with me, I just don't see it happening.

Chapter 3
Kai

Sunshine is fucking annoying. Now I don't have anything against sunshine normally, but right now there's a particularly diabolical ray of the piss golden light blinding me while I'm trying to sleep. I shift, trying to reposition away from the light, and immediately roll off the edge of whatever it is I'm sleeping on and land hard on the floor, almost crushing my tail and scuffing a horn.

"Mother fucker. God damnit."

That's right; I crashed on the couch last night after I got home from *Blue Moon*. This town is seriously lacking in proper nightly entertainment. At least there's a bar with adequate liquor and bartenders. Sadly, most of the females in town know who I am, and I returned home alone. Which is probably why I only made it as far as the couch.

Small towns are the worst. Though coming into town early for the equinox did serve to entertain more than I expected. Helping Hunter beat down the elf and his posse was the most excitement I've seen in this town in years.

Coming to stay at my family's place a few weeks early had been unplanned. My mother had called and all but commanded me to attend the autumn equinox. Originally, I was going to refuse to attend but after ending the conversation the idea kept nagging at me. Something told me I should go, so I booked a first-class ticket on the next flight out of Greece and headed home.

When I arrived there was an influx of shifters and even a few humans for the full moon. I met a visiting female shifter and happily assisted her through the blood moon. Then I got to beat the shit out of a few non-human scum, which was just as thrilling.

But now? Now I'm fucking bored out of my mind. There's still another almost two weeks until the equinox. My parents, and the majority of my siblings, won't arrive until closer to the day. Until then I'm on my own with no one to distract me from the sheer boredom of this small town.

Sure, there's the lake. I could go swimming with some friendly mere's, and have some fun but that would only fill one day. What would I do with the rest of my time?

Growling in frustration I crawl to my hands and knees and sit back on my heels. Rubbing my eyes with the palms of my hands I clear the sleep from them.

The living room is dark—except for the bright ass sunshine beaming in through the slits in the curtains. There are a few items of clothing strewn across the back of the chairs and couches. Dirty cups and empty take-out containers clutter the kitchen counters, the trash can overflowing where it sits against the wall because I'm too fucking lazy to take it out. To be fair I'm used to room service taking care of things like trash and laundry.

Pocket Full of Posies

There has to be someone in town my parents usually hire to work for them while they're here. Maybe I should text them to find out. Though if I do, my mother will know I'm here and probably show up way earlier than planned. And I definitely do not want that to happen.

Fuck. I'm going to have to clean up myself, aren't I?

I stand and survey the space trying to gather enough energy to actually clean. My tail flicks behind me in agitation and brushes against a pile of something I'll no doubt have to clean up as well.

"Guess I should get started," I grumble under my breath. "Maybe just the trash." I wrinkle my nose as I get closer to the mountain in the trash can. "It is starting to smell."

I manage to force myself to take out all the trash and at least start a load of dishes in the dishwasher.

"Look at me, being all domestic and shit."

When that's finished, I shower and slip on a pair of loose jeans remaining shirtless, slipping my tail through the custom-tailored slit in the back so I don't have to cram it down the pant leg. Not that any human can see it anyways. Why hide it? I'd rather be comfortable.

Strolling through our spacious and professionally decorated vacation manor, I find myself in the kitchen rummaging through the fridge searching for edible leftovers in the remaining takeout containers. Thank fuck they have Dottie's here. Her food can rival any Michelin star restaurant in the world.

Looks like there's some bacon and cheese fries left. I pull it out and transfer it to a plate placing my hand flat on the bottom. I generate heat in the palm of my hand. Not sparking a flame, just infusing my hand with heat like a hot plate until the cheese is melted and gooey once again. Sometimes having fire abilities is awesome.

I'm halfway through my breakfast of champions, when I hear the front door slam and then the voice of my younger brother call out through the house.

"What the fuck man? Can you at least pick up your dirty underwear? Gross."

I laugh around a mouth full of fries and wait for my little brother to make his way to me in the kitchen. He strolls in moments later glaring at me with false indignation.

Endo is the youngest of all my siblings, and the one I'm closest to. We're the black sheep of all the kids. The ones that give our parents the most headaches. I'm rather proud of that fact. They're so uptight and snobby I'm glad I'm not like them.

Both Endo and I possess a lot of similar traits, thanks to our mother passing on her animal magic abilities. She's an animal and water nymph with more sea-like attributes, but without her blood we wouldn't have our own animal traits. Not to mention our ability to speak to animals and sense their presence.

Although we both possess physical animal attributes they differ greatly between us. Where I have crimson hair and tiger stripes across my body with a tail to match, Endo has short russet suede fur with white deer spots along his neck and chest, his hair almost golden. I know he also has a deer tail too, but he keeps it tucked away. It was a source of teasing from the boys growing up.

Endo is cute, like an adorable little doe, with soft features and attributes of docile animals that tend to be prey. I, however, have attributes of predators, giving me sharper, harder features. We may be physically different but extremely similar in our dislike of family status and forced socialite behavior. Being the cream of the crop is neither of our preferences. We'd both be completely happy never participating in social events ever again.

"What the hell are you doing here so early? Whenever mom does manage to force you to attend, you usually show up hours before the celebration," he says in greeting.

Leaning my elbows on the kitchen island, I shrug and go back to eating my fries.

"No reason, just felt like it."

Which is true. I have no idea why I'm here or why I came nearly a month before the equinox. If Endo knew how long I've been here he might die of shock.

"What are *you* doing here so early?" I retort.

"Mom tasked me with getting the house ready, which I thought would be an easy task since it has supposedly been empty for months. I see now we've had a squatter who doesn't know how to use one of the multiple washing machines."

Endo picks up a piece of clothing, a shirt I think, between his fingertips and flicks it onto the pile on the floor.

"I was gonna get to it. Be happy I just cleaned the kitchen."

He looks around the kitchen, the flattening of his lips telling me he doesn't believe me. I may not have mopped or wiped down the counters, but the trash can is empty, and the smelly take out containers are gone. I call that a win.

"Sure you did. Anyway, back to why you're here." Glaring at me he raises an eyebrow and waits for an explanation.

"Told ya, just felt like it. Was getting bored partying with horny water nymphs and meres in Greece and thought I'd spend a little quiet time in the middle of the forest in Montana, with no night clubs and where half the town is related."

"Very funny. You're fucking hilarious."

"Thank you. Next time you should come with me to Greece. Nude beaches everywhere." I sweep my hand wide emphasizing my point.

Endo sits on a stool on the opposite side of the white marble island and smirks.

"Maybe I will. I could use some time away from the family."

"Mom been pressuring you lately?" I ask.

Our mother can be quite demanding sometimes, and as the youngest he sometimes gets the short end of the stick. Especially when I've practically amputated myself from family affairs. I still get sucked in, case in point my current presence in Snowberry. But I'm older, pushing ninety, and have had plenty of time to manipulate and strategize my freedom.

Compiling my own money, separate from the family accounts I have access to, allows me to slip away when our mother tries to nail me down. I still use the family money for a good number of things. I'm not built for day jobs. So, I continue to assuage my parents by attending events here and there, showing up and doing my duty just enough to keep in their good graces and under their radar.

Poor Endo is barely twenty-five. He hasn't managed to put strategies into place yet to escape our parents' control. At least he has his own place so he doesn't have to live under the same roof as them. If he were within reaching distance, he may not have any freedoms.

We'll eventually get him there. With my help he'll be as free as me by thirty.

"Yeah. She's been on a mission lately." He narrows his eyes at me, his tone turning curious. "Have you spoken to anyone in the family recently? Heard about what she's been up to?"

"No." I shake my head but am feeling nervous now at the seriousness in his tone. Standing up straight I stare down my younger brother who is now giving me a look that says *you are not gonna like this*.

Pocket Full of Posies

"I hate to ask, but what did she do now?"

Taking in a deep breath Endo releases it in a long exhale. Not a good sign.

"She's on a mission to get you and Keiko mated. She's been sneaking away and plotting. I'm pretty sure she's made her picks but hasn't told anyone who they are yet."

The heat that is always present in my veins, thanks to my fire magic, chills to an icy frost. She's nagged me about finding a mate for years and has been relentless about it at times, but she's never gone so far as to pick out a mate for me. If she's to the point where she's gone in search, and found, a female she believes will be my perfect mate, I am well and truly fucked.

Mom arranged my older brother Ren's mating to a well-bred female with a pristine pure-blooded heritage. My older sister Airi managed to pick her own mate but received mother's approval first. Now it seems me and my younger sister, Keiko's time has run out.

Fuck, fuck, fuck, fuck, fuck.

"How much time do I have?"

"I think she plans on revealing her at the equinox."

"Shiiiiit."

My elbows smack down hard on the marble countertop, and I drop my face into my hands.

"If I leave now do you think I'll be able to outrun this?"

"Probably not," Endo says with obvious defeat. Which means even if I leave, she'll probably still announce my future mating ceremony with whichever female nymph she has deemed worthy.

"Why didn't anyone tell me?"

"Because you never talk to anyone. Plus, it's all hearsay. Gossip from eavesdropping and conjecture. We don't know anything for sure, other than she's been sneaking away and has been heavily hinting at wanting you mated." Endo reaches over and snags a french fry from my plate and chews, waiting for me to break down.

"Why does she care so much about me being mated? She already has two mated children and they're happily fulfilling her weird obsession with bloodlines by having the exact number of children she tells them to. Why does she need me?"

Removing my face from my hands, I step away from the island and begin to pace the massive kitchen, appetite gone. I run my hand through my long hair and stroke one of my curving horns absentmindedly, trying to devise a way out of this.

Is there a way out of this? Once mom makes up her mind, there's usually no getting out of it. There's a good possibility that if I were to publicly snub her mate choice for me, I'd no doubt be disowned and lose all access to the family's money. And as much as I hate the family "business" I do appreciate the family money. I can only sneak by for so long.

"What do you think I should do?" I ask Endo, continuing to pace and coming up with nothing.

"Not a clue man. Short of bonding yourself to someone else before she can announce it, looks like you'll be finding out who your mate is at the equinox."

I scoff. "Yeah right. Like I'm gonna find a female, let alone a full-blooded nymph, because you know she won't accept anything less, to agree to form a permanent mate bond with me in a week, in Snowberry."

Endo shrugs and eats another fry. *Yeah, just wait till it's your turn, you won't be so disinterested then.*

"I need to clear my mind. I'm gonna go for a walk and get some fresh air. Maybe the answer will come to me then."

"Whatever you say bro. I'll be here, but I won't be cleaning up your dirty underwear. You're gonna have to do that yourself," Endo calls to me as I make my way to the back doors leading to the acres we own behind the house.

"Yeah, yeah. I'll do it later," I call back over my shoulder as I slip on my shoes.

"You better!"

Chapter 4
Kai

The cool forest air brushes against my bare chest, a reminder that the equinox is not far off. A day that I wasn't looking forward to to begin with but now am dreading. If my mother has chosen a mate for me, once that announcement is made, it's as good as done. I have to do something to keep her from forcing some uptight prissy female on me.

There's always the option to run. I have money; I could just disappear. If she can't hold her money over my head to control me, she has no leverage. Thought that money can only last for so long. It still won't stop her from hunting me down, badgering me endlessly, and trying to force a mate on me until I break. She's probably as thick headed as I am. She won't stop until she gets her way.

A nymph mate bond has to be entered into willingly. Verbal vows spoken aloud and truthfully. If she were to force me to bond and I didn't want to, my words would relay that, and the bond would fail. She knows this, we all do. Which means she would be on my ass until I submitted and went willingly.

"Ugh," I groan out loud, kicking a pile of newly fallen leaves. I've ventured north into the woods behind the house, and the lack of modern society is staggeringly obvious.

It's been a long time since I've been surrounded by nothing but nature. The only sounds are the breeze rustling the leaves and the quiet crack and scurry of animals in the distance. My nymph abilities allow me to connect with animals. I can sense them from a distance and can instinctually understand them when they "speak" to me. It's not so much exact words, but a knowing of meaning. Sometimes specific words make their way through, especially with the more intelligent animals. Creatures like sprites and pixies who don't speak any known human languages, I can understand more clearly. Full sentences and definitive words.

Now, I can sense the sprites that live in the most uninhabited areas of the forest and change direction, heading for them. Sprites can be comforting and cute. Maybe they can lift my spirits and help me figure out an answer to my growing problem.

Shoving my hands in my pockets I continue internally cataloging my options, little as they are. Accept my mother's choice and mate a female I may hate and be the family's puppet for the rest of my life, not a great choice. Find a suitable female to mate before my mother can announce her choice, which would irritate her but also assuage her at the same time. Then there's the option to just say no, reject my mother's chosen one and deal with the blowback. Which I figure will turn out the same as if I just left; never ending demands to do as she says, threats of disownment. If that doesn't work there's always guilt. My mother is great at getting her way. Even when I was younger, I couldn't do anything but submit to her will. The *freedom* I currently possess is because I yielded to her controlling ways and manipulated my way into a position of unimportance.

Apparently that status is no longer valid, since getting me mated has now become the most important thing in her mind, for some god-awful reason. I don't know what bug climbed up her ass and set her on this path of deeming it time for me to find a mate, but it's cramping my style.

What I need is a way to get her off my back indefinitely. Suddenly, Endo's offhanded suggestion of finding a replacement mate before my mother can force one on me isn't sounding so bad. Iit would have to be a bogus relationship. There's no way in hell I'm actually bonding myself to another indefinitely. But if I could find someone to lie about being my mate to get her off my back, I could at least buy some time to figure out a more long-term solution. Because lord knows as soon as she finds out I'm not mated she'll be on me like flies on shit.

"Fuck. I should just knock up a human woman. Maybe then she'd disown me, and I could be free from all this bullshit."

I'd need to syphon off money into my private account before that though, to ensure I can support myself for years to come without folding and giving in to her demands.

Wouldn't that be nice though? To be free from the demands of my altruistic family and our centuries old tradition of only mating with other nymphs. There's not a drop of human, fairy, shifter or other blood in my lineage. I've heard of distant relatives and ancestors having chosen non-nymph mates or spouses, but those individuals were disowned from the family, removed from family history, and none of their descendants are allowed at events. Not that any of them want to attend anyway.

It's disgusting really, how prejudiced my family is. Like me,

I know there are relatives who don't fully believe in the whole *'pure-blooded protect the bloodline'* nonsense. Others either allow their elders to choose for them or pick someone who fits the ridiculous list of requirements out of some weird sense of duty or guilt manipulation.

Personally, I love all types of people. Human, non-human, mix breeds, half-breeds. Preferably those who don't fit my family's messed up list of attributes.

I wonder if there are any humans in town who know about non-humans that I could convince to pretend to be my secret lover, now pregnant with our half-breed love child? That would shock my mother into a fit for sure. I would love to see that.

Up ahead I sense a rather animated and chatty sprite. Nymph hearing is superior to most, being our most important sense. Even this far away, where I can't see the sprite, I can hear it. It sounds like it's boasting about its most recent acquisitions.

There are sprites that sneak into town and "find" items they bring back to their nests and hollows. Their curious nature insisting they explore, even against their better judgement.

This one sounds like it's listing off things and sharing its new treasures with another.

"Look, look at this one. Isn't it nice? So soft and pretty. And this one, it makes the sunshine change colors."

The sprites strange language translates in my head clearer than most I've heard before. It must have more contact with people than most to speak so similarly to us. Usually, their thoughts and sentences are more blunt, simple and direct. Not conversative.

"Oh yes, that one is very pretty. I don't think Larken is going to be very happy you broke into *The Closet Carousel* again, though. I'm going to have to go into town now and apologize, and pay for this fabric," a soft feminine voice replies to the sprites chattering as if she knows exactly what it's saying. Perhaps another nymph with animal magic?

Curious who this possible nymph holding a full conversation with a sprite could be, I extend my claws and silently climb the nearest tree, hoping to get a bird's eye view of the female and sprite.

If there were any birds nearby, I could actually get a bird's eye view by connecting with them and seeing through their eyes, but climbing a tree and making my way closer is more than enough.

I only need to leap across half a dozen trees before I come upon the female. There below me stands a petite female wearing frayed denim short overalls, standing on bare tip toes, reaching into a tree hollow and rummaging around. I can't completely see the sprite, but I'd guess it's inside the tree, where it must keep its hoard.

"Oh dear, and a cup from the *Ugly Mug*. That one I'm going to have to take back, Delphi. You can't keep that."

"*What? Can't have? But it's mine I found it.*"

"I know you want to keep it, but you can't. Arthur collected these for years from all over the world. He's very proud of his collection and they'll notice if one is missing."

The sprite makes a whimpering whining sound, like a pouting toddler. It's kind of adorable, the back and forth these two are having. I'm still not sure if the female can understand the sprite or just knows it well enough to deduce what it's saying.

Inspecting the girl further, I see sunflowers and slivers of green in her chestnut brown hair. Hair that's thick and lush, looking silky soft to the touch, falling in soft waves down her shoulders. Shoulders that are barely covered with tiny cap sleeves, leaving her neck and arms exposed. Green markings swirl on her skin that a human would assume were tattoos but I know better. She's an earth nymph, they always have green markings or skin, the flowers in her hair only confirm this further. Although her skin tone is different from most earth nymphs, who tend to be shades of green or even dark earthy brown, her skin is like soft toffee or a creamy latte.

That's when I notice the curling twitch of a tail peeking out through the bottom of her shorts. It's small and petite like her, barely reaching her knees with more of her green markings at its end. It's cute and my tail responds, wrapping around my leg and twitching when hers does.

Smiling, I crouch on the branch and latch my claws into its bark, holding me still to watch the fascinating female below me. She soothes the sulking sprite and pulls it from the hole in the tree. Its plump, furry body wrapping around her like a child holding onto her neck, playing with the flowers in her hair.

These two have obviously formed a bond, solidified over time, to become so familiar. They've spent time together, learned each other, and created a natural bond. A bond that I realize I don't possess with anyone.

I wonder what it's like to feel such a thing.

The pair step away from the tree and the female turns, and I'm finally able to see her face. Soft features, with full pink lips and unnaturally emerald, green eyes almost too large for her face, make her look sweet and innocent, nearly taking my breath away. The complete opposite of the women I'm used to spending time with. Sweet and innocent don't mingle in the circles I do.

The girl smiles and giggles quietly, the sound like fairy bells dancing in the wind, entrancing me. Forcing my body to remain completely still, I watch her.

The sprite fusses with her hair as she reaches up to the egg-

Pocket Full of Posies

shaped hanging nest, checking its structure, a pink dinosaur mug gripped in one hand, but my focus is on her and not what her hands are doing. It's on the hair the sprite is moving and the flowers that seem to be changing and growing. New blooms blossoming next to the sunflowers. Something small and purple that looks like a star. I'm not versed in flora, so I have no idea what they are.

The fussing sprite reveals her ears and they're still pointed but shorter with a more rounded point. That's when I realize why she seems so different from other earth nymphs, she's a half-breed.

Perhaps my prayers have been answered, because I don't recognize this girl. I've never seen her around town, but from her conversation with the sprite, it's obvious she's a resident. *So, who is she? And how have I never seen her before.* I would have remembered those eyes and lips. The cute little tail.

If I've never met her, it's highly unlikely anyone in my family has. Especially if she's a half-breed.

She seems young. Definitely attractive. Maybe I could convince her to be my nonexistent baby momma. At the very least, perhaps a serious girlfriend that I plan to bond with. The fact that she's half human could possibly get me disowned, and the thought makes me smile. This could be more enjoyable than I anticipated.

Waiting until she's done with her inspection of the nest, I position myself on the branch and leap from it, landing on the ground with a soft thud. It's still loud enough for her to hear, and she whirls around, her hair fanning out wildly before settling around her shoulders again. A cute high-pitched yelp squeaking out of her pretty pink lips.

The sprite, who was inside its nest, scurries out and leaps onto the female's head, squealing in disapproval.

"Who are you? Go away! I will bite you."

The female pulls the sprite off her head and holds her close to her chest, cooing into its ear and petting its blue and white striped fur until it calms.

"Hello," I say calmly with a smile I like to call *the panty dropper*. The female only scowls at me, her mouth falling open slightly in confusion. That's not the usual response I get when meeting a female for the first time, shirtless, and not even wearing a glamour.

"Who are you and why are you creeping around? What do you want?"

Okay, so not the best first impression.

"I'm Kai. And I wasn't creeping, just out for a walk. Heard you talking with the sprite and thought I'd say hello. Maybe offer my assistance." I give her another toothy grin, this time trying to make it more casual and friendlier.

Her furrowed brow smooths out, but not completely. Those emerald gems search the immediate area from side to side before resettling on me.

"So, you're here alone?" she asks, her voice conveying her distress and uncertainty.

Can't she hear the truth in my tone? Can't she tell that I'm not going to hurt her? Maybe her human half diminishes her nymph hearing? I try again, infusing my tone with my sincerity.

"Yes, I'm alone. My family owns some land nearby and I needed some air. Went for a walk and stumbled upon you." I keep my hands loose at my side in as unthreatening a pose as possible.

This time her posture relaxes, and she appears to hear the truth in my words.

"Oh. Are you part of the Kingsley family?"

It doesn't sound like she's judging me for my family, just

simply curious.

"Yes. My parents own the land and house. I'm just in town for the equinox celebration. And yourself? Are you a local?"

She pinches her lips together before answering, almost as if she doesn't want to tell me. The blossoms in her hair shift again. The tiny purple star blooms and sunflowers change to what look like irises and white peonies.

Why are the flowers in her hair changing?

"I'm Daisy. I live just on the other side of your family's land. My brother and I run the local flower nursery and gardens there."

"Daisy." I roll her name across my tongue, and it suits her. Suits the little blossom of a female in front of me. "It's nice to meet you, Daisy. And who might your friend be?"

I turn my attention to the sprite in her arms, who doesn't seem to want to rip out my eyes and bite me anymore. It's watching me with curious ebony eyes that shine with the magic inside.

"This is Delphinium. Delphi for short. She's my friend."

"It's nice to meet you Delphi."

The sprite, Delphi, cocks her head at me and chirps.

"Are you friend?"

"Yes. I am a friend."

Delphi extricates her little body from Daisy's hold and, using her abilities, hops through the air, bouncing off invisible bubbles until she lands on my shoulder. Scurrying up to my head she settles between my curved horns. I can feel her tiny little hands gently hold them like handles.

"I like your horns, and your hair. You smell nice. I like you. You can be Delphi's friend. And Daisy's."

A deep chuckle bursts from my lips and I watch Daisy, who is watching Delphi with open curiosity. I can only imagine how

I look with the sprite on my head using my horns as handlebars.

"Well thank you Delphi. I like you too."

"You can understand her?" Daisy steps closer to us, and the scent of wildflowers and fresh cut grass washes over me. It's intriguing.

I suck in a lungful of the scent, categorizing it in my mind as hers and find that I like it. It makes the fire in my chest burn hotter.

"Yes," I answer in a voice I don't think I've ever heard from my lips. "As an animal nymph, it's one of my natural abilities. Sprites are easier to talk to than some lesser intelligent animals, like squirrels. They are annoyingly illiterate."

Daisy smiles and bites her bottom lip, probably to stop herself from laughing. The flowers in her hair change once again, the peonies remain but the irises are replaced with multicolored carnations. The way they change so frequently throughout our conversation is fascinating.

"I wouldn't know. I've never talked to a squirrel before."

"Don't waste your time. They're dim witted and only care about finding and storing nuts. The conversation gets quite boring very quickly."

Then, she does laugh. Her face lighting up with mirth.

"I'll keep that in mind."

"So, what's a pretty little blossom like you doing way out here? And shoeless?" Pointedly I look down at her bare feet. The falling leaves and light underbrush covering the forest floor don't seem to bother her in the least.

Her toes curl into the ground as she fidgets, still holding the pink dinosaur mug in her hands, and before she even speaks, I can hear her shyness.

"I was checking on Delphi's nest before winter sets in. I wanted to make sure it was sturdy and ready for the snow."

"And the cool temperature doesn't bother you? Aren't you cold?"

"Not really. I'm used to it. I'll probably have to start wearing pants soon though. I wait as long as possible because it's uncomfortable for my—" Her words abruptly cut off and her face falls, as her gaze drops to my tail lazily swaying behind me.

It curls forward, brushing against my jeans, appreciating her attention on it. Sometimes it has a mind of its own, reacting on instinct. Hers in response curls up inside her shorts, hiding out of view, her cheeks darkening with...embarrassment? Is she embarrassed by her tail?

"Um, I just don't like wearing pants is all. Winter is my least favorite season."

"Mine too."

Her downcast eyes jump back up to mine, a hopeful expression on her pretty face.

"Really?"

"Yeah. I also have fire abilities, from my father's side, and I'm partial to the warmth. Snow and I don't get along."

"I would imagine not."

"It tends to be very wet. Ruins a lot of shoes."

"You should try not wearing shoes then. I highly recommend it."

I look down at her feet again and smile at her wiggling toes.

Daisy is not what I expected to find out in the middle of the woods. I don't think I would have ever noticed her if we weren't alone with no distractions. She's short, quiet, and a little meek. She would have blended in and disappeared in a crowd. Which is a shame, because eyes like hers shouldn't be overlooked. And her smile is more genuine than the gold of my necklace and the many earrings decorating my pointed ears.

Ears that compared to her dainty ones feel larger than they ever have before.

"I'll keep that in mind."

Delphi finally tires of playing with my horns and makes her way back to her nest, shuffling around inside, rearranging her treasure trove.

"May I escort you back? I know I wouldn't mind the company."

Daisy blushes again at my request but nods once. Stepping closer to her I put all my flirting seduction skills to use, brushing her hair out of her face, which is ridiculously soft, and tuck it behind one daintily pointed unadorned ear.

Nymphs historically have the longest and most elegantly pointed ears of all the non-humans, and we like to decorate and adorn them. I myself have no less than a dozen jewels, cuffs, and precious metals on mine. But hers are completely bare. Not a single piercing or cuff.

I make a mental note that buying her jewelry could be a good way to soften her up. If her family can't afford it, she will melt for me if I give her a diamond studded earring. The kind that curls around the lobe and up her delicate helix. The mental image has my cock twitching in interest.

Ears also happen to be a very erogenous zone for nymphs, and I have a particular attraction to them, and her short, but gently pointed ears with shifting green swirls, are particularly enticing.

My mouth waters, wanting to lick and suck on them. My fingers linger as they curve around the tip sliding around the shell before I force myself to pull away.

"You are very attractive, Daisy. I wouldn't want anyone to take advantage of you."

"Oh, well, thank you?" She phrases it like a question. Like

she's never been told about her obvious beauty before.

I give her a small, closed lip smile, not wanting to overwhelm her with all of my charm at once. "You're welcome. Shall we?"

I gesture back in the direction I came from, and she rolls her lips between her teeth, nodding in agreement. No doubt not wanting to speak because I'd be able to hear whatever she's feeling in her tone.

Slowly I lift her empty hand and rest it in the crook of my elbow, lining our bodies up, side by side. My wandering tail brushes against the bare skin of her calf, and I can see her visibly shudder at the touch. Her pouty lips part on a soft exhale. She wasn't expecting me to be so forward, and I can tell she's surprised but also interested. Possibly aroused?

Maybe I won't have to convince her to fake date me at all. Maybe I can just woo her enough for her to want to date me on her own. I've had short meaningless relationships before. This wouldn't be any different. And I wouldn't have to explain all the details of my mother's meddling to her and worry she might slip up in the act.

If she's this malleable and already leaning towards interested, perhaps we can both get something out of this. She gets to be with me and enjoy all that I offer, including sexually, because damn if I don't want to lick her toffee skin and play with her pretty little tail. And I get a built-in barrier to my mother and her mate bonding schemes.

If she thinks I'm desperately devoted to my half-human girlfriend, she'll either be so pissed she stops talking to me and even disowns me, or at least backs off and drops this cockamamy idea of me mating whomever she's chosen.

Either way win, win, win. This may be my most ingenuous idea yet.

Chapter 5
Daisy

A boy is talking to me. A half-naked, extremely attractive, nymph male to be exact. From what I can see there's nothing boyish about him, other than his...nope nothing. I've got nothing. He's all masculine male from my point of view. Which at this very moment is mere inches from his toned bicep.

His skin is a creamy ivory, banded with jagged crimson stripes, like a tiger. There's even a few framing his face along his jawline and temple. Sharp piercing red eyes steal glances down at me as we walk. The gold and gems on his ears glittering every time we walk through a ray of sunlight, matching the single gold chain around his neck and rings on his fingers.

I'm not sure if he's flaunting his wealth or if he just likes jewelry. His family is wealthy, it could be normal to him to wear so much. Most nymphs, including my brother, have multiple piercings in their ears and wear dangling ornaments. He offered to help me pierce mine years ago, I never wanted to though. My ears and their inadequacy have always been a source of embarrassment. I don't want to show them off or draw attention to them. Especially since I can't glamour them around humans. It's better to just hide them under my hair and forget about them.

That's hard to do when Kai literally put them on display, practically causing me to melt under his touch. No one has ever touched my ears. And his touch was warm and extremely enjoyable. So much so, I haven't even bothered to brush my hair back over my ear to hide it like I usually would.

Kai cradles my hand in his elbow like a gentleman and I don't know what to do with my fingers. My palm feels clammy, and I try not to touch him too much, but his other hand reaches up and presses down on top of mine, trapping my hand between his and his arm.

Any cold I may have felt is instantly warmed under his touch. His body radiating a steady heat. I absorb it like a flower in the sunshine, leaning towards him on instinct. I can feel my flowers blossoming and changing in my hair with my erratic emotions. Apparently so does Kai because his eyes stray to the top of my head and for once I have no idea what flowers are there.

"I like your flowers. They keep changing."

"Yeah, they do that sometimes." No way am I going to tell him they reflect my emotions and which ones they represent. He can already hear the emotions in my voice, he doesn't need to see them changing in real time on my head.

"I like your red hair. Mine's such a boring shade."

"Nonsense. I think it's perfect. Brings out your eyes. Besides, red would clash with your flowers."

Kai gives me another dazzling smile and even with my diminished abilities I can sense the truth in his words. He really does like my hair, and my eyes.

Pocket Full of Posies

I turn my attention back to the path in front of us, trying to ignore my racing pulse. I don't know how to deal with a male speaking to me like this. Complimenting me and smiling at me so much *while shirtless*.

Guys rarely talk to me. Everyone rarely talks to me. That could partly be my own doing. Ever since dropping out of public high school to be homeschooled, I've become a homebody and recluse. Only going into town when necessary.

Guess I'll have to go into town now, I realize as I grip the quirky pink dinosaur mug in my hand not currently curled around tight muscles. Or I can just give the mug to Tobias to take back to the shop avoiding the need to go into town at all. Yeah, that sounds like a better plan.

Sooner than anticipated, we reach the edge of the wooded area, and I can see the gleam of my greenhouse not far beyond. The time passing faster than desired. When we step across the threshold to the grassy fields behind the outdoor gardens, Kai's appearance shimmers as his glamour slides effortlessly into place. For a brief moment his human appearance flashes, lacking his stripes, horns and ruby eyes. In their place he's glamoured a plain white t-shirt, bare skin with *no* stripes, and hazel eyes. His red hair remains mostly as it is but lacking the other worldly brightness.

In either form he's beautiful, attractive. I, on the other hand, reach up and tuck my exposed ear back inside my hair, letting it drape across the side of my face, double checking my tail is securely hidden within my overalls. Realizing there are a few people at the nursery that could see us, I force my hand away from his arm and take a healthy step away.

He may have been kind to me so far but he's still a Kingsley, and they're known for their dislike of humans and half-breeds, at least when it comes to their personal lives. Working with them is one thing, socializing is another. Members of his family have purchased flowers from us in the past for their many fancy parties, but not once have they invited me or my family.

Equinox celebrations are different, they're public, open to any non-human who wishes to attend. But the private events they hold at their mansion, only the select invited few are allowed. I doubt Kai would want to be seen walking so closely with me.

Does he even realize I'm half-human? Should I tell him? Probably. It would end any ideas he has about speaking with me again.

Kai notices my distance and sudden quietness. He stops walking and turns to face me, hands loosely tucked into the front pockets of his jeans. Jeans that sit low on his hips, drawing my attention to his narrow waist and the curving v of muscles there. His human glamour conceals his bare chest with a t-shirt, but to me I still see his true shirtless self, which does not help the situation.

"Something wrong, Blossom? I thought we were getting along rather well." His tone conveys his confusion, but also his interest.

"Do you know what I am?" I blurt out before I lose the tiny bit of nerve I possess.

"You're a beautiful female I met in the forest," he answers smoothly as if that's the only correct answer.

I blush at the compliment but steel my nerves, I can't let his flirting distract me. I have to tell him, no matter how much I dread the look of disgust and revulsion I know is coming with my confession.

"I'm an earth nymph, but I'm also half-human. I'm a half-breed." The words come out weak, and no matter how many times I've heard them before or thought them in my head, the sound of them still makes me shrink in on myself.

"So?"

His one-word response has my head popping up to glare at him. That's all he has to say? So?

"So? You're family..."

"What about my family?"

"They hate half-breeds."

Kai growls and his playful smirk drops. "My family may have their...ideals, but *I* don't hate anybody. I don't care if you're half human or half yeti. It doesn't matter to me either way. I'd still find you distractingly beautiful and completely intriguing."

His words have my mouth gaping open like a dying fish. How am I supposed to respond to that? I have no idea. Most of the time I have no idea how to reply to others in conversation, now I'm completely lost.

"Did you already know?"

"I guessed as much when I first saw you. It doesn't change anything." His tone is truthful.

"Oh, well, okay then. I just thought you should know."

"I don't see why it matters, but thank you for telling me. May I continue escorting you back now?" he asks, extending his hand out once again.

He may be comfortable with me being a half-breed, but that doesn't mean I'm comfortable waltzing into the greenhouse hand in hand with him.

"Sure."

I cross my arms over my chest and tuck my hands in tight, clearly indicating I won't be taking his offered hand. He lets it fall to his side, brushing off the denial easily and falling back into step at my side. This time a proper distance away.

"Do you have plans for the rest of the day?" he asks after a moment of silent walking.

"I have work to do in the nursery." When I don't elaborate, he raises an eyebrow at me. "I'm preparing bouquets and centerpieces for a wedding later this week."

"Well, that sounds more entertaining than my plans. I'll help."

"What? No, that's alright. I don't need any help."

"I'll help anyways. I'm very good at observing and complimenting. I can just watch and offer my praise."

That's a strange thing to offer, and I don't like being watched or complimented. Both make me nervous.

"No, no that's okay—"

"Nonsense. I'm helping. Come on, it'll be fun."

This is not fun. Having Kai watch me arrange the centerpieces has every hair on my body standing on end, and when he compliments my work, it only makes me second guess everything. Even so, I've managed to move on to the bouquets. I give Kai a pile of spare flowers I deem unworthy of a bridal bouquet and show him how to properly bind them together.

"How about this? Does this look okay?"

Kai holds up a small grouping of flowers that I wouldn't normally put together, but somehow, he manages to make it look good.

"Yes, those look great."

Kai picks up some floral tape and pulls off a generous portion, far too much for the small bundle he's made. He tries wrapping the stems like I showed him, but the green papery tape gets stuck on itself and within seconds is a tangled mess. He'll have to start over again.

"Here, let me help."

I reach across the wooden work table we're sitting at in the back of the greenhouse and pluck the sticky tangle from his fingers, extricating them one by one from the trap he's captured them in.

"Thanks. I guess I'm not very good at this part," he chuckles, letting his long fingers linger on mine a beat too long while grinning at me.

He's been like that the entire time we've been here, sending me heated glances and easy smiles. Every time my ears heat up I have to turn away to hide my blush. He's being extremely friendly, and I don't why.

I can't quite reach across the table to help him properly, so I walk around to his side, picking up the floral tape and pulling only an inch or two free.

"You have to start with a short amount and pull out more as you work it down the base, wrapping it as you go."

Sticking the end of the tape to the top of the stems, just under the blooms where they gather, I start slowly wrapping the stems, Kai's hands bumping into mine where he attempts to help.

"That sounds dirty. You know that right?"

"What?"

I look up into his sparkling ruby eyes and think back to what I said. Oh wow, that did sound dirty. And from the grin on his lips, he's enjoying my blunder.

"Anyway," my voice comes out high pitched and squeaky as I turn back to focus on our work, "you can't use too much, or you'll end up with a mess like before. Just use a little at a time. And make sure to wrap it tight, but not too tight." I rattle on more instructions trying to ignore his knowing chuckle.

Kai shifts off the stool he's sitting on and stands, moving behind me to wrap strong arms around either side of me, placing his hands over mine. They still in their winding and my entire body tingles under the warmth of his looming presence behind me.

"Keep going. I want to make sure I get this right," he murmurs into my ear, his warm breath rustling my hair.

Clearing my throat, I try to focus on the task at hand, literally, but I can't speak. Whatever caused me to ramble before has now turned my tongue to stone. Together our hands wrap the stems and I reach for the short strand of ribbon I precut for him. He holds the small posy of flowers while I crisscross the ribbon a couple of times before tying a bow, Kai's finger holding the knot without asking. The entire episode takes place in complete silence.

Once it's finished, Kai's hands rest on the table at my sides and I turn in the circle of his arms, holding his posy, a small bouquet of mismatched flowers; one petite pink peony, a few stray jasmines, and even a daisy. All mixed together with stray strands of long grass and leaves.

"Well, here you go. All done."

I hold up the posy for his inspection, imbuing it with my magic. The blooms perk up and open their pedals, releasing their floral scents. He doesn't move, other than his eyes, to angle down to where I hold it in the small space between us, lips parting to flash his pointy canines.

"Perfect. You should do this professionally."

The joke eases my tension and I relax, leaning against the table behind me. Just as I think Kai is going to release me from his hold and step back, his tail caresses my ankle. Circling and sliding up to my calf.

Pocket Full of Posies

Parts of me that usually remain dormant, except when I'm alone, spark to life. My nipples instantly harden as a breath catches in my throat. If I weren't holding onto the flowers for dear life, I fear I might have reached out and ran my hands up the bare expanse of his chest.

What in the love of mother earth is going on?

I don't have the slightest clue, but I need space, distance from Kai and his skin and heat and musky man scent. Oh crap, he smells so good. How had I not noticed before?

"Here you go," I say an octave too loudly and forcefully thrust the flowers into his chest, forcing him to remove a hand to grab them before they fall.

With his arm removed, I have a clear path of escape and take it. Quickly scurrying back to the opposite side of the table, picking up a flower and cutting its stem before placing it in the vase where I have the flowers for the bouquet arranged.

"I've never made a bouquet before," Kai muses, turning the flowers in between his fingers. "Maybe you could hire me on? You know, for the busy season. I'm sure everyone would love my work. Look at this, I'm a floral genius."

He is in fact not a floral genius, but I appreciate his dedication to trying. Tucking his masterpiece into the back pocket of his jeans, Kai claps his hands and rubs them together like a villain mastermind.

"Ok what's next, I'm on a roll here."

"Well first off what you just made is called a posy. You might want to get the terminology right before you go announcing yourself as a floral genius."

Kai looks at me quizzically, his lips quirked to one side. "Posy? Isn't that a flower?"

"No. A posy is a small bouquet. So, what you have right there is a pocket full of posies." I point to the flowers poking out from his back pocket. It really is ironic he happened to tuck them in his pocket.

"Like the song?"

"Exactly like the song. Except that was referring to bubonic plague victims that carried around posies in their pockets to cover the smell of their rotting flesh."

Kai's eyes go comically wide, and I've managed to make his jaw go slack for once. I bite my lips between my teeth to stifle a laugh. I don't think there are many people who can catch Kai off guard.

"You're joking right?"

"Sort of. It hasn't been proven, but there were speculations about it. I kind of like the creepy history of it."

"You're a little weirdo, aren't you?"

"Only when it comes to plants and flowers."

Over Kai's shoulder, I see Sage round a wall of hydrangeas. He does a double take and stops dead in his tracks. His expression shifting from relaxed to confused, then enraged. I follow the trajectory of his glare and realize he's staring daggers into Kai's back. He must know who he is, or at least his family, because I've never met him before today. But I also hide out in my greenhouse and avoid social interactions altogether. Not a big surprise I didn't know who he was when we first met.

Kai catches my distant expression and turns in his seat, catching Sage's glare before he drops it to a flat expression. Turning back around Kai gives me a sheepish smile.

"I think I've taken up enough of your time. I'll come see you again soon though. You can tell me more stories about nursery rhymes that have disturbing historical origins."

He stands and smirks at me once more, flashing a fang, then he's gone. Strolling past Sage and out of the greenhouse with the posy of flowers still sticking out of his back pocket.

Pocket Full of Posies

"You shouldn't be hanging out with him, Daisy. I know I told you to make more friends but not him." Sage sits in the stool Kai just vacated and doesn't look happy one bit.

"Why? What's wrong with Kai? He seemed nice to me."

"Oh, he's very nice. With every female he meets. He's a relentless flirt and slut. If he's being friendly, it's because he only wants one thing from you."

My tail tightens around my waist and I try to see Kai as Sage sees him. Yes, he is very flirtatious, but as for being a slut? I couldn't say. I don't know his past. And so what if he is? There's nothing wrong with having numerous sexual partners. Some of us aren't lucky enough to even have one sexual partner. Not that I choose to still be a virgin at twenty-three. Well, in the sense that I've never been with a real male. My secret toy collection doesn't count.

"And what exactly is it you think he wants from me? All he did was walk with me and then make a few flower arrangements."

"Huh," is all he says. Like it's completely unfathomable a guy like Kai could be interested in me for any reason *other* than casual sex. "I still don't like him. He'll only end up hurting you in the end."

"Well, I liked spending time with him."

Sage also doesn't like that. "Just promise me you'll be careful, Daiz. He has a reputation and I'd hate to see you become part of it."

I stare at the flowers in the vase, ignoring Sages pleading eyes, and mindlessly move them around. We sit in silence for another minute before Sage gets up to help a customer and leaves me to stew in my thoughts of everything that happened today with Kai. Particularly when his tail stroked me.

Chapter 6
Kai

Stepping back into my family's house hours after I left, I find my brother sitting on the couch watching TV, some action movie with loud explosions that he has to pause in order to be heard.

"You're back. Where the hell did you go for so long?"

I cross the wide living room and plop down on the couch next to him, my head falling back onto the plush cushion.

"Finding my new mate."

"Excuse me? I don't think I hear you right. Your new mate?" Endo sits up straight and stares at me, his chocolate and gold eyes gleaming.

"Yeah. I took your advice and found myself a mate before mom could choose one for me," I casually declare while kicking off my boots and dropping my feet onto the coffee table. Mom would cut off my ears if she saw the way we behave in the house when she's not around.

"You're serious? You actually found a female nymph to

agree to be your mate? How?"

Pursing my lips, I bob my head side to side. "Not exactly. I'm not actually going to bond with her, and she hasn't agreed to be my mate."

"I'm confused. How is she your new mate then?"

"She's not. I'm just going to tell mom she is. There's no reason she has to know that."

Endo shakes his head and leans back into the couch. "You're a piece of work, you know that? Does this poor girl even know what she's getting into?"

"Probably not. Oh, and she's a half-breed."

"What?! Are you out of your mind?" Endo practically shrieks, and I recoil at the shrill sound, his voice ringing in my ears. "You can't tell mom you're planning on mating a half-breed. She'll disown you."

"One can only hope," I mutter under my breath while fingering my ear trying to regain my hearing.

"You want to be disowned? Truly?"

"It wouldn't be the worst thing in the world. You'd still talk to me, wouldn't you?"

"Of course, I would. It doesn't matter to me if they approve of you, never has."

Of all my siblings I've been closest with Endo since he was a child. My older brother and sister have always been the golden children, the apple of our mother's eye, doing everything right. Keiko, my younger sister who was born in between me and Endo, is the opposite of anyone in our family. Daisy reminds me of her, quiet, reserved, sweet as sugar.

Endo's always been more like me; enigmatic, extroverted, bit of a flirt, but in a calmer softer way. He's always the one to tag along when I go out and join in on any fun to be had. No matter if our parents disown me and never speak to me again,

I know Endo will always be there.

"So, who is this poor half-breed girl you've managed to pull into your scheme?"

"Her name's Daisy. Works at a flower nursery right next door. Who knew the answer to my problem was so close?"

"Daisy? As in *Daisy's Gardens*?"

"Yeah, that's the one. Cute little blossom. Found her in the woods, with a sprite of all things."

Endo doesn't speak, and at his unexpected silence, I look over to him. The face he's giving me is not one of approval at my ingenious idea to spurn our mothers' plans, in fact it looks downright disapproving.

"What? You don't think it'll work?"

"I have no idea if it'll work, but I do know Daisy. She's a sweet girl and doesn't deserve to get caught up in our family drama." His tone says it all, disapproval indeed.

"How do you know Daisy?" Suddenly I'm very interested in how my little brother knows my blossom. When did he meet her? Did he flirt with her? Did she laugh and smile at him like she did me?

"Some of us actually go into town for more than drinking at the bar. Mom likes fresh flowers in the house. I go to Daisy's sometimes to get them. She's helped me out a few times. You really think I put all those arrangements together myself?"

Honestly, I never gave two thoughts to the flowers in the house, or any decorations for that matter. I just figured some employee or hired help took care of it all.

Thinking of Daisy's emerald, green eyes and ever-changing flowers, I recall the posy in my back pocket and lean forward, carefully extracting it from where I partially smooshed it by sitting on it. A few petals fall from the askew blossoms, but all in all it survived my ass crushing. Bringing it to my nose, I take a deep inhale and an image of Daisy blushing instantly pops into my head and a new feeling I haven't experienced before takes me by surprise. Longing. I want to see her again.

"Just be careful with her Kai. Daisy isn't like the girls you pick up for one night, or party with. She's an introvert, and from what I've seen, barely goes into town. She's not a woo girl. She's the kind you take home to mom. Well, if your mom were anyone but our mom. She's the girl you keep, the one you actually mate bond with. Just remember that."

"You're getting all worked up for nothing. I'll spend some time with Daisy, make mom think we're gonna bond, and have a little fun in the process. After the equinox is over, I'll let Daisy down easy, leave town and mom will either disown me or forget the whole thing and move on to intruding on someone else's life." My explanation is exactly the plan I came up with in the forest, but the words settle differently in my mind than they did before.

"Oh, you mean like mine?" Endo scoffs.

Sooner or later mom will set her sights on Endo and his relationship status as well. Not yet though. He still has a few decades before it matters. Lucky bastard.

I chuckle and spin the flowers in my fingers, marveling at the perfect bow Daisy tied in the ribbon.

"Maybe you can find yourself a sweet little half-breed to mate and get disowned too. Then we can celebrate the equinox properly in Ibiza."

Endo grins and all worries that my foolproof plan will fail flies out the window as we list all the things we plan on doing while in Ibiza for the spring equinox and or summer solstice. Both sound good.

After we—okay Endo—cooks dinner, I slink off to my assigned guest room, one that I've only slept in about half the time I've been here. The bed is unmade, and my clothes are strewn about the room, hanging on the edge of a hamper, the back of a chair, a lamp shade. I'm not the cleanliest of people. Why bother folding and hanging clothes, when they're just going to end up back in a suitcase when I leave to move on to the next place?

For the last, I don't even know how many years I've been moving from place to place. Leaving only once I got bored and needed a change of scenery. There's no one place I call home or that I return to for solace. I like to be active, moving, disconnected. I don't like being tied down; it makes me feel restless, useless. As soon as the equinox is over, I'm out of here. The smaller the town, the quicker I feel the desire to leave.

Resting the posy on a clear spot on my dresser, I realize now I have something to fill my time while stuck in this backwater town, Daisy. Daisy the flower blossom whose cheeks turn the prettiest shade of pink when I flirt with her. I like flirting with her. I'm going to enjoy pretending she's my future mate. And if I can manage to keep her none the wiser, all the better. She doesn't need to know all the details. To her this will be a short fling and nothing more.

Stripping off my pants, I crawl naked into my bed and stretch wide, my feet dangling off the edge. Stroking a hand over my horns and through my hair, I run it down my chest and lower, adjusting myself, noticing I've managed to get half hard while thinking of Daisy.

This may turn out to be the most pleasurable equinox celebration I've had with my family in years.

Chapter 7
Daisy

I barely slept last night. Every time I closed my eyes, I kept picturing Kai with his half hooded ruby gaze and the sensation of his soft fur tail caressing my skin. My imagination kept playing that part on repeat, elaborating on its journey up my leg until it slid up my shorts and stroked other parts of me.

I've never been so turned on by the thought of a male in my life. There's something about Kai and his blunt confidence and flirtatious nature that intrigues me. I know I should heed my brother's warning and forget about Kai, but forgetting about someone like Kai is like forgetting there's a sun in the sky. You can't, his presence is blinding and demands attention.

Kai's promise to come see me again is still playing over in my thoughts when I spot a familiar head of light brown hair making her way through the greenhouse.

"Calliope!" I call over the hedge of greenery and her head whips in my direction revealing the black rim of her glasses and bright kind brown eyes beneath.

Calliope is a human who works at the bakery in town. As far as I know she has no idea about the non-human world and until something changes to allow her to know, I have to keep my non-humanness a secret. Which is a shame. Calliope is the sweetest human I know, and not just because she always smells like sugar and frosting. I doubt she would tell anyone about non-humans, she's not that kind of person.

"Daisy!" Calliope calls and waves back at me, finding her way around the tangle of hanging vines.

We hug warmly when she reaches me, and I instantly feel more at ease. She's never questioned my "tattoos" or commented on the flowers in my hair, or even mocked my lack of shoes. She's the only person I've ever met who's instantly accepted me for me and never made me feel awkward or uncomfortable.

Kind of like Kai, my mind reminds me. I feel like this around Kai, plus a healthy helping of desire and lust. Let's not forget that little tidbit.

"I'm so glad I found you. You're awfully busy today. Something special going on I'm not aware of?" Calliope pushes her glasses up her nose and glances around at the abnormally full greenhouse.

I follow her line of sight and realize almost everyone present is a non-human, but Calliope doesn't know that or that they're all preparing for the equinox celebrations.

"Um, well, you know how people get when the season changes. Alternating their summer displays for fall colors and blooms. It always happens around this time of year. We're all very into seasonal decorations."

I try to play off the influx of customers on a Wednesday as nothing of note. To me it isn't, we expected as much so close to the equinox. Before I met Kai, I was expecting to see Endo or maybe Julia (the Kingsley family's personal assistant) picking up flowers for their pre-equinox party. They always have one and it's usually one of those two who come seeking the best blooms in season for the event.

    I don't know who Endo is to Kai. I never asked how he was related to his family, and we never spoke about his relatives in much detail. I got the impression he didn't like to. So, we spoke on easier topics like flowers, decorations, and the upcoming celebrations.

    "Oh. Well maybe I should do the same. I don't want to be the odd one out in town," Calliope jokes.

    She's only lived here for about six months now. She moved here when her great aunt died and left her house and all her possessions to Calliope in her will. Instead of selling it off and leaving with the money she decided to move here and live in her great aunt's house. She's still not sure if she's going to stay permanently but has no plans to leave any time soon thankfully. Although she was here during the summer solstice, she didn't see any of the celebration preparations, as most humans aren't supposed to. Summer is also our smallest celebration. People tend to come here for autumn and winter because of the changing leaves and snow and go to warmer, more southern locations, for spring and summer.

    "Nonsense, you're not the odd one out in town, I am. Everyone already loves you."

    "They love my baking. That's all."

    "No, that's not all. You possess the ability to befriend everyone you meet, whereas I manage to always make people uncomfortable."

    "Stop that Daisy, you do not. You just need more practice being social. If you'd go into town with me more, you'd see that."

"No thank you," I shake my head and back away instinctually. "I don't do well in town."

"Because you need practice. Come into *Sticky Buns* any day and we can just sit and talk and enjoy a warm sticky cinnamon roll." Calliope gives me her award-winning smile and big doe eyes and even though I probably never will, I agree.

"Fine. But don't hold your breath."

She laughs and thankfully drops the subject of trying to assist in practicing my nonexistent socialization skills.

"So, what brings *you* in today? If you're not changing your seasonal decor?" I ask, more comfortable talking about her than me.

"Oh, Sage called and said the tea leaves were ready for pick up."

Among our many flowers and floral arrangement services, we also grow green tea, black tea, and chamomile for the businesses in town as well as for individual sales. We also grow a selection of flora that pair well with tea that customers can use to make their own, like hibiscus, when in season. For customers and friends like Calliope and *Sticky Buns*, we also pick and dry the leaves and petals.

Currently we have a batch of black tea leaves that are ready. Getting into the fall, the non-floral and light flavors become more popular. Meaning my cinnamon and allspice will be getting low soon.

"Yes, I have it all ready for you at the house. Why don't you come up with me and I can get you some fresh cinnamon as well."

"I would love that. There's nothing like fresh cinnamon to make everything better."

My cinnamon comes from a Cinnamomum verum tree my mom brought back from one of her trips to Sri Lanka and planted in our greenhouse. I've nurtured and cared for it ever since, harvesting many years of cinnamon sticks from it to sell to the locals, and use personally. It's a bit of a treat having it fresh nearly year-round.

    I guide Calliope out of the greenhouse and through the back towards the house I've called home my entire life. To me it looks like a cottage from a fairytale, but with modern amenities. It's a white two-story, with a curved roof and pale-yellow shutters, complimented by the creeping vines we've let grow up the walls. We make sure to tend to them and the house, so they don't overpower the wooden siding and affect its structural integrity. We like having the plants around but we also like having a safe place to live.

    The house is off limits to customers, but Calliope is more than a customer, she's a friend. This isn't the first time I've invited her into my home, and it won't be the last.

    Stepping up to the front door I use a soft shoe cleaner to brush off the dirt and debris from my feet before stepping over the threshold. Calliope does the same without question.

    I quickly procure the tea jars and help arrange them within the canvas tote Calliope brought. She's short like me but with curves I've always envied. Where I'm lanky like a stick-bug with breasts smaller than a peach, Calliope is soft curves with an hourglass figure and breasts that actually create cleavage. She hefts the bag onto her shoulder, and I grab a bundle of dried cinnamon sticks to add to her haul.

    When we reach the front porch again, I offer Calliope a seat and to make her a cup of tea before she goes back into town. I may be socially inept, but I have manners. Plus I'd like to spend a little time with my friend. As Sage so painfully pointed out, I have very few.

    Calliope sits in one of the many chairs cluttering the porch.

We like to sit out here throughout the day and have a wide variety of comfortable chairs to choose from. Calliope chooses a wooden rocking chair, while I go inside to get the tea kettle and cups. I return minutes later with a small tray laden with tea making instruments.

"How have you been?" Calliope asks as we prepare the tea.

"Fine."

"Nothing unusual happen lately?" Calliope's tone changes and I hear a very clear and distinct curiosity in it.

Looking up from my steeping tea, I inspect my friend closely. She's holding her teacup in both hands, rocking her chair idly. But there's something in her shifting gaze that says this is more than her average inquiry into my boring life.

Leaning back in my rocking chair, I tuck my feet underneath me, rearranging the long flowing skirt I chose to wear today. Tucking it neatly around me to cover my legs and tail. The temperature dropped today from yesterday and I even put on a thin cropped sweater to keep out the growing chill.

"Why? Is there something specific you are referring to?" I ask with narrowed eyes watching her closely.

"Well, I heard you had a special customer yesterday. A rather handsome and flirty male customer." She doesn't outright say his name, but I know she's referring to Kai.

"How did you hear that? It was literally less than twenty-four hours ago."

"If you ventured into town more often, you would know how quickly gossip spreads. I heard it this morning from Jimmy, our delivery boy, who heard it from his sister, who heard it from Larken, who said she was told by Donna, who saw you two canoodling over flower arrangements in the greenhouse."

"Wow. People really need to find better things to fill their time with."

Pocket Full of Posies

"So, it's true? You were canoodling with Kai Kingsley, the infamous playboy?" Her eyes go wide, and she leans forward in her chair expectantly, hoping for gossip confirmation.

The last thing I want to do is be a part of the town gossip, but Calliope looks so excited I can't lie to her.

"We weren't *canoodling*, we were just talking. He was helping me with some bouquet orders, that's all. Nothing scandalous or worthy of gossip, so everyone can just cut that out right now."

Calliope looks absolutely thrilled at the partial confirmation. I have a feeling this isn't going to stop her curiosity.

"And what do you mean *playboy*?" I ask, trying to redirect the conversation to get a few answers of my own. She seems to know more about Kai than I do, and I can't deny I'm curious about him.

"He's a player. A relentless flirt and philanderer. He's already gotten a reputation in town, and he's only been here for like, what, two weeks, maybe a month? From what I've heard he goes to *Blue Moon* almost every night and hits on any female who will give him attention. Gone home with a few too."

This information sours the tea in my stomach. I already knew he was a flirt, but this blunt explanation of his activities so close to home, is far less tactful than Sage's was yesterday. *I'm not special.* The thought surprises me with how much I wanted to be special to Kai. A realization I'm just now having, and it seems like a rather inappropriate time for my heart to give a heavy kick in my chest.

Calliope notices the change in my demeanor, including my lack of reciprocated enthusiasm about Kai's playboy status.

"Oh, I mean...he seems like a nice guy. Very friendly. Everyone who speaks about him doesn't have a negative word to say. Maybe people are just overexaggerating to make better gossip. You know how people can be. Making things greater than they are."

She's trying to assuage my discomfort, I can tell by her tone; it's filled with regret. Although I know she's probably just saying it to make me feel better, she does have a point. You can't always believe everything you hear from others. Kai may indeed be a flirt, that I can vouch for, but that doesn't mean he's a womanizer who sleeps with every female he meets. After all, people were saying we were canoodling or making out, when in reality we were just talking.

"Right. Can't always trust those gossip chains. Too many interpretations of the truth."

"Exactly. I haven't met him personally yet, only seen him around a few times, so I can't say what kind of guy he is. You've spoken to him, spent time with him. You would have a better idea than anyone what kind of person he is."

The more we talk the less dejected I feel. Because she's right. I spent time with him, not them. They're just making up extravagant stories that make good gossip, none of which has been confirmed. The Kai I met was open, friendly, nice, and yes there was flirting, but he didn't act like a womanizing sex fiend.

There's nothing wrong with having an active sex life. He's an adult and the women are adults. They can make their own choices, and their choices are no one else's business.

Feeling more confident in my original presumption of Kai's character, I relax into my rocking chair and sip at my now cooled tea. The warm bitterness of the black tea soothes the unease in my chest. As if on cue, knowing we were talking about him, the male himself rounds the greenhouse and heads straight for us.

I sit up straight in my seat and watch as Kai casually and unhurriedly makes his way towards us.

Pocket Full of Posies

"Is that him?" Calliope stage whispers to me.

Unable to remove my eyes from Kai, I give Calliope a short nod. He's wearing a shirt today, a real one. The black material is tight on his lean frame, and somehow it feels more revealing than when he was shirtless. Maybe because I know what lies underneath? It's like a secret between us, that again makes me feel special.

Every part of me is on high alert and my nipples respond, turning to points that brush against the soft material of my sweater. I'm not wearing a bra or an undershirt and I'm now regretting that choice. If I were at least wearing another layer, perhaps it would help protect me from his heated gaze. Highly unlikely as it only seems to grow hotter the closer he gets.

My breaths turn shallow and I'm squeezing my legs together under my skirt. *What the actual hell?* This is not a good response to just seeing him from a distance. I'm going to need to get my shit together asap.

"Oh, my goodness. He is really focused on you, isn't he?"

I assume the question is rhetorical because I don't respond.

"I wish a man would stare at me like that." I can hear the slight jealousy and longing in Calliope's voice and am shocked to hear it. No one has ever been jealous of me before.

Kai finally reaches the porch and stops halfway up the few steps.

"Hello."

That's it. That's all he has to say for my heart to jump into my throat and my pussy to clench with want. Oh holy hell this isn't good. And apparently Kai can see all the internal turmoil I'm going through as he gives me a slow once over, his eyes lingering on my chest.

Oh my god he can see my nipples.

I should move to conceal them or shift to force his gaze

away, but I don't. I let him look his fill for as long as he likes. I think I like his attention on me.

We probably would have remained there in silence for an eternity had it not been for Calliope thankfully breaking the sexual tension.

"Hi. I'm Calliope."

Kai's eyes drift away from me and to my friend sitting next to me. His lips stretch into an easy smile. It doesn't appear lude or suggestive, as one would expect from a playboy. It's natural, friendly, like he smiles all the time. I think he does. He seems like a happy guy to me.

"Hello Calliope, I'm Kai. It's very nice to meet you."

He steps all the way on to the porch and reaches out to shake Calliope's hand, bringing with him his warmth and bonfire smell. As an earth nymph, fire is my natural enemy. It burns forests and kills plants, but I can't help but be drawn in by the scent of it coming off of Kai.

Once the introductions are over, Kai leans against the short wooden railing across from us, hands shoved in his pockets and eyes once again glued to me. His smile remains in place but softening, right along with his posture. He's completely comfortable and relaxed, whereas I'm wound tight as a spring ready to pop at the slightest breath.

In his reclined position, Kai's muscles flex and stretch, his tail resting lazily on the porch's wooden planks. Calliope can't see it with his glamour in place, but I do. He is a sight to behold, vibrant red hair, polished ebony horns, the gold adorning his ears and hands. Kai carries himself differently than the local boys, all swagger, confidence and sex appeal. It's not hard to understand why females are drawn to him.

Calliope's voice breaks through the haze of sexual longing I'm aiming at Kai once again. I'm gonna have to work on that.

"Didn't you say you wanted to go to *Tall Tail* to get a new book Daisy?"

"What?" Finally breaking my gaze away from Kai, I turn to frown at Calliope. What is she talking about?

"The other day you said you had no good books to read and wanted to check out *Tall Tail Books* for something new. Maybe Kai could accompany you into town?"

Oh no, she did not just say that.

Instantly Kai's face brightens with delight.

"I would love to escort you into town, Daisy. I'm bored hanging around the house with only Endo for company. Maybe I need a good book as well."

"Oh, I don't know. We're awfully busy today. Sage needs my help," I argue, hoping the excuse I've used more than I can count to avoid town, actually works this time. It doesn't look like I'm going to have such luck.

"I think your brother can manage," Calliope says without hesitation. "Pretty sure I also saw one of the local high schoolers you hire on occasion helping out today."

She gives me a cheeky grin and I know I'm going to lose this battle.

"Come on Blossom. Let's play hooky for the afternoon." Kai reaches out a hand waiting for me to take it.

Between Kai's outstretched hand and Calliope giving me the *don't you dare say no to this hot man* eyes, I know they won't give up until I agree. Reaching out one hand I slip it into Kai's and let him pull me to my feet, bringing our bodies inches from one another. He doesn't step back or give me space, just gently removes the teacup from my other hand and places it on the table.

Looks like I'm playing hooky today and going into town... with Kai.

Chapter 8
Kai

I could kiss that Calliope girl for placing such a perfect opportunity to spend time with Daisy right in my lap. I won't though. If I'm going to be kissing anyone, it's going to be Daisy. That's not the type of gossip I want spreading around town.

I happen to be partial to the quiet, half human, earth nymph. Imagining more and more what I'd like to do to her distractingly tempting mouth.

Today Daisy has covered herself with a long flowing forest green skirt and creamy ivory sweater, and again no adornments or jewelry. The flowers in her hair are calmer than before, remaining the same without the constant changing; a yellow daisy, white jasmine and a few small light purple blooms I don't know.

Although her skin is concealed under the fabric, she must not be wearing much under it, because the hard points of her nipples are still visible through her sweater. I want to reach out and pinch them but restrain my impulse. She's still too shy and timid around me. I'll have to work on that. I want her soft and accommodating, pliant and accepting of my touch and affections when I reach for her. I don't want her shying away from me, I want her reaching for me as much as I do her.

The thought of having her under me and yearning for me has my zipper tightening against my groin. I don't readjust myself; I don't care if she or anyone else sees the evidence of my arousal. As long as Daisy knows it's because of her.

We walk into town, and I make sure to keep close to Daisy, brushing my arm against hers every chance I get. When we cross the street, I make sure to place a hand low on her back to direct her, and take any opportunity given to touch her. By the time we reach *Tall Tail Books*, I feel like our walk has been a strange form of foreplay and my cock is ready to go for the main event.

I ignore it, no matter how hard that may be. I'm trying to woo Daisy and convince anyone who sees us that we're an item, not seduce her for a quick fuck. Although fucking is not off the menu. I will gladly fuck Daisy in any way she wants me to, but not until she wants it. I may be a borderline sex addict, but I never sleep with a female who doesn't agree to it first.

A bell jingles overhead as we enter the bookstore. Glossy wooden shelves line every available space, packed to the brim and filling the small store to bursting. Meres and their collections. They always get obsessed once they've discovered their treasure of choice. It's obvious this is a mere owned establishment, and whoever they are, they have a massive thing for the written word.

Elegantly hand painted wooden signs hang from chains, labeling the isles genre. Fiction, non-fiction, history, cooking, children's, science, young adult, religion, and romance. The light inside is dim, spines of books illuminated from vintage sconces and fixtures. A few golden rays slip in through the two front windows, most of which are blocked by gauzy curtains. The place smells of paper, ink, and celibacy.

Daisy smiles shyly at the mere with shimmering kelp green scales working behind the counter, a young male who looks us each over with a welcoming smile. For once I don't smile in return. My usually friendly demeanor faltering as I watch the male check out Daisy's backside as she walks by. When he looks to me, I give him a narrowed eye glare telling him that yes, I did see him checking her out and no, I do not approve.

Moving in closer to Daisy, I place a possessive hand on her hip that I convince myself is just because I'm trying to sell the image of us together, not because I want to slip a finger under the short hem of her sweater and feel her soft skin beneath. It's all for show. It's all so the gossip does what it's supposed to and gets back to my mother, solidifying my ruse. The way my body reacts to her nearness and the soft inhale my touch elicits has nothing to do with it. Not. At. All.

"What kind of book are you looking for, Blossom?"

Daisy shrugs an indifferent shoulder, but I don't believe it. "I don't know, just something new."

"Well, I have no idea what's new, so you'll just have to tell me if my picks are ones you've already read."

Daisy nods. She doesn't like to talk much when other people are around I notice, because yesterday she was very chatty with me when we were alone. So, in an attempt to get her talking, I pull a book off the shelf as we pass, holding it out for her inspection.

"How about this one? It looks interesting." I have no idea what book I picked, but she turns to look at it and the corner of her lips pulls in a smirk.

"If I were curious about the history of the US quarter, I'm

sure it would be riveting."

I look at the book in my hand and realize I pulled some sort of history of US currency book. I snicker at myself. "Okay, maybe not that one."

For the next book I pay a little more attention to my choice. "Here, you can read about homesteading. Seems like something up your alley."

She gives me a lopsided grin and cocks her head at me playfully. *There's the Daisy I remember from yesterday.*

"I don't need to read about it, I already know how."

"Of course you do, because you're the amazing Daisy of *Daisy's Gardens.*"

"I wouldn't call myself *amazing*," she says, with such a quiet disbelief that it tears up my insides to know she doesn't believe she's amazing. Whoever told her such nonsense deserves to have their ears clipped and nose broken.

"I would."

Daisy looks up at me through thick lashes and that self-deprecating tone I heard vanishes with her appreciative eyes and ruddy rosy blush.

"Thanks," she practically whispers as we round a shelf and find ourselves in the romance section.

"Now this is my type of genre. Which one do you think has all the naughty stuff in it? Do they have picture books? I'm a visual learner."

I reach out and start fingering through the titles, choosing one with a couple on it where the woman is swooning and the man is looking at her like he would burn the world down for her, after a good fucking of course. "Ooh this one looks promising."

I flip it over and read the blurb on the back. It's about some Irish lord who must marry to keep his family lands and finds himself marrying the first girl that comes along, even if she's his arch nemesis's daughter.

"This one could be good. I feel like there'll be a lot of calling her lass and dirty talk in Irish."

I turn to Daisy for her approval and where I expected complete embarrassment, I find only a guilty knowing expression.

"That one's okay. A lot of brooding and sexually charged arguments because they really want each other but can't admit it. However," My eyes nearly bug out of my head knowing she's actually read this book as she steps up to the shelf, bringing our personal spaces together. "don't bypass the cartoon covers. They look sweet but often have as much, or more *naughty* parts than the bodice ripper covers. And no one suspects when you're reading it."

Daisy pulls a pastel pink cover book from the shelf showcasing a cartoon couple kissing and embracing innocently, and hands it to me.

"Try this one, I think you'll like it."

I raise an eyebrow at her and take the offered research material, because that's what it's just become. If she's read this and is recommending it, that means she likes whatever happens in it. Fuck if I won't read this entire thing tonight.

"Thank you. I think I will."

"And if you ever want to read anything closer to non-humans, there's plenty of monster and alien romances. They don't get it all right, but at least there's more details that make it feel more real."

Again, she smiles but bites on her lips to contain it. With my free hand not clutching the most important reading material I'll ever purchase, I reach up and cup her cheek, running my thumb across her lips until she releases it. It's pink, plump and glistening. I rub away the wetness and relish in her dilated pupils.

"I will definitely keep that in mind."

Daisy's eyes shift back and forth between mine then lift to slide along the curve of my horns. I can only imagine what she's thinking about. Grabbing them, using them as leverage to pull her body up mine. I can think of a dozen or two ways she can use my horns to bring herself pleasure. I wonder if one of these monster romance books she's referring to has a character with horns. Maybe she has a horn kink.

I can see the tips of the green vine markings poking out from her collar curl tight and then extend. Most likely reacting to her emotions. Kind of like I think her flowers do.

In the small space between shelves our bodies are pressed close, and I take the opportunity to bring our chests together, just letting her nipples graze my shirt. My cock pulses hard in my jeans and I expect I'll be jerking off tonight, while reading this book and thinking of Daisy.

"You are surprising in a way I could have never expected."

Daisy doesn't respond to my confession. She knows I'm not lying, that I mean every word. Because I wasn't expecting her, I don't think I could have ever prepared myself for her and the way I react to her.

That unfamiliar longing feeling washes over me again and I don't know what to do with it. I don't know what I'm longing for. Daisy is right here in front of me, looking at me with *please bend me over and fuck me* eyes. What more could a male want? Something. Something I can't name, but something.

"Do you have any more book recommendations? I'm suddenly finding myself in need of more *stimulating* reading material."

"Sure. Romance books are kind of my guilty pleasure. Sage

says I should stop reading about romance and go out and find some instead."

"Although I agree with this Sage person, you should go out and find it, I also don't think you should feel guilty reading what makes you happy."

"Sage is my older brother, and I'm not sure how he would feel about you agreeing with him. He's not your biggest fan."

"Well, I'm yours, so he'll have to deal."

Daisy looks up at me with such open admiration, that *something more* feeling crashes over me like a tsunami again. A heavy feeling of realness and solidity settles in my stomach and the sensation feels oddly like attachment. In an attempt to shake off the all too real emotions growing in my chest, I revert to my default setting, comedic flirting.

"For instance, I love reading porn magazines. Very riveting articles on masturbation and the female orgasm." I give her a wink to top off my lewd sundae.

It makes her giggle and the dense, almost viscous sensations lessen enough for us to return to our previous flirty banter.

"I imagine such an article would prove extremely lucrative."

"I wouldn't know, haven't been able to test out their theories yet. Are you volunteering?"

"I don't know. Who's demonstrating? If you can get Henry Cavill to teach the class, I'll be the first to sign up."

Daisy elbows me playfully, getting more at ease in my company and not as bashful when I make crude jokes. I always wanted a female who could take my perverted sense of humor and throw it right back in my face.

"I don't know, he's awfully busy these days. You might just have to settle for little ole me."

Daisy sighs dramatically. "Oh, well, in that case." She scrunches her nose in mock disapproval giving me an exaggerated once over and makes an *eh* gesture. "I guess you'll have to do."

I step in close and practically purr in her ear. "You know you wouldn't be disappointed, little blossom. I'll make you bloom for me, over and over and over."

Her lithe body shivers against mine and I hold back the praise sitting on the tip of my tongue. I wonder what type of sexual partner Daisy would be. Is she the praise kind? Loving every word of affirmation. Or a submissive, liking to be dominated and controlled? Or would she be the one in control. Thinking of letting my little blossom command and control me is intriguing enough for my cock to give an approving twitch in my pants.

Stepping back out of my reach, Daisy visibly forces herself to refocus. Straightening the hem of her too thin sweater and fidgeting with the book in her hands, we're finally back on even footing. Her flustered and aroused, and me hard and wanting to fuck. Safe space, known space. Space where I know how to handle the feelings curdling inside my gut.

"Perhaps we should keep looking. I still haven't found a new book."

"Okay then," I turn to face the shelf and peruse the titles that are both pun filled and suggestive. "Which one of these haven't you read yet?"

Daisy points out about a dozen books and I choose the ones with the most suggestive titles, tucking them under my arm with the book she first gave me. The one she's already read.

I pay for all six of our books even though Daisy tries to pay for hers, but I won't allow it. My family has more than enough money to buy her a few books. Plus, wooing, remember? Buying gifts is only step one.

When we leave the bookstore, I make sure to drape an arm

around Daisy's shoulders and hold her tight to my side. The top of her head just reaches my shoulders, and she fits perfectly in the circle of my arm. It feels oddly comfortable walking down the street with her tucked against me, seeing everyone we pass do a double take. Not sure if they're more shocked by me or Daisy. Could be the whole combination of us together that's baffling them.

Internally I shrug because I don't give a damn what they think about us, just as long as they tell everyone they know.

"So, what other kinds of books do you like to read, Daisy?"

"All kinds really."

"Just not the history of the US quarter?" I joke.

"Maybe not that one. But I do like history books. It's fascinating to read about the people and events that shaped the world, even if they are missing a large chunk of it."

She's referring to the non-human history of course. We all know this. Our history has been greatly fantasized into myths and legends, everyone forgetting the truth of it all. Especially since we began living in hiding. It was easier for the humans to pretend it was all make-believe instead of reality.

With the growing interest in fantasy books though, I wonder if the human world isn't ready to start believing again. That, however, is not my concern. I don't worry about educating ignorant humans on the truth of the world and convincing them thousands of years of their history is wrong. I'll leave that to some fairy who has lived through it all.

My only concern is Daisy.

"What about you? Do you read much? Were you serious about the porn magazine thing?" she asks so earnestly. I don't know that I've ever had a non-joking conversation about reading porn before.

"I read on occasion, more of a movie person myself. And

weirdly yes, I have read articles in porn magazines before. People joke about it but sometimes they can be quite illuminating."

"I'll have to keep that in mind next time I'm looking for something new to read. Medical textbooks just don't do the body justice. Though I suppose that has to do with the fact they're all about the human body. Even though we are nearly similar physiologically, where it counts."

"Is that so? I'd like to think I'm superior to most human men."

"I'm sure you do."

"What? You don't believe me?"

Daisy looks up at me through one squinted eye, the sun hitting her in the face as we head down the street back towards her house. She looks so relaxed and perfect under my arm that I nearly stumble watching her lean closer to me.

"I believe you," she says quietly, and my heart nearly triples in rhythm.

"Good," I clear my throat and tear my gaze away from hers, focusing on the road ahead of us. "Because if you didn't, I might have to prove myself, and then you'd be ruined for any male for the rest of your life."

Daisy laughs and the sound calms my nerves.

What the actual fuck is happening to me? I bought a girl romance novels, am walking with my arm around her and *not* trying to grope her ass. Though I very much want to grope her ass, and other parts of her.

Daisy's sweetness has drawn me in and captured me so thoroughly, I barely realize my desire to spend more time with her is genuine and not just driven by my need to deter my mom.

"Well, we wouldn't want that, now would we?"

"No, we most certainly wouldn't." *Because I plan on leaving in a few short weeks and you will be with other males after me.*

And that thought has me stewing in a funky uncomfortable contemplation the entire way back to her house.

When we arrive, I shake off the funk and focus on Daisy, on making an impression that makes her want to see me again. We're standing at the end of her drive, and I make sure she can't walk away just yet, holding both her shoulders to keep her facing me.

I've been controlling my tail's wild desires the entire time we were in the bookstore, but now I release my hold on it, allowing it to move freely as it desires. It immediately wraps around Daisy's ankle and slides up her skirt until it reaches her knee. The back of it is smooth and the tip of my tail lingers there. It makes my dick hard.

"Can I see you again? Soon."

"S-sure. I don't think Sage would approve but…"

"Sage doesn't matter, only you do Blossom."

With the knuckle of my finger, I lift her chin to angle her just right, before leaning down and brushing my lips against hers, intending to give her a tiny taste, just a sample. Something to keep her interested. The touch is barely a kiss, but it ignites the fire that lives in my blood. A demanding urge and need forces me to press harder, to take more.

Daisy gives in, just as greedy for it as I am. Our kiss becomes demanding, pressing hard before pulling back to suck and lick. Daisy's passion nearly knocks me on my ass. I hadn't expected her to be so…everything.

Her body presses into mine, erasing the last inches of space and when her soft pliant body melts against my hardness, I almost break. An inferno sparks to life in my chest, heating my entire body. A reaction only Daisy has stirred in me.

My cock is rock hard and grinding into her small frame. She has to feel it, there's barely any fabric between us with her mediocre layers. It doesn't seem to deter her, only spur her on more, because she's the one who deepens the kiss. Sliding her tongue past my lips and tasting me. She tastes like honeysuckle and tea. Sunshine and spring. I wonder if the rest of her tastes the same.

At thoughts of stripping her bare and having my way with her, I manage to muster enough strength to pull free of the kiss that will haunt my wet dreams for the rest of my life. Resting my forehead against hers, I try to catch my breath and force myself to be the gentleman my family has always tried to make me.

"Maybe next time Blossom. For now, why don't you go read your dirty books and think of me?"

I try to come off cocky and cool, but I'm breathless and feel like I'm standing on a seesaw.

"Okay," Daisy breaths against my lips and I almost lean in to kiss her again but manage to control myself.

I pass her the bag of books and she pulls out the one she picked for me and hands it to me, putting very much unwanted space between us. My body doesn't want her to leave. My tail latches on to her thigh and I can feel the heat radiating from the holy land between her legs. Good fucking lord, I bet if I slid up just a little farther, I'd encounter evidence of her own arousal.

I groan thinking about it but force my tail to release her. It takes a second for it to comply but eventually it does, reluctantly, and only after I tell myself we can feel her again tomorrow.

"Thanks," I mumble hoarsely. "For the book recommendation. Not the kiss. Although I liked that too, I wasn't thanking you for that. I mean."

Fuck. I've never stumbled over my words before with a

female. I need to take a step back and regroup.

"You're welcome. For both, just so we're clear."

Fucking, fuck, fuckity, fuck. I need to leave, *now*.

"Okay, well I'll be back."

"I look forward to it." Daisy's smile is sheepish but dripping in innuendo and lust. This girl has a hidden side, and I suddenly want to find out all about it.

"Yeah, right. Me too. Okay. Bye."

I turn on my heel and blindly walk in the general direction of my house, not paying any attention to anything. Replaying that fucking kiss and her sultry look in my mind, I don't immediately notice the additional vehicles parked in the driveway when I return home.

Chapter 9
Kai

My two sisters, who couldn't be any different from one another, have arrived. I completely ignored them last night, wanting to dive into my new romance book and desperately needing to jerk off. Talking to my sisters would only have killed my hardon and given me excruciating blue balls.

It took me a few minutes to figure out the one-handed read, but once I did, I think that book was better than porn. Far more graphic and detailed, way more intimate and sensual than the bad acting and gorilla grunting you get from online porn. I kind of wish I'd made her pick out one of those monster books. Even so, the book, plus my imagination and placing Daisy in the position of the main female lead, made me nut harder than any other solo session I've had.

This morning I'm better prepared to deal with my sisters. Freshly showered and rested after a late night of reading, and more than one intimate encounter with my hand has given me a little pep in my step.

"Good morning siblings," I greet, walking into the kitchen where three of my siblings are in various stages of making and eating breakfast.

"You are here. I was beginning to think Endo made the whole thing up. And I hear you've been getting familiar with the locals," Airi, my older and very pregnant sister says.

Wow, small towns really are something else, aren't they? I've done far more provocative things in my time abroad and not once has anyone ever commented on those escapades, but you take one local girl out to a bookstore, and everyone's interested.

"Nice to see you too, Airi. I've been great. How have you been?" I retort sarcastically.

We're not exactly the warm and cuddly kind of family, but it's fun to irk my sister. She's a rare mix of fire and water magic. Her temperament is just as stable, fluctuating from hot headed to go with the flow, depending on her mood. Today seems to be leaning towards hot headed.

Airi brandishes a sharp, dark eyebrow at me, her crimson markings flaring on her pale blue skin.

"Don't sass your older sister. Especially your pregnant older sister. I'm as likely to burn off all your hair as I am to give you a polite greeting."

Which is to say very likely. She's done it before.

"Don't you dare touch my hair. I've got it just the length I like it." I give my hair a little dramatic toss for good measure.

"I think your hair looks lovely Kai."

"Thank you, Keiko."

My youngest sister, and the only one of us with an ounce of humility and tenderness, crosses the kitchen to give me a genuine hug. It always seemed to me like the more children our parents had, the less they were like them in personality and disposition. The oldest two very much subtle clones, me the middle child wavering between their righteous stubbornness and actual emotions, then the two youngest who are as far from our family's typical spawn as possible.

"I'm so glad you were able to make it for the celebration. Mother and father will be so pleased to see you."

"Not once they get the bill from the house I rented in Greece."

Keiko only smiles, not at all capable of believing anything bad about anyone, including our parents. Keiko is too kindhearted. A trait none of us know how she got. Being a water nymph, she's already predisposed to being calm and chill. Our mother is a water and animal nymph, and although she possesses a chill calm that could put ice in your veins, she's never been as easy going as Keiko.

"Still, we're all happy to see you. It's been too long. Will you be staying through the equinox?" Keiko asks in her gentle voice; one I've never heard higher than a conversational pitch. It conveys her happiness and joy. I always love being around Keiko. She's grounding in a way that always frightens me in any other situation.

"Of course. It's why I came after all."

"And bringing a date, I assume?" Airi interjects. Looks like my plan is already working. If Airi's already heard about Daisy and is asking about her, mom will know in no time. "If the scant information I've been able to pry from Endo is true."

I look to Endo who gives me a blank stare. He wouldn't have told her the part where none of it is true, at least the mate bond part. Not sure if he actually told her that bit either. Might be better to save that part until mom arrives and I can tell her directly. Convincing my parents and extended family I'm planning on bonding with Daisy is one thing. Starting rumors in the town where she lives and has to deal with the aftermath when I leave, is another.

"Yes. Her name is Daisy, and she's an earth nymph." For a moment I contemplate if I should reveal Daisy's half human status now to my sister. It was always my intention, that was the reason I pursued her in the first place, isn't it? I'd rather they hear it from me than learn about it later. This way I can control the situation. "And half human."

Leaning a hip against the kitchen island I wait for my sister's inevitable disapproval. Unfortunately, she's bought into my mother's ramblings of pure blood importance and tainting the line bullshit. It doesn't come as explosive as I expected. It could be the pregnancy hormones, because Airi laughs. *Laughs.* Like hysterically as if I've just told the funniest joke in history.

It takes her a full two minutes to calm down and stop laughing, wiping the tears from her eyes and holding her rounded stomach.

"Oh man. I thought you were serious for a minute there. You wouldn't dare bring a half-breed as your date to an equinox celebration. Not even you're that stupid."

My jaw flexes under the strain of the effort it takes me not to bark out all the things wrong with not only her statement, but her beliefs. Daisy is ten times better than the majority of pure-blooded nymphs I've met in my life. She would never laugh or belittle another because of their mixed blood or family. Just look at how she's easily accepted me with who I'm unfortunate enough to be blood related to.

Crossing my arms over my chest, I decide to convey my disapproval of her in a different way, a way no nymph can ignore. "I guess I am that stupid."

Airi freezes at my words, absorbing all the emotions I

allowed to imbue that short statement. Disgust at her prejudice, anger at her blatant dismissal and disregard for myself and Daisy, and the protectiveness over Daisy that's been growing since the moment I met her. I knew there would be prejudice. That was the point in dating Daisy. But I find I hate seeing it directed at Daisy now.

Her expression goes flat, then her features pinch in displeasure, and I want to smack the look right off her face. "Well, I'm sure mom will just love that. You'll be disowned before the equinox and then we won't have to deal with your ridiculousness anymore." Airi stomps from the room, undoubtedly, to call mom and tattle on me.

One hurdle down. The next one will be mom and that one won't be so easy to clear. Her disapproval won't be as swift and fleeting. It'll linger and she'll try to convince me that her way is what's best for everyone. She's wrong of course, and I'm more than willing to let this play out all the way to my disavowal from the family. This family can suck it for all I care. I am so done pandering to their sensibilities and outdated ways.

I should have done this years ago. The feeling is freeing.

Endo sighs and returns to eating his omelet, while Keiko doesn't even flinch at our sister's outburst or my announcement.

"I'm sure she's a lovely girl."

"She is. I think you two will get along great."

"Then I look forward to meeting her."

Keiko's kindness smooths out the wrinkles in my anger caused by Airi. I knew it would be an unpleasant experience using Daisy to force a severance from my toxic family. It's only now just dawning on me how much I'm going to have to protect Daisy from them, and I will. With whatever small amount of decency I possess, I'll use it to ensure my blossom remains as sweet and happy as she was today, and not let their derision taint her.

Over my dead fucking body, will I let that happen.

Daisy

"And then he kissed me!" I tell Delphi. I've been regaling her with the story of Kai and I's adventure to the bookstore yesterday and she appears to be hanging on every word.

Delphi's little fanged mouth drops open as if shocked by my revelation.

"I know right? I couldn't help myself, I had to kiss him back. His lips were so soft and warm, I just melted into them. I've never been kissed like that before. Like if he didn't do it right that second, he may disintegrate from the lack of my touch. It was…" I sigh loudly, "amazing."

It's midafternoon and all day I half expected to see Kai strolling through the gardens and was only mildly disappointed when he didn't. Okay I was very disappointed when every male I heard wasn't him. I want to see him again but thought better of knocking on his door. I don't know who else is staying there with him, or how friendly they are. They are still the Kingsley's and I don't want to risk encountering one who is less than accepting of non-pure-blooded nymphs.

I hadn't thought about the fact that his family normally doesn't associate with us. Being with Kai is so different than with anyone else. Sometimes it's a little hard to think straight around him.

Delphi crawls over my lap and plucks a grape from the bowl on the table next to me. Sitting on the back porch my view is of our private gardens and the forest beyond. I decided it was time for an afternoon snack break and when I saw Delphi sniffing around the tree line, I decided to sit back here so I could visit with her out of sight.

I grab a few grapes and pop them in my mouth, sitting back in the bench swing hanging from the back porch rafters. It creeks quietly as I listen to the sounds of the forest and tune out any of the chatter from the nursery on the other side of the house.

The soothing sounds lull me into a hazy doze while Delphi crawls into my lap and curls up inside my oversized cardigan. She tucks in and we both settle for a peaceful nap in the balmy autumn afternoon.

Nearly silent footsteps rouse me from my half-asleep state not ten minutes later and I open one eye to see flaming red hair appear from around the side of the house. My heart instantly picks up its lazy beating, waking Delphi when I shift to get a better look.

She perks up and makes animated noises that sound excited to see Kai. She likes him almost as much as I do. Jumping from my lap she bounds towards Kai and scurries up his leg and around his body like a tree trunk stopping only once she's in his arms at his chest patting her little clawed fingers across his cheeks. Kai smiles and laughs.

"Hello Delphi, it's nice to see you again too. Have you been behaving yourself lately? No? Well, I can't blame you for that. I don't like behaving either," Kai chats with Delphi as he carries her all the way to me on the porch.

Pulling the sides of my cardigan together, I readjust my tail up my back and over my shoulder, the most comfortable way to carry it when wearing fitted denim jeans, the knitted coverage easily concealing it.

"You are not an easy girl to find. You know that?" he says in greeting, his eyes sparkling like flickering fire.

"No. I never leave so it should be fairly easy to find me."

"I searched every bush and corner of your greenhouse before I thought to check the house. If you weren't back here, I was going to start knocking on doors to find you. This would be a lot easier if you just gave me your cell number. Then I could just text you to find where you're hiding."

Delphi leaps from his arms and positions herself on a stool next to the bench swing. Kai makes himself comfortable next to me, sitting back in the seat as if he's done this a hundred times before.

"Wow, this is a really nice view. Your land is beautiful. I guess I shouldn't expect any less from a talented earth nymph like yourself and your brother."

I blush at the compliment. He's always doing that, and I don't always know how to respond.

"Thank you, but I don't have a cell number to give you."

Kai turns away from appreciating the backyard to frown at me. "What do you mean you don't have a cell number? Don't you have a cell phone?"

"No."

"Seriously? I didn't know there was anyone left in the world who didn't have a cell phone. How do people get ahold of you?" Kai asks this as if I have tons of friends constantly trying to reach me. When in reality, I don't think anyone has called for me since mom and dad last called to check in on things a few weeks ago.

"We have a landline, but no one ever calls for me," I admit.

Kai's frown only deepens. I distract myself by picking at a stray thread on my sweater. At least today I have on something thicker to conceal my reaction to Kai's virility.

"What have you been up to today?" I ask, doing what I do best and redirecting conversation away from myself.

"Mostly dealing with my family. A few more of my siblings arrived last night. My sisters."

"You don't sound very excited about them being here."

"One of them I'm happy to see. She's the best of us all. You remind me of her. The other, not so much. She's far too much like our mother, and let's just say is a handful on the best day and a knife in the back on others."

I don't have any sisters and my relationship with Sage is nothing like what he just described. Their family dynamic is way different than mine.

"I see."

"But don't worry, I won't let them keep me from seeing you, Blossom."

Kai reaches up and caresses the flowers in my hair. From my periphery they look to be geraniums and of course fucking jasmine. Thank goodness he doesn't know jasmine's mean I'm sexually aroused.

Fuck, what if my brother sees me with Kai and then notices the flowers? Does he even know what they mean? *It's okay. Just get it together Daisy. Think about something else and maybe stop staring at his throat and broad shoulders, and definitely do not look down into his lap.*

Trying to compose myself I alternate looking at his face and out to the yard, hoping the jasmines fade soon. Before I have a chance to formulate a thought the back door bangs open and Sage stomps out, not looking happy at all.

Delphi leaps from her stool in surprise and hides under the bench swing. I can feel her little hands holding on to my ankles protectively. She knows Sage won't hurt either of us. I wager the banging of the back door scared her is all.

"What are you doing here?" he sneers at Kai, who thankfully doesn't flinch at my brother's harsh tone.

"Just came to see Daisy."

"Why?"

"Am I not allowed to? She's never told me to leave before."

My brother scowls and prowls closer, arms crossed over his chest, the calm sage color of his skin darkening in anger.

"What do you want with my sister? Sleeping with all the single humans in town wasn't enough for you? You just had to get your hands on the innocent half-breed, didn't you?"

"Sage!" I gasp in horror and embarrassment at the vehemence in his words. I've never seen him like this. He's usually a pacifist, hates confrontation of any kind. And I've most certainly never heard him refer to me in such unpleasant terms.

"What? It's true. He's just looking to put another notch on his belt so he can brag about it to his friends, and maybe even rub it in his family's face." He turns his ire from me to Kai and continues. "I know how males like you operate and I will not let you drag my sister through the mud with you." Sage points an accusing finger directly at Kai, who to his credit doesn't flinch.

"I have no intention of dragging Daisy through the mud, as you so eloquently put it. She's a beautiful, smart, and interesting female, and I could care less if she's a half-breed. I don't let things like that decide how I treat a person," Kai speaks in a level but firm tone, meaning every single word he speaks. He can't fake that and Sage knows it.

Jumping from my seat I place myself between Kai and Sage and face off with my brother. He's taller than me and easily looks over my head at Kai, who I can sense standing as well.

"Sage, that is enough. You don't know what you're talking about."

"Unfortunately, I know exactly what I'm talking about. Even if he speaks pretty, flattering words."

"No, you don't."

At the stubborn tone in my voice, my brother stops scowling at Kai and looks down at me. Face still stern but questioning.

"You've never spoken to him or spent time getting to know him. You're judging him based on rumors, gossip, and predetermined beliefs based on who his family is."

Sage's face drops, along with his arms, in shock and defeat, realizing he's doing the very thing he always told me not to.

"We don't judge people without getting to know them first, right?"

He grumbles and looks down at the ground, his face twisting in regret.

"Right?"

"Right," he finally admits. Looking back up at me he sighs, and one corner of his lips pull in a faint smile. "When did you become the reasonable level headed one? I thought I was supposed to be the big brother giving you guiding life advice, not the other way around."

"Sometimes we can forget our own advice and act purely on instinct. Especially when protecting a family member, and I love you for that. But you have to remember I'm also an adult and can make decisions for myself."

Sage glares at Kai who remains silent and still behind me. Hopefully not doing anything to make me regret my words. I don't think Kai is what people see him as. He's more than what they see on the surface level, he just doesn't like to share it with everyone. His extroverted, outgoing personality masks his inner gentleness and vulnerability. I've seen it in the moments between us when no one else is looking. The layers beneath his outer shell.

"Fine. But I'll be watching him very closely." To Kai he adds, "Daisy is my only concern, her happiness and safety.

Do anything to risk either and I'll make sure you never touch another female in your life."

I look over my shoulder to see Kai nodding his head in agreement, a stern determined look on his face. "I would never intentionally hurt Daisy, it's the last thing I want."

Sage stares at him a few moments longer before accepting his words and the emotion he heard within them. Not a lie. Sometimes being a living lie detector comes in handy. Both male's postures remain taut but far less aggressive now.

"What are you doing here today?" Sage asks again, far more calmly than before.

"I wanted to ask Daisy to dinner at Dottie's tonight. If that's okay with you?" Kai doesn't sound condescending or patronizing, he's actually asking Sage's permission to take me to dinner, and my heart warms.

Shifting from foot to foot, Sage appears taken off guard by the honesty in Kai's tone. I give Kai a beaming smile and try to hide my pleasure. I'm sure my flowers give me away but neither male is looking at them right now, only each other. Each sizing the other up, both finding they reluctantly like the other, I think.

Sage nods and Kai visibly unclenches, letting out a quiet breath. Was he worried Sage would stop me from going out with him? For the first time in my life, I actually want to go out with a guy and no matter what Sage said I would have, one way or another.

Looking to me, Sage smiles and places a strong hand on my shoulder. "You're my little sister Daiz, I have to be the big brother sometimes. I just want you safe and happy."

"And I am both of those things. Don't worry, if he steps out of line, you'll be the first to know."

At that he grins, a little maniacally, far more calm and

relaxed than when he first burst out of the house.

"If I don't have to castrate you first, maybe you could come over for dinner sometime? Have a proper introduction, maybe prove my sister right?"

Kai looks shocked at Sage's offer, but that's just how he is. Willing to admit his wrong and make it right, or at least try to. He's willing to let Kai prove himself to be more than his rumored reputation.

Kai stutters for a moment, looking as if he's never been invited over for dinner before.

"Sure. I'd like that," he finally says.

"Good. Tomorrow night then?"

Tomorrow is Friday, a prime evening for going out to the bar and picking up girls. Sage is testing him already. It's strange to have my big brother testing a male for his right to... what? Court me? Date me? I have no idea where this is going but I'm just going to let it take its natural course and find out.

"Tomorrow sounds perfect."

Sage seems satisfied with Kai's dinner acceptance and gives me a kiss on the top of my head before returning back inside the house without another word.

"Well, that was..."

"Intense?" I finish for Kai.

"Something like that. I don't think I've ever had a showdown with a big brother before. It was oddly nice."

I chuckle and shuffle on my feet, folding my hands inside the sleeves of my sweater.

"Nice? Why was it nice?"

For the first time since we met, Kai blushes, his cheeks reddening, complimenting his crimson stripes. "I've never had to *meet the family* of anyone I've dated. It's nice to see a family that's protective of one another out of love. I kind of like it.

Gives me more reason not to fuck up."

Realizing what he's saying, my heart flutters and a heated knot forms in my stomach. *I am different from all the rest.*

Taking the few steps to Kai, I reach up on my tip toes and press a tender kiss to his cheek, which he wasn't expecting either.

"So, you mentioned dinner at Dottie's?" I ask coyly. I've never been the bold one, but I feel braver around Kai. Like I want to be more outgoing and playful.

Kai smiles and rests a hand on my back, his thumb stroking up and down, a sensation I still feel through the knit of the cardigan.

"I'd take you anywhere you wished, if you kiss me like that every time I see you."

"Just a peck on the cheek? That's not asking a lot."

"Seems like a fair price to me."

The knots in my stomach snap and become butterflies flying up my lungs and throat, choking me with their beating wings.

"Come on, Blossom. Let's go get dinner before your brother comes back and chops off my tail."

Delphi takes that opportunity to hop from her hiding spot and plop her fluffy little body directly between us, forcing Kai to release me and hold her or risk dropping her. Of course he catches her. She chitters wildly at him.

"Sorry Delphi, you can't come with us. Maybe you can join us tomorrow when I come over for dinner though. How does that sound?"

Delphi responds in her sprite language I can't understand.

"Alright then, it's a date." Kai sets her down and she stands on her hind legs looking up at us both.

"I'll see you later Delphi. You can hang out in my room and

if you're good I'll bring you back something from Dottie's."

At the promise of treats, Delphi's ears perk up and she hurries over to the back door where she expertly opens it and squeezes her fluffy butt inside.

Kai and I both laugh at the sprite's antics.

"Are all sprites like her?" Kai asks. "I haven't spent much time with them and now I think I'm missing out."

"I don't think so. I think she's just like that from spending too much time with me."

"Doesn't sound like a bad thing."

Kai lets his words, and their meaning, linger in the air and I have to clear my throat and force myself to look away or we'll stand here all night like this.

"So, dinner?"

"Of course. Lead the way."

Chapter 10
Daisy

The walk to *Dottie's Diner* goes much like the walk to *Tall Tails*. Kai casually touching me and directing me, when we reach Dottie's parking lot, his hand finds its way to my waist. I can feel eyes on us, I know people are curious and nosy. But when Kai leans down and whispers in my ear, I completely forget them.

"You okay, Blossom? This isn't too much for you, is it?"

"No, I'm fine. I'm not going to break down or freak out, I just don't know how to behave in crowds or public places."

Kai leans in close, engulfing me in his warmth and strength instantly easing my anxious fidgeting. His nose brushes against the tip of my ear through my hair and it sends a shiver through my body that coalesces between my thighs, forcing my thoughts away from my awkwardness in public interactions and directly on his lips nearly against my skin. I can hear his deep inhale and smothered moan.

"You can't walk into Dottie's smelling like that, little

blossom."

"Like what?" I ask breathlessly, needing desperately to know what caused him to moan like that.

"Like you're looking for a male to fuck. You have me now Daisy, no need to attract every male in the diner. I'll gladly take care of any need you have."

His words are like hot honey coating my skin and absorbing into my pores. If he expects me to be less aroused after that statement, he is out of his mind. If anything, it revved me up even further.

"Saying things like that, doesn't exactly help," I scold him with little fervor. My protest more of a whimpering plea.

"Well then you'll just have to stay close to me, so everyone knows you're mine."

"I am?"

The proclamation is said with such simple frankness, I can barely comprehend the words. Two simple words that when put together have such great meaning. *You're mine.* How have we made it to this point in only a few days of knowing each other? Is it always like this with others? Am I just not experienced enough with relationships to know the normal process?

"Of course, you are, Daisy. I never expected to find you when I went walking through the forest, but I'm thankful that I did."

I may not be able to hear every minute emotion, but even I can tell he's surprised by his own words and how true they are.

We stand there in the parking lot, pressed close together and breathing in each other's air and scents, only getting more aroused with every passing second. Half an hour ago I was excited to be going on a dinner date with Kai. Now I wish I had said no and kept him at home in my greenhouse.

Pocket Full of Posies

Kai presses a chaste kiss on my lips, not lingering long enough to get pulled in by the overwhelming yearning I know we're both experiencing.

"Come on, let's get you fed."

"Uh huh," I nod wordlessly, trying to calm my racing heart.

By the time we make it to the front door I've managed to force myself into a semblance of calm and collected. At least as much as possible with my social anxiety. An anxiety which doesn't seem so overbearing when standing next to Kai and held in his strong embrace.

We're greeted by a young girl working as the hostess tonight and sat in a booth. Kai gestures for me to sit first and then slides in next to me, resting an arm on the vinyl cushion behind us. Instantly my body loosens and I'm able to ease into a comfortable position. It's as if Kai knew I needed him close to ease my nerves. Secure between him and the wall, I feel safe and protected.

Since it's been an indeterminate amount of time since I last ate at Dottie's, I pluck up a menu and start reading it over.

"Oh, my goodness. Daisy?" The astonished and delighted voice of Becca, a fairy who works as a waitress at the diner, draws mine and Kai's attention away from the menu. "I haven't seen you in here in ages, and with Kai Kingsley to boot. The two of you are a sight for sore eyes. I thought Donna was pulling my leg when she told me about you two. I'm glad she wasn't. You look perfect together. Why didn't I think to pair you up before?"

Becca rambles on in her good natured and animated way, her pink wings fluttering behind her to match her gesticulating hands. From what I hear from Sage and Tobias, Becca is a bit of a matchmaker, or at least attempts to be. Reports are she has yet to be successful in her pairings. One more well-known mismatch being when she tried to hook up Hunter, our mayor, with his own cousin. I cringe considering who she would have paired me with, given the chance.

"Good evening to you too, Becca. What's good on the menu tonight?"

Becca lists off the evening's specials, some fancy cut of steak being the most expensive and attracting Kai's interest.

"Perfect. We'll have two of those, medium, with grilled mushrooms and loaded baked potato."

Becca stops midway through writing the order on her notepad and stares down at Kai. I do the same, giving Kai an apologetic smile. He notices both of us and looks back and forth before settling on me.

"What? You don't like steak? They have fried chicken or spaghetti if you'd like."

I stall, trying to figure out the most polite way to tell him I don't eat meat, without making him feel humiliated in front of Becca. In my delayed response and fumbling, Becca blurts it out for me.

"Daisy is a vegetarian. She doesn't eat meat at all. Shouldn't you know that if you're dating?"

I want to correct her that we're not dating, but I also don't mind her thinking we're dating, because I want to date him. I've never dated before and I think I'd enjoy it with Kai.

"Oh, I'm sorry, Daisy. I didn't mean to assume."

"It's okay, we haven't really talked about it, so how would you know?"

"We have a delicious stuffed pasta shell and red sauce with fresh parmesan if you're in the mood for Italian," Becca offers, easily smoothing over any discomfort.

"That sounds great. Thank you."

Before Becca can roll away on her skates, which look like a

ton of fun, Kai stops her with a lifted hand.

"Wait. I'll have the same thing as well."

"You don't have to change your meal just because of me. I don't mind if other people eat meat."

"No, it's okay. Stuffed shells sound appetizing." Kai gives me a reassuring smile and the hand resting around my shoulders squeezes gently.

"Alrighty. Two stuffed shells coming right up. Anything to drink?" Becca asks.

Instead of immediately ordering Kai looks to me and waits.

"Iced tea?"

"With lemon." Kai adds.

Becca rolls away on her skates, with a huge smile plastered on her face, to put in our order.

Turning to face Kai, I fiddle with the frayed hem of my jean shorts under the table. "You didn't have to do that. I don't mind if you want to eat a steak."

"I didn't do it for you. I told you, stuffed shells sounded better than a steak." He shrugs and acts like he didn't just change his entire order to match mine on purpose. He acts all cool and tough, but really he's a softy.

"Okay, sure."

"Have you always been a vegetarian?"

"For a long time yeah. I think ever since I met Delphi when I was a kid. I couldn't imagine eating another creature that was as sweet as her."

Kai's thumb brushes over my shoulder and the movement shifts the neckline of my cardigan enough for his finger to connect with my skin. My attention instantly focuses on that touch, but Kai just continues talking as if this is nothing new.

"How old were you when you found Delphi?"

"About ten. She was just a kit, and I heard her crying.

She was all alone and when I asked mom if we could bring her home, she said yes. We made a house for her on the back porch so she could learn to live outside like a normal sprite. We didn't want her becoming completely dependent on us. That wouldn't be fair, when she is likely to outlive us all. Well, except maybe Tobias."

Talking about Delphi puts me at ease, and it gets easier to talk to Kai without my heart practically leaping out of my chest through my throat.

"And who's Tobias?"

"He's Sage's husband and mate. He's a fairy. You'll meet him at dinner tomorrow night."

"Is he the one who works at *Ugly Mug* and tells you what coffee you need to order?"

"That's the one." I laugh and relax even further.

"And he lives with you and your brother Sage?"

"Yeah. He and Sage moved back to Snowberry when I was born. We've always been a pretty close family. Tobias is just as much my brother as Sage is."

"I wish my family was more like yours," Kai admits quietly, his voice becoming wistful.

From the little information I've managed to pick up on, Kai doesn't seem to get along well with his family. He mentioned siblings. He has at least two sisters and I still don't know how Endo is related to him.

"You mentioned your sisters weren't your only siblings. How many do you have?"

"Total, there are five of us. I'm the middle child. Two older and two younger. Ren is my oldest brother, Airi my sister after him, then me, then Keiko, my favorite sister, followed by youngest brother, Endo. I'm closest with Endo but would choose Keiko's company over any of them any day."

Pocket Full of Posies

Well, now I know how he's related to Endo. Since non-humans don't always have physical similarities to our siblings, it's not as easy to spot familial resemblances.

"Wow. That's a lot of siblings. Must have been crazy in your house as a kid."

Kai scoffs. "Not really. We're all so far apart from each other in age, that by the time the next was born the previous was already grown and on their own. Not to mention we spent more time in exclusive non-human boarding schools, than at home. My childhood was filled with rulers to the knuckles and many hours spent in detention. If you couldn't tell, I was a bit of a troublemaker."

Kai gives me a mischievous grin and I can tell he's recalling fond memories of all the trouble he got into in school. I had issues in school as well, but mine involved getting bullied by kids, both human and non-human. Being introverted and unable to glamour made me the strange kid in school, which also made me an easy target for childish taunts.

I know now none of them were being truthfully malicious. It's just what kids do. But still it was enough to make me ask to be homeschooled. I didn't have to hide my markings or ears, explain why the grass was literally greener where I sat in the field for lunch, or why I was talking to the flowers. With my parents, Sage, and Tobias I had more than enough educated and intelligent individuals to teach me everything I needed to know.

"What about you, Blossom? Were you a troublemaker? I bet you drove all the boys crazy, didn't you?"

I laugh with little humor. "Not even close. I left public schooling before my second year of high school to be homeschooled. I didn't fit in with the other kids and it was just easier for me to stay home."

"Why is that?" Kai asks, his normally blazing red eyes a soft garnet as he watches me, so engrossed in our conversation.

"I don't know if you've noticed, but I don't glamour myself around humans. I can only hold one for a short period of time, which made it difficult to go to school when I was younger because I couldn't conceal my ears or my markings. I guess I'm just lucky that my features present as more human and people just assume my markings are tattoos."

Kai watches me, and I can feel his tail lazily twitching against my bare leg under the table.

"So, your parents were your teachers?"

"And Sage and Tobias. Tobias is really, *really* old so he knows a lot of stuff. He was my history and language teacher."

"You speak other languages?"

I blush at his continued interest in me and am given a moment of reprieve as Becca returns with our tea and lemons. Kai removes his arm from the back of the booth to squeeze the lemon and stir in sugar.

"So, you were about to tell me how many languages you speak," he probes, once he gets his tea just the way he likes it.

"You are relentless, aren't you?"

He shrugs and smirks, sipping his tea through the straw, but never shifts his gaze away from me. I sigh and give in to telling him more about myself, the little there is to know. But only after taking a long slow drink of my own tea.

"I am fluent in Italian. Tobias wanted me to speak the language of love. He also taught me Latin and Greek, but I forgot those almost as immediately as he taught them to me. And I also know a little Norwegian. Tobias spent a lot of time there and said I should know a language that isn't as common. Not that I've ever had a reason to use them, other than to converse with Tobias."

"So, you've never travelled outside of Snowberry?"

"Never."

"Why not?"

At risk of sounding like a broken record and repeating myself and the reasons I was homeschooled, since they're the same main reasons I don't travel, I take the easy way out.

"Just haven't. Don't really feel the need to."

"Not even to put that love language to use?" Kai's voice is filled with mirth and teasing, as is his expression.

"Not yet."

"I love traveling, I've been to Italy many times. Would you be interested in traveling to Italy someday? Maybe I can be your guide."

"I haven't really thought about it but, yeah, I think if given the opportunity I'd like to visit other places. But it's not high on my to do list. I like staying home, seeing to my gardens and flowers."

"We're opposite in that way. I like to always be on the move, travelling. I rarely stay in the same place for more than a few months. I think I've lived in almost every country at least once."

"Why is that?"

Kai falters at my question. I don't think anyone has ever asked him that before. I don't think he's ever considered why himself. His eyes fall to the glass of tea in his hand on the table as he considers his answer.

"I think at first it was to escape my parents, and the restrictions of my family. But after a few years, they didn't care anymore where I was or what I was doing. Yet I continued to move around. My family isn't known for being overly affectionate and emotional and I think every time I got too close and comfortable in one place with anyone, it scared me.

I don't know how to handle serious emotions. If you haven't noticed yet, I use humor and flirting to lighten situations and avoid serious conversations."

He chuckles and shakes his head, his fire red hair brushing against his cheeks and curling around his charcoal horns. His appearance is all fire and heat with sharp features and strong lines, but inside, he's just as fragile as I am.

"I avoid conversations altogether," I admit, which has Kai turning to look at me, the edges of his eyes softening. "I don't even try to talk to people. Instead, I hide out in my greenhouse and behind my flowers, so I don't have the opportunity to get involved with anyone."

"You talked to me."

The smile that stretches across Kai's face is beautiful in its authenticity. It's not flirty or seductive, it's real and boyish, giving me a glimpse of the unguarded male underneath all the posturing and flirting.

"Well, that's only because you befriended Delphi. If she hadn't liked you, I would have strangled you with vines."

My attempt at humor actually works, his posture and demeanor eases and I feel his smile settle into my soul when he looks at me.

"I didn't know your abilities included villainous superpowers. Are you practicing to be in a comic book?"

"Maybe. I was partial to Poison Ivy."

After breaking the tension of the serious conversation, we talk easily, the conversation flowing naturally. Starting at my abilities with plants and earth, then his abilities with animals and fire. In the middle of it our food arrives, and we talk while eating. Kai asks about my parents, and I happily tell him all about my botanist human mother and earth nymph father and how they met and married. Deciding to move to Snowberry when they found out my mother was pregnant with me.

Being a hybrid child is filled with unknowns. They had no idea if I would be more human or more nymph and what that meant for my future. They wanted to be somewhere safe and accepting of non-humans. Apparently, no matter where you go there's always people who will judge you no matter what. At least here in Snowberry I know I won't be ostracized for being half-human among the local non-human community. It was really only an issue when I was a preteen and teen trying to fit in with the humans.

Now that I think about it, it's been years since I last heard anyone make a negative comment or remark about me in any way. Maybe I should take Sage's advice and get out more. Perhaps I should consider Kai's offer to visit Italy. Tobias would surely approve of me getting to use my Italian.

Why shouldn't I? I've done nothing but hide out in my gardens in fear of what could happen. Not paying attention to what is happening, to life going on around me, and me letting it.

A strange new sense of purpose and optimism grows in my chest. Maybe next time I'll say yes, instead of using the excuse of working at the nursery to avoid social interactions. The time I've spent with Kai has shown me that maybe I can go out, at least minimally. I'm not going to be performing in the holiday talent show anytime soon, but maybe I could attend and watch. From the back. Baby steps, okay. I'm only capable of so much at a time.

Being so engrossed in Kai I haven't been paying attention to those around us, which I normally would. I'd be worrying about who's looking at me, what they're thinking, if they can see my ears, what my flowers are doing. I haven't thought of one of those things since sitting down with Kai though. As such, I don't notice Hunter and Lottie approaching our table until they're standing right in front of us.

"Hello Daisy. It's nice to see you outside your gardens for a change." Hunter smiles at me and I feel a little awkward but nothing as uncomfortable as in the past.

"Hi Hunter. Nice to see you, and you too. Lottie, right?" I ask to confirm I wasn't remembering her name incorrectly. It has happened before. Sometimes I zone out when people talk to me, and names just slip through the cracks.

"Yes. It's nice to see you again. How is everything at the nursery? Are you all as busy running around preparing for the equinox as we are?"

I relax and smile. This is something I can talk about without bumbling through my words and sounding like a moron.

"Yes. We'll probably even have to bring in a few of our part time employees to help out soon."

"I'm so excited to experience my first equinox. Hunter says it's quite a party. Are you going to be there? I'm told it's a very important celebration for—" she pauses and looks around before whispering and mouthing exaggeratedly, "Nymphs and fairies."

Lottie smiles wide and dances a little on her feet in excitement. She's only just recently discovered the non-human world and is already taking to it better than I ever have. Being a pop star, she's had a lot of practice with large crowds, singing on stage and being the center of attention. We're not supposed to know all this, but because Tobias was asked to help deal with the elf problem, we know a little more than the rest of the town. Lottie used to be a famous pop star. Like *'travel the world and perform for millions of people'* famous. I would die if I had to perform on stage in front of that many people.

"Oh, um, I'm not sure. I haven't been before, but my brother always wants me to go with them."

"I'd be happy to take you." Kai interjects. "I was going to ask you anyway."

Shock has me momentarily speechless. No one other than my brother or family has ever asked me to go to the celebration with them.

Only minutes ago, I had internally decided to do more in the community and already that declaration is being tested. Here's my opportunity to participate in a social event. One that Sage has been trying to get me to attend for years. It's not much more than a giant party in the woods, with food, music, and dancing.

Non-humans of all kinds come and set up tents and campsites where they congregate and hang out. But Lottie is correct. These types of celebrations are highly attended by nymphs and fairies. Shifters have their full moons; we have the solstice and equinox. Many of us have close connections to the earth and animals when it comes to our abilities, so we celebrate the earth and the changing of seasons. It's something we've always done. I don't even know how long ago it started. The lack of historical documents recording non-human history accurately means we have no idea where some of our oldest traditions came from.

The equinox celebration lasts nearly forty-eight hours. Beginning at dawn on day one and ending at dusk on day two. Spending two whole days and one night in the designated celebration area. An area that fairies in town mark off with their magic and conceal from human eyes, as well as human interaction. Forming a barrier that acts like a force field, keeping anyone of non-human blood out. It also creates a glamour of an empty quiet forest, so non-humans can be comfortable in their true form without a glamour or worry they might say or do something a human might see and freak out over. People use their abilities freely, fairies fly overhead, magic is present in nearly everything. Or at least so I'm told. Not ever having experienced it, I can only imagine what it's like.

But I want to experience it, I realize, and with Kai.

"I didn't realize you two were so close," Hunter says, breaking my dazed stare at Kai.

Kai looks up at Hunter who stands like a mountain over us still sitting in the pink and teal vinyl booth. He doesn't show it but somehow, I can sense it in his micromovement shifting on the seat, he's insulted by Hunter's insinuation.

"It's a recent development. That doesn't make it any less sincere."

Hunter narrows his eyes at Kai and tilts his nose into the air sniffing. Shifters use their advanced sense of smell to sense changes in a person's emotions. It's not as precise as a nymph's ability to hear lies but they can smell if someone is feeling guilty or deceitful and draw conclusions.

Kai straightens his spine and sits tall and proud. He's not going to back down from Hunter though I imagine if Hunter asserted his alpha power, he wouldn't be able to fight it. I really hope they don't start fighting in Dottie's over me. I really wouldn't be able to show my face in town ever again if that happened.

"Time with someone doesn't determine the significance of the relationship with them. Wouldn't you agree?" Kai raises an eyebrow in question.

Shifting an arm around Lottie's waist, Hunter grunts, and poor Lottie looks completely lost at their conversation. I'm not. Shifters scent their mates and know instantly they're meant to be together. Sometimes it doesn't happen right away or at their first meeting but once it does happen almost nothing can stop them from being with each other. It's an instinctual connection. Nymphs choose. We form permanent mate bonds, but we can do it with anyone of our choosing, shifters cannot. Hunter understands how important a person can become in a short amount of time, his current relationship with Lottie proof of that.

Lottie and her bright blue eyes ignore Hunter and Kai's male posturing and focus on me. "So, what do you say, Daisy? Are you going to come with Kai? I think it's going to be a lot of fun. It would be a shame if you missed it."

It's going to happen again in a few months for the next equinox, but I don't point that out. Apparently, this equinox is going to be something special. And for the first time in my life I want to go.

"I'd love to go with you, Kai."

Kai's head whips around so fast his red hair flutters with the momentum. Blazing ruby eyes burn into me and I feel the heat of his stare all the way to my bare toes and the tip of my tail that curls around my shoulder under my sweater.

"Really?" he questions in astonishment.

"Really. I want to go."

"Perfect." Lottie claps her hands excitedly. "We will see you there then. Come on Hunt, let's leave them alone to enjoy their dinner." She pulls at Hunter's arm directing him away from the table.

"Enjoy your meal," he says nodding at Kai and then me, smiling wider before following Lottie's insistent directing to leave us alone.

When they've returned to their own table on the opposite side of the diner Kai's posture eases and he slyly looks over at me, a lopsided smile on his face.

"You know we are going to share a tent at the equinox."

A blush instantly heats my entire face and neck. I most certainly had not thought about sleeping arrangements.

"Well, you'll just have to make sure there are two beds then."

His grin only widens. "I most certainly will not. You're going to have to cuddle with me all night to stay warm, and clothing is optional."

I smack him in the chest and try to cover up my embarrassment with a laugh. This equinox could very well be the most important of my life, if for nothing more than the possibility of losing my virginity.

Chapter 11
Kai

Tonight is the night I have my first dinner with the family of a girl I'm dating or interested in dating. I guess we haven't solidified that yet. Even though I'm telling anyone in my family who asks that we are, Daisy and I haven't named what's between us. Because there is *something* between us. This is going so much farther than pretending.

Logically I should end it now. Give up this whole farse. But in my heart, it's no longer a farse. I can sense real emotions growing for Daisy and I don't want to leave. Not like I usually would. In the past whenever I'd start to feel a growing connection or bond with anyone, lover or friend, I would leave. I would never let things get real.

I want something real with Daisy. For the first time in my life, I'm not going to run away from my emotions. I'm not going to push them down and pretend they don't exist or cover them up with partying and the playboy persona everyone believes me to be. And the first step to doing that is dinner with the family.

Ironic since I'm currently ignoring my family. Everyone except Endo and Keiko. Airi keeps trying to pry but I brush her off. Dodging her, and now my cousins that have arrived, is fairly easy with how huge the house is. I call it a house but it's a mansion. Something like twenty rooms and twice as many bathrooms. I never cared to count or pay attention and am thankful for the extravagant opulence offering reprieve.

Sneaking out of the back door to go to Daisy's, I pass by Endo. He gives me a knowing look and just smiles as I gesture with a finger to my lips for him to be quiet. Shaking his head, his shoulders shake with silent laughter. I'm not sure if Endo approves or disapproves of how attached I'm becoming to Daisy. For once I hope he approves.

If this continues with Daisy, I'll most likely be disowned, and if not, I'll disown myself. Being part of this family has never given me anything of significance to better my life, except for Endo and Keiko. I hope that no matter what happens, I will at least retain my relationship with them.

I arrive at Daisy's house, and this time I don't have to wander around checking every nook and cranny to find her. I know exactly where she'll be. Striding up the front porch steps, I check the collar of my shirt and sleeve cuffs. This is the first time I've put effort into my appearance, not just to attract a female but to hopefully impress those important to her. Choosing a white button up and dark wash jeans, I hope it's nice enough but not too nice. I'm not trying to flash my wealth, they don't care about that.

Two seconds after I knock on the door, it swings open and Sage stands there in front of me with a shit eating grin on his face. I can only imagine what he has in store for me tonight. Or I guess I can't, since I've never done this before.

Pocket Full of Posies

"Evening, Kai. Glad you could make it tonight."

Oh yeah, he's going to do everything he can to make me as uncomfortable as possible tonight. Too bad it's not going to work. I've had decades of preparation attending uncomfortable family events. There's nothing he could possibly do that could make me flinch.

"Sage. Good to see you again. I'm happy to be here." I reach out a hand in offering and he takes it. Giving me a cursory once over.

"I'm sure I don't have to tell you that Daisy is very important to us and we're not going to go easy on you. If you do or say anything that leads us to believe you have anything but honorable intentions with her, we will make sure you never have contact with her again. Daisy is too sweet and forgiving to be taken advantage of by anyone. Am I understood?"

"I can't promise I'll be honorable, it's not in my nature. But I can promise I won't hurt her. That I'll do everything in my power to make her happy. That I'll do anything she demands of me. I've never...wanted to be better for someone, and I'll admit this is all pretty new to me too, so I might fuck up. But I'll try."

Sage's studies me closely and offers a nod, hearing the truth not just in my voice but written on my face. "Alright then. I suppose that'll have to do. Come on in."

Stepping back, he gestures with one arm for me to enter and I quickly step over the threshold. The interior of the house is just as charming as the exterior. Filled with potted plants and colorful art on the walls. There's a variety of nicknacks that look to be from multiple different countries and even eras. Pieces that could be hundreds of years old displayed under glass.

We pass by a room lined with bookshelves and an oversized armchair by a large window that looks well used, occupied with a tousled throw blanket and pillow. I can picture Daisy curled up there reading her naughty books.

I follow Sage through the older style home that boasts a central hall with doorways into separate rooms. We end in a large dining space just off the kitchen with a set of stairs leading up to the second floor. Bounding down those steps, barefoot as always, is my blossom. Dressed in a sweet cornflower blue dress that brushes her thighs and an ivory cardigan, Daisy looks as innocent as a bunny and the part of me that lacks propriety instantly wants to do naughty things to her in that dress and prove she's not as innocent as she looks.

"Hi," she says the one word greeting with such breathy fondness, I nearly fall to my knees at her feet.

"Hello. You look beautiful tonight."

Daisy blushes and the flowers in her hair bloom larger, daisies and a peony. She always looks like she's wearing a crown of flowers, and it makes me want to buy her a real crown. The visible green markings on her neck and legs shift as she walks the last few steps and stops directly in front of me. I can see how that might have been troublesome in public school with humans and unable to glamour.

"Thank you. You look handsome as well."

We stare at each other in silence, never breaking eye contact and I completely forget there are other people present until a voice breaks through our connection.

"Hi Kai, I'm Tobias. I know we've met in passing at *Ugly Mug* but it's nice to formally meet you."

I turn to face Tobias, a tall pale lavender skinned fairy with matching silver lavender wings, long white hair that's pulled half up, and eyes so light they're practically white. From his coloring alone I can tell he's old. Probably close to a millennia. It doesn't appear his years have dampened his disposition though.

Tobias smiles wide and sincere, extending his hand out for mine. I shake it and am happy he doesn't do the normal male posturing of squeezing as hard as possible to try and assert dominance. He's completely confident in himself that he doesn't need to resort to rudimentary intimidation tactics. I instantly like him.

"Nice to meet you too."

"Would you like something to drink?" he asks.

"Shouldn't you be telling me what I need to drink?" I retort jokingly, knowing his affinity for telling customers what type of coffee they will order.

Tobias smiles and I can see I've already gotten on his good side.

"Touché. I'd say you could do with...a glass of red wine."

"Sounds great."

"Perfect."

Tobias goes into the updated kitchen and pulls down a bottle from a built-in wine rack and begins to open it and pour four glasses.

"Tell me Kai," Sage begins, while Daisy guides me to sit at the already set dining table. "How old are you?"

The question takes me by surprise. Age isn't of great importance to non-humans since we live for so long and remain in our physical peak for most of our lives. To us age *is* just a number. Meaning nothing more than how much life experience you have.

Daisy sits in the chair next to me while Sage takes the one directly across from me, both waiting for my answer.

"Eighty-seven. Why?"

"Daisy is only twenty-three. She's still young, even among non-humans. I just want to make sure you're aware of that."

Daisy's age is no surprise to me. She's obviously still young, but that doesn't mean she's not an adult.

"She's also half-human and as such we don't know how long her life expectancy will be. I don't want her wasting her time."

"Sage," Daisy grumbles at my side, obviously embarrassed at her brother's blatant discussion of her right in front of her.

Reaching under the table, I slide a hand over her knee and squeeze reassuringly. Her scowl at her brother immediately drops and turns to delight directed at me, and with that bolstering my confidence, I turn to face off with her protective big brother.

"I completely understand. I wouldn't want to waste her time either. But if she's willing to give me even a second of it, I'll gladly accept it."

Tobias enters and places a wine glass in front of each of us and takes one for himself, sitting in the seat next to Sage. Why do I feel like this is going to be a good cop, bad cop situation?

Before any more interrogation can take place, Delphi's plump furry body bounds through an open window and lands directly in my lap.

"Hi friend! You're here. You wanna see what I found?"

"Hi Delphi. I would love to see what you found."

"Look, look."

Delphi reaches into her fur, most likely having a pocket like a kangaroo, and produces a neon orange golf ball. Holding it up in her little hand, she pushes it into my face for inspection.

"See? See? So bright and pretty. Like tiny sun."

"Oh yes, that's very lovely. I think it'll go well with your nest. Don't you?"

Delphi falls into a long-winded one-sided discussion over the best place to put it in her nest, and I look up to find Tobias grinning and Sage glaring suspiciously at me.

"You can understand her?" he asks.

"Yes. She's quite chatty. I met her when I first met Daisy."

"How *did* you meet Daisy? I'm curious how the two of you crossed paths and ended up here."

How we met isn't anything dubious, but Sage may question my intentions out in the woods alone. Confessing my original plans for Daisy feels dirty and deceitful, especially since my feelings for her have changed so drastically.

"My brother just arrived in town to prepare the house for my family's arrival and was threatening me with cleaning duties. So instead, I escaped out the back and went for a walk in the woods. I heard Delphi and Daisy talking and followed the sound, finding them inspecting Delphi's hoard and nest."

Sage cocks a brow at me. "And you just thought, wow what a great opportunity to flirt with a pretty girl?"

"Basically, yeah. I'm not going to lie. If I see a pretty girl and want to talk to her, I usually do. I'm not a shy person."

"Now that you're with my sister, are you going to continue to talk to unknown pretty girls in the woods?"

His question instantly offends me. I understand his protectiveness of Daisy but am insulted he would think I would ever do such a thing to her.

"No. I told you I wouldn't hurt her, and that includes emotionally. Being with Daisy is a gift that I don't intend on squandering."

"*Delphi likes Kai. Wants Kai to stay, play with Delphi. Know you speak true. Like Daisy a lot.*"

I wish the others could understand Delphi. Sprites don't lie, they sense things within others we can't even fathom. To have a sprite speak highly of me in such a warm way would definitely prove to Sage I have no ill intentions with his sister.

That may have been my initial motivation, but how we came together means nothing now that we're here. Now that my feelings are progressing towards something real. I know Daisy's are true. She would never feign attraction and affection just to lead a person on. She's too pure for that. She acts on instinct, there's nothing fake about her.

"I think Delphi approves of him," Daisy states softly, while petting Delphi's colorful fur. "And if she approves of him, maybe you can too?"

Daisy looks to her brother and his mate. Tobias has already accepted me, I can tell. Sage is the hold out, still wanting to hold on to his preconception of me and finding less and less to do so.

"Fine. I suppose if Delphi likes him, I can give him a chance."

"Thank you, Sage."

Sage smiles at his sister and lets out a loud exhale, his posture relaxing.

"Well, now that that's done. Would anyone like an appetizer? I made stuffed mushrooms."

Daisy hums in delight and excitedly helps Tobias bring over the couple plates laden with vegetarian appetizers. Noticing the obvious lack of meat, I wonder if this is the norm or if Sage wanted to test me again to see how I would react.

I dig into the offered bites and happily devour the delicious food. There doesn't have to be meat included in a dish for it to be good, and I'm pretty sure I see Sage's lips twitch with approval.

Pocket Full of Posies

Daisy

Dinner goes surprisingly well. After Sage's initial harshness, he eases up and we're able to have a pleasant evening. By the end of the night everyone is joking and laughing like old friends. Kai is more relaxed, draping an arm over the back of my chair and remaining physically close to me.

After dessert and an elongated play time with Delphi and her golf ball, Kai asks if we can go for a walk before he heads home. I offer to walk him home but he says he doesn't want me walking back alone in the dark. It's nothing I haven't done before but Kai refuses, stating a walk through our gardens and greenhouse is more than sufficient.

"I had a lot of fun tonight," Kai admits sheepishly as we slowly make our way, hand in hand, down the flattened gravel paths between rows of manicured plants and bushes.

"Were you expecting not to?"

"I wasn't completely sure if I would or not, since your brother seemed to hate me."

"He doesn't hate you."

"Not anymore. I worked my charm on him, just like I did you."

He's not wrong, Kai is a very charming male. Confident and sure of himself and his words, he could charm a swarm of man-eating piranhas with little effort.

"I wanted to warn you...about my family, since you're probably going to see them at the equinox. They're not the friendliest."

"I've heard they don't like hybrids very much," I offer, hoping to ease his concerns. I know what I'm getting into with him and his family. I have no misconceptions about being accepted easily by his family.

"True, but specifically human half-breeds. Most of the family, especially my mother, have a particularly abhorrent set of beliefs when it comes to tainting the family with human blood."

What he's telling me is nothing I didn't already know. It's something I've dealt with my whole life, although sheltered and safe here in Snowberry it's always been a concern for me and my family.

"I know Kai. You don't have to worry about explaining. I've heard it all before and know how people can be. I may have some insecurities about my human side, but there's nothing I can do to change that. And if others can't accept me for who I am, that's their problem, not mine."

I repeat the words my family has spoken to me on so many occasions and I think I'm finally starting to believe them. Some people's prejudice will never go away. I learned that while I cannot control the actions of others, I can control mine and I refuse to let them have that power over me.

Kai stops next to the dwindling rose bushes and grips my hand tight in his, an appreciative and supportive smile tugging at his lips.

"I'm glad to hear that, Daisy. I still wanted to warn you that they might say some unpleasant things, but know that I won't stand for any of it. If they say anything to you and I'm not around, I want you to tell me, okay? I won't tolerate them mistreating you in any way."

"Okay," I agree.

"Good. Now, do you think we're far enough away from your house to not be seen by your brother so I can kiss you?"

My cheeks go hot, and my heart rate beats rapidly in my chest, nearly pounding out of my ribs. Our previous kiss was spontaneous and unexpected. I didn't have time to freak out and get nervous. All I had to do was fall into his kiss. Now, with him asking me and looking like he could devour me, I feel a little weak in the knees.

"Um, maybe. I don't know. I never checked."

Kai looks over his shoulder and I follow his gaze realizing where we're standing the greenhouse conceals us from the house.

"Looks like that's a yes."

Kai turns back to me, and his lips pull up in a wicked grin that has that place between my thighs pulsing, and the butterflies in my stomach flying.

Pulling me by the hand Kai presses our bodies flush and wastes no time leaning in to claim his kiss. Soft hot lips press firm to mine. His heat washes through me, starting at our locked lips and venturing all the way to my bare feet, toes digging into the cold ground.

My body instinctively molds perfectly to his and my eyes fall shut allowing me to feel *everything*. The press of his hand to my back, holding me tight. The growing bulge in his pants as he presses into my stomach. His hair in between my fingers as I circle his neck and cling to him. The slick of his tongue as it slips through my lips searching for mine.

Wetness gathers between my legs, my pussy growing needy. Fuck. I don't think even my largest dildo will satisfy the desire he's stoking in me. I don't think I've ever felt desire as raw and demanding as this. Consuming my entire being and washing every thought from my brain that isn't *more*.

Kai groans into my mouth and his hands grow impatient and exploratory, cupping my ass and even grazing the base of my tail that sends a pulse of vibrant electricity through my spine. *Well, that's new.*

"I can't wait for the day I can strip you naked and worship your perfect fucking body. Taste every inch of your skin and play with that cute little tail of yours."

To emphasize his words Kai's tail climbs up my leg, and where before he stopped at my thigh, this time it keeps going. Searching, until it finds the wetness at my core. I shudder and whimper as the velvety tip of his tail strokes my slit and gently presses against my clit. *Oh, fuck yes.* I've read about tail play in books but never experienced it and it is so much fucking better than anything I could have imagined. There's something unbelievably erotic about being stroked and caressed with his tail while his hands knead my ass and subtly shift me to spread my legs wider, lifting me gently almost onto my toes.

"Do you like that, Blossom? Like my tail teasing your wet pussy?"

Kai's words are like lighter fluid to a barbeque, forcing my arousal to flame and surge higher. Again, experiencing something I've only ever read about has a greater effect than I could have ever imagined.

"Answer me, Blossom. Do you like my tail on your pussy? Teasing your sweet hot clit?" Kai asks again, his tone slightly more demanding but still drenched in lust.

"Y-yes. I like it," I stutter out. "I also like your horns," I admit in a drunken lust haze.

Then I do something far bolder than I thought myself capable of and reach up to stroke his horns. Gripping tight at the base I glide my hands up and back all the way to the tips before returning to the base, where I stroke the smooth base with a fingertip. Kai's hips buck into me and his nails dig into the flesh of my ass. The tail between my legs spasms and jerks as he momentarily loses control.

"Fucking hell, Daisy. You have a hidden temptress inside

you I very much look forward to bringing out."

While I still grip Kai's horns, he leans down and claims my mouth again. Barely controlled hunger emanating from his lips with low growls.

His lips trail across my jaw to my ear, where Kai brushes away my hair to expose the moderately elongated shell. He runs his finger around my lobe and all the way up and around the tip, sending pleasant shivers through me. Which he only intensifies when he traces the same pattern with his tongue, nipping at the pointed tip with his teeth.

I moan and rub myself shamelessly against him, reveling in the press of his cock against my pelvis.

"I fucking love your ears, Blossom. I want to mark them with my teeth and line them with gold. Would you let me, Blossom? Can I give you something to wear on these perfect ears?"

"I guess so. But they're not pierced."

"They don't need to be."

Reaching up to his long, graceful ear he removes a small gold cuff. One that doesn't require a piercing but hugs the outside of the ear. Kai delicately places the cuff around the bottom uppermost part of my ear nearly to the tip, squeezing it so it hugs snugly and won't fall off.

Kai groans when it's in place. "Fucking perfect."

With another lick, he tastes my ear and prods my new jewelry with the tip of his tongue. His lips pressing wet kisses to my neck and throat until he finds his way back to my lips.

This kiss is slow and exploratory, and I take the opportunity to do a little exploring myself. My hands drift down from his horns to trail light fingers over the long point of his ears, brushing against the dangling chains and spinning studs. The sensation is apparently too much for Kai to focus any longer, his tail abandons my pussy to coil around my thigh and hold tight. His lips break our kiss, as he breathes heavily and presses his forehead to mine.

"Easy there, Blossom. Keep that up and I won't be as gentlemanly and will take you right here in the grass."

As tempting as that sounds there's no way I'm going to have sex, for the first time, somewhere Sage could easily see us. Doing it outside in the grass doesn't bother me one bit. Fearing my brother or his mate could walk up on us at any moment, does.

I drop my hands from his ears and grip his shoulders instead.

"I should head home. Don't want to embarrass myself."

I look up at him and furrow a brow. What is he talking about?

"If you keep touching me, I'm very likely to come in my pants at this point."

Oooooh. Looking down between us I get a decent view of his straining jeans. He's practically fully extended towards me, at least as much as the material will allow. I can't help but bite my lip at the sight, desperately wanting to see the source of that bulge.

"That doesn't help either."

I chuckle and look up at him through my lashes. "Sorry."

"No, you're not, and I welcome your teasing, just not tonight. I desperately want you Daisy, but I want to do this right. I don't want to rush it. When it's the right time, I'll have you, and you'll consume me."

With a tender touch, Kai brushes my hair back from my shoulder and ear, stroking the flowers around my temple and smiling.

"Tell me something, Blossom. Do these flowers change

based on your mood?"

Even without saying so, he's figured out my flowers. I suppose when they change so frequently around him, he had to figure it out at some point.

"Yes."

"Are you going to tell me what any of them mean?"

"No."

He snickers at my flat-out refusal, not at all deterred.

"That's fine. I'll figure it out myself. I think I know what these ones mean." He taps one of the flowers, I'm not sure which one is there at the moment, but I have a pretty good guess. "But I'll have to wait to confirm my suspicions till another day."

With a kiss to the tip of my nose, Kai extricates himself from my hold, sliding my hands from his shoulders and down his chest where he catches them in his and places another kiss on each one, then flipping them over and repeating the gesture on my palms.

"Until then sweet blossom, sleep well."

I watch as Kai wanders off into the darkness towards his family's house and I stand in the crisp evening air letting my heated flesh cool before returning home and trying to satiate my constant sexual desire for Kai.

Chapter 12
Daisy

The tropical blooms are starting to go dormant now that the weather has gone cold. Even I had to put on a pair of long overalls and a sweater today. My feet remain bare, and I decide to stay inside the greenhouse. Coaxing the moss on the ground to grow and thicken, I create a padded soft carpeting to keep my feet warm as I stand behind the worktable we worked at the first day I met Kai.

I'm not assembling bridal bouquets and centerpieces today though. Instead, I'm working on transplanting a few succulents. Using clippings from the large jade and carefully repotting them in small clay pots. Succulents don't do well in cold weather, but inside the greenhouse they'll root and grow over the winter and be ready to sell in spring.

For two days Kai showed up at the nursery and followed me around, attempting to help as I worked. He's friendly with people but not *overly* friendly or flirtatious with anyone. Well, anyone but me. Any chance he got he would lean in close to my ear and whisper things that made me blush, then he would lick or kiss or gently suck on my ear before pulling away and leaving me panting.

It's not all sexual. There were plenty of times we sat in comfortable silence or Kai let me ramble on about the importance of proper soil for specific plants without complaining I was boring him. He was also very helpful in trimming the larger bushes and moving some rather pesky large rocks.

Sage seems to be warming up to Kai more. Chatting with him when we sit together to have lunch or nodding approvingly in passing. Kai's always surprised when it happens but tries to cover it up with his blasé attitude, but I can tell he secretly likes it.

Today, however, he hasn't shown up like he had before. I shouldn't be expecting him to wander in with his usual swager at any moment. It's not like he's an employee or has any purpose to be here every day. But I am a little bummed when I don't see him.

I tell myself he doesn't have to be here every day. I'll see him when I see him. We didn't make plans or schedule anything. This is normal behavior between two—*dating?*—adults, right? I don't know if we are dating or not since I've never dated anyone before. It kind of feels like we are but I don't want to assume. I'll just wait till Kai brings it up.

With all the orders and influx in business, we've brought in our part-time workers to help out. Mainly high school aged kids wanting to make a little spending money. There's one shifter, a human, and a fairy. Meaning we have plenty of people to work with customers, so I don't have to.

Tobias joins me at the table, leaning on his elbows to watch me work. His lavender wings flutter behind him flashing veins of silver in the light as his piercing white eyes watch me closely. I know he's watching my colors, it's something I'm used to. Not only because all fairies can do it, but because I've been around Tobias my whole life. Fairies can see emotions as colors surrounding a person like an aura. Tobias watches as the colors of my aura shift with my emotions, though I have no idea what my colors have been lately with all the emotions I've been going through. I'm sure it's clear to Tobias watching me, seeing my colors is a lot easier to understand than feeling the emotions they represent.

"What are you doing here so late?" I ask to distract from his inspection of my colorful emotions.

Not only can he see and understand my shifting flowers, but he also sees my emotions as colors around me. It's like a double whammy I can't escape from. Thankfully he's always been a lot easier to talk to about things than Sage. Where Sage is all protective big brother, Tobias is the calm, nonjudgmental one.

Usually, he's at *Ugly Mug* by now working the morning shift, since it's the busiest.

"Working the closing shift today. Not going in for a few more hours. What about you? Any plans?"

"No."

"You waiting for Kai to show up?"

I look up at him through my lashes and notice his far too perceptive smirk. He liked Kai from the beginning. I wonder if he saw something in his aura. Should I ask him? Would that be weird? Intrusive?

I go back to filling the pot with soil and sticking the clipping in its center. I contemplate lying and telling Tobias that no I am not waiting for Kai to show up. But what's the point?

"Maybe. He's been here nearly every day so I just kind of

thought he'd be here again today."

"I'm sure he will be eventually. I saw a few cars arriving this morning heading towards his house so he might be busy with his family."

Oh. I hadn't considered that. It makes sense. I knew they would be showing up soon since the equinox is only a few days away. Kai and I even assembled the floral arrangements for the house. Endo helped pick them up and take them back. I didn't go. I thought it would be intrusive to go into their family home without a proper invitation.

I nod, accepting Tobias's reasoning.

Kai probably won't be by for a while then. I feel strangely claustrophobic knowing I'll be spending the day in the greenhouse without him. I've never felt confined by my greenhouse before. The sensation is odd and I'm not quite sure what to do about it.

"I like Kai," Tobias announces with absolutely no prompting.

"Okay." I really don't know how else to respond.

"I know what people say about him, but that has nothing to do with what kind of a male he is, or how he feels about you."

"How he feels about me?"

"Mhm." Tobias nods his head, his long snowy white hair falling over one shoulder at the movement. "He's quite taken with you, smitten even."

"Is that so? He's *smitten* with me? I think your age is showing Tobias." I tease him only because talking about Kai's feelings for me makes my heart beat like a hailstorm on a tin roof.

"Maybe, but it's true. His colors change when he's looking at you. Lots of pinks and purples."

From the many times I asked Tobias what all the colors in a person's aura means, I know pinks are affection and adoration, and purples are, well they're sexual attraction and horniness. Knowing that Tobias knows me and Kai are sexually attracted to one another is beyond embarrassing.

"But there was also golden honey yellow. He's always happy when he's around you. You make him happy, and he makes you happy."

"I suppose he does," I admit.

"Don't let Sage's overprotective nature make you think you can't feel for Kai the way you do. He just wants you to be happy, and if Kai makes you happy, he's happy. We just want to make sure Kai is being honorable, which we would do with any male who showed interest in you."

His voice is honest and pure, true as always. Tobias is one of the most honest and considerate people I know, and he's never lied to me. Even with the hard topics he always manages to be candid without being cruel.

"Thank Tobias."

I finish potting the plant in my hands and set it to the side with the others, brushing my dirty hands off on my pants. Looking around the greenhouse I remember something Calliope said to me when she came by to pick up the tea for *Sticky Buns*.

"You know, I think I'll go visit Calliope at *Sticky Buns* today."

My declaration shocks Tobias almost as much as it shocks me. I don't think I've ever decided to go into town for no reason and without external motivation. Like my brother plotting in order to get me to do a grocery run.

"I think that's a wonderful idea."

Not ten minutes later I'm perched on my sunshine yellow bicycle pedaling down the street towards *Sticky Buns*. Generally, I walk everywhere but with the colder temperature, getting there a few minutes faster—and keeping my feet off the chilly ground longer—is worth hopping on my rarely used bike.

Parking outside *Sticky Buns*, I prop my bike against the brick wall. I don't bother with a lock, no one steals bikes in Snowberry. With the sheriff being a shifter, he can sniff it out in less than an hour. Plus, everyone in town is super friendly and polite. I'm starting to think all the speciesism I thought others believed is all in my head. It's hard to break old habits but I'm trying. Because I'm realizing I may be wrong.

Stealing my nerves, I lift my chin and walk into the bakery. When I walk into a public place, I always assume every eye there is going to turn and stare and judge, everyone going completely silent and waiting for me to move, then internally commenting and questioning why someone like me would be there. What really happens is; I walk in and only the two people nearest the door glance at me for a half second before returning to their own drinks and pastries, the light upbeat music playing over the speakers doesn't screech to a halt but keeps playing. No one glares or does anything. Perhaps if I just lifted my eyes and looked around when I went out, I would realize that more people smile as I pass than frown, and no one cares that I'm here. Because I'm just another customer. Just another person drawn into the sugary goodness of *Sticky Buns*.

When I get close enough to the counters lining the back half of the space, Calliope spots me from where she's sliding a full tray of cookies into the display case, a smudge of flour on her cheek and all over her apron.

Her hair is pulled back into two low pigtails, the length curled at the ends with a matching white bow barrette on each. When she sees me, she pushes up her glasses with one finger, smudging the lens with the same white flour on her cheek.

"Daisy! You're here."

Calliope rounds the counter and greets me with a giant hug

that transfers some flour onto my overalls. We laugh and she tries to brush it off, apologizing between smiling giggles.

"I wasn't sure you would ever take me up on my offer, but I'm really glad you did. Come on, pick something out and I'll get us some tea and we can sit."

"Is that okay with your boss? You won't get in trouble?" The last thing I want to do is get her in trouble with her work.

"Not at all. She lets me take my breaks whenever I want. Plus, I can always threaten to quit, which she would never let me do because she loves my baking too much. She said she would kill to keep me in her kitchen. I think I'll be fine."

I didn't realize she had become such an asset to the bakery. Not surprising, she is the most talented baker I've ever met. Which isn't saying much as I haven't met many, but still, she is the best.

Calliope drags me to the counter, and I point out a few cookies and a cupcake decorated with fall-colored leaves and thick creamy frosting. Sitting at the table she indicates, I wait quietly, looking around the shop and people within. Becca and her mate Julian sit at a table near the window staring into one another's eyes like they're about to start making out at any moment. Fynn is sitting alone in the furthest corner reading a book and nursing a cup of tea. Lifting his eyes as Calliope passes, he watches her make her way over to me. He only drops his gaze when he realizes I've caught him watching her.

The plate Calliope sets on the table is filled with cookies and my cupcake, two cups of steeping tea next to them.

"Thank you. These look delicious."

"Wait till you taste them."

I nibble on the edge of a warm gooey chocolate chip cookie and watch Calliope prepare her tea. Now that I'm here I don't know what to do. Do I ask how her day is going? Do I tell her about mine? Should I compliment her cookies? Wait, I already did that. Ummm...

We sit in silence, while I internally panic on what to do and try to remind myself not to talk about vegetation of any kind. Calliope smiles at me and sips her tea and I take another bite of cookie, tapping my finger on my thigh under the table.

"I like your flowers today."

"What?"

Calliope's compliment startles me and for a moment I don't know what she's talking about. Then I see her incline her chin towards my head and realize she means the flowers in my hair. Since I don't know what flowers are currently blooming, I decide to just roll with it.

"Thank you."

"So, what made you decide to come in today?" Calliope sets down her teacup and watches me with an unassuming expression. Friendly and open as usual.

"I don't really know. Just thought I would. Trying something different I guess."

Setting down the partially eaten cookie, I pull my teacup to me by the rim of the saucer it sits on and remove the metal tea infuser, making sure all the liquid is drained before setting it on the edge of the plate. The tea is a dark amber and tastes of cinnamon and honey. The warm heat of it chasing away any lingering chill from my bike ride over.

"I used your cinnamon to make the tea. Do you like it?"

"Yes, it's very good."

"You know you can talk to me the same here as we do at your house. There's nothing different about being here."

Except for all the people around us. But they're all focused on their own plates and cups.

"I just don't know what to talk about."

"How about your new boyfriend?" Calliope teases with a grin and playful poke at my elbow.

"He's not my boyfriend...I think."

"Oh, he is so your boyfriend. He spends every day at the nursery following you around with a dopey smile on his face."

"He does not." Kai has spent a lot of time at the nursery, just this morning I was depressed when he didn't show up right after opening.

"He so does. Anyone who sees the two of you together can see how much he adores you. It's cute."

Cute is not a word I would choose to describe Kai. Sexy, handsome, inquisitive, touchy, silly, and even sweet but he outgrew cute a long time ago.

"Why don't we talk about something else?" I suggest, covering my blushing face with the expertly frosted cupcake and shoving half of it into my mouth.

"Okay. Like what?"

"Like what you're going to enter into the Christmas baking contest this year, because this cupcake is *amazing*," I mumble around a mouthful of the most delicious cupcake I've ever eaten.

I may not attend the contest, but Sage and Tobias always bring me back a bag full of goodies, and this cupcake would put them all to shame.

"Oh, I don't know about that." Calliope blushes and readjusts her apron around her waist, attempting and failing to brush away more flour.

"I do. Because you would definitely win."

"Well, I have been working on my peppermint recipes. They would be perfect for Christmas cookies or cupcakes."

I can see Calliope's wheels turning as she stares off, her eyes unfocused as she mentally catalogs the possibilities. Her smile slowly grows as she seems to get more comfortable with the idea.

"Maybe I will, but only if you come to the contest and taste them."

Hm. Maybe suggesting she enter the contest wasn't such a good idea. Now she's going to make me come or miss out on her baking. As long as Kai comes with me, maybe I could go to the holiday event I've only seen from afar. It's still a few months away. Maybe by that time I'll be more comfortable around people.

In my newly formed pledge to be more social and put myself out there more, without fear of what others think of me, I give her my best smile.

"Okay then. It's a deal."

Stretching out my hand, Calliope shakes it once and we both break into smothered giggles at our ridiculousness, but the laughter eases my tension, and I relax.

Our conversation flows easily over the next hour as Calliope goes over her recipes and I do end up talking about flowers. Specifically, the ones me and Kai assembled for him to take to his family's house.

Chapter 13
Kai

My mother has arrived. Thankfully, with my father and oldest brother Ren in tow, along with his mate and devil spawn. For the first hour she paraded around the house criticizing the floral arrangements Daisy and myself put together. Most of her complaints are with the ones I assembled. I make sure she doesn't blame Daisy and complain about her ability to others or Endo since she originally tasked him with this job. She already thinks less of me, so why not add it to the list? It's only going to get longer when she finds out about Daisy.

Everyone finally settles in and returns to their own business. Leaving me and Endo with our parents as they linger in the living room and den, letting their personal assistants unpack their suitcases and put everything in its rightful place. That always bugged me. What kind of person can't even unpack their own suitcase? Naomi Kingsley that's who.

Naomi is a very proud female. Born into a millennia long

pure blood family line. Elegant and beautiful with her mix of water and animal attributes, with powder blue skin and delicate midnight indigo markings, her hair a silvery white that matches her short nub horns that she polishes to a pearlescent shine. With ears that stretch into multi pointed fins, she was the diamond of her generation, raised to be the upper echelon of non-human society. Which is oddly similar to human societal standards. All about family names, blood lines, education, and financial status. Just mix in a helping of non-human holidays and species-specific bias and you get my family history.

"I'm so glad you were able to squeeze us into your busy schedule of drinking and women," my mother states in a flat tone, as if she isn't hiding ulterior motives to wanting me here. "It's been a while since you attended an event with the family. It would be even better if you came to New York to attend other events, not just seasonal parties in the woods."

Sneaky female is already trying to influence my decisions and sway me to accept her choice of mate for me.

Now is the time to tell her about Daisy, to put my plan to work, but something prevents me from speaking the words I had practiced when I first came up with the idea. Flat out telling my mom I've already promised to bond with someone else, a half-breed named Daisy, and there's nothing she can do to stop me. But the words stick in my throat. I don't want to tell my mother about Daisy. I don't want her to know her, meet her, even speak her name. She isn't worthy of the beauty and joy that is Daisy Rosenfeld.

I'll figure out a different way to get away from my mother's meddling. Keeping Daisy away from her and the family won't last forever, especially since we're going to the equinox celebration together. At least there, there'll be hundreds of people to use as a buffer to hide from them.

Pocket Full of Posies

Airi already knows about Daisy, I'll just let her and mom gab with each other about our relationship and who she might be. But I won't lie and tell anyone that me and Daisy are going to form a mate bond, at least not yet. The future may hold a mate bond between us, but not until we decide to do it together.

Until then everyone can speculate what they want, and I'll just have to tell mom no. No, I will not bond with the female of your choosing. No, I will not return to New York to meet her to decide. No, you cannot spend time alone with Daisy. No, I don't give a damn if you cut off my access to your money. Because Endo was right, Daisy is too good to be put in the middle of our family. She's definitely too good for me, but for as long as she wants me, she can have me. I'm a greedy male, and I want all of Daisy.

Set on my new plan, I set out to manage my mother as I usually would and try to keep the Daisy talk to a minimum. If Airi has spoken to her already, she's probably going to have questions. I'll just have to do what I do best, skate over topics and give vague answers.

"I don't think so. I'm not a fan of New York. Nor am I a fan of anyone who attends those events."

"You seem to be a fan of the local girls here though. One in particular as a matter of fact. There's even talk of you mate bonding with her."

Well fuck.

I turn to face Endo, because he's the only one who could have told anyone that. He raises his brows at my glaring scowl, like *I thought that's what you wanted me to tell them?* Perhaps I should have clued Endo in on my change of plans and feelings towards Daisy before our parents arrived.

"Nothing like that yet, but it is serious," I say to her while trying to convey to Endo to keep his mouth shut from here on out. He rolls his eyes and shrugs at me, yielding to my wordless demands. Poor guy, I'll have to explain everything when we get a minute alone.

"Oh? So, you don't plan on mate bonding with this female?"

"I didn't say that." I don't elaborate, it's none of her business.

"So, you are bonding?" Mom narrows her eyes at me and glares. I can tell she's getting frustrated and that makes me grin.

Leaning back against the armrest of the couch—something I know drives her crazy—I cross my ankles and shove my hands in my pockets. The picture of calm and collected.

"Maybe."

"For goodness' sake Kai make up your mind. Are you, or aren't you?"

"Yes."

She throws up her hands in frustration, widening her eyes at my father for assistance. He sighs, wanting to be involved in this conversation even less than I do. Crimson eyes a mirror of my own round on me. I look most like my father in coloring and appearance, although my features lean towards animalistic predator, and his are more square and classically handsome. His red markings more like living flames than stripes.

"Don't sass your mother, Kai."

"I'm not sassing her. I'm just answering her questions."

"We both know what you're doing, and we both know how it'll end. Just give her what she wants and make this a whole lot easier for us all," he demands in a low stoic voice, one that might have worked on me as a teenager but has absolutely no effect on me now.

"No. I don't think I will."

My father growls in frustration and I smile wider. If she gets upset over how I answer her intrusive and personal questions or decisions I make about my life, that's her issue. And if she wants to let it bother her, she can, but I won't.

"Kai, you cannot be serious about this local girl. About this…ugk, half-breed." She sneers at the last words adjusting the cuffs of her silk blouse, and the fur along my tail and back of my neck stands on end, ready to defend my blossom.

"Yes," I sneer right back at her. "And you will desist referring to her as half-breed. I won't tolerate it."

She raises a white eyebrow at me but doesn't argue.

"And will I be meeting this female?"

Not if I can avoid it. I'm sure she'll attempt to at the equinox, no doubt try to scare Daisy away. My mother would chew her up and spit her out given the chance, and I don't plan on giving her one.

"She'll be attending the equinox celebration with me."

"Not the party before?"

The party she's referring to would be the uptight cocktail party she throws at the house a few days prior to the actual equinox. All her highbrow friends and a few locals they deem worthy in attendance. Originally, I was going to bring Daisy, but now I don't want her anywhere near it.

"No. I don't even know if I'll be attending."

"Oh, you must. If this female is worthy of my son's undivided attention, the least you can do is introduce me to her."

"And why is that? You hate hybrids of any kind, especially human. Why would I bring Daisy around for you to torment?"

"Daisy?"

I realize my mistake too late. I let her name slip. *Fucking hell.* I let my anger overpower my rational calm and Daisy's name just flew out of my mouth.

"I may have standards for my children and their partners but that doesn't mean I don't want to meet her because she's part human."

I highly doubt that. She's probably planning something awful, and I won't take part in it. My tail twitches at my feet, agitated. I'd rather be anywhere but here. I'd rather be with Daisy in her gardens watching her talk to the flowers and plants.

Thinking of Daisy and her sweet smile and lighthearted kindness, calms some of my fury and discontent, allowing me to reply with less venom than before.

"You don't need to meet her. I don't need your approval of her and if I can manage it, she'll have as little contact with you as possible."

If the look on her face is an indication, she wasn't expecting that. My mother always gets her way, always gets what she wants, and is never told no. Well, she better get used to it because she's about to start hearing it a lot.

"Don't you think she should have a say in that? Maybe she would like to meet your parents. Perhaps you should ask her? Offer her the opportunity to say no or yes."

I would rather shave my head, and anyone who knows me knows how much I love my hair. I'm about to tell her as much but pause. I could tell her I'll talk to Daisy, and the day of the party just tell her she said no. Done and done. It'll keep her off my back and make her think I'm bending to her will. Making my mother think she's getting her way is always the best for everyone involved.

I give her my most sardonic smile, fangs and all. "Of course, Mother. I'll ask her. But if she says no, I won't force her, and you'll accept that."

"That's all I'm asking for. Even if she doesn't attend the

party, I would love for you to stop in. Even if just for a minute. Indulge your mother who hasn't seen you in a year."

A mother who also doesn't contact me unless it's to try and manipulate me into being her puppet. A mother who's never once asked about the women I've dated before now. A mother who last showed any genuine emotion towards me when I was five years old.

"I'll think about it."

Standing, I don't bother saying goodbye, I just walk out the back door and head straight for Daisy's.

Chapter 14
Daisy

Who knew spending an hour in town, eating cookies and talking about nothing in particular with Calliope would be so enjoyable? I sure as hell didn't. When I return home, I'm even smiling, not feeling one bit awkward about my adventure to *Sticky Buns*. I smile even wider when I realize Kai is waiting for me on my porch. Shirtless. His horns gleam in the faint sunshine, and every exposed crimson inch of him appears to burn brighter under my wandering gaze.

"There you are, Blossom. I was wondering how long I'd have to wait before deciding to go into town and find you myself."

"Hi. I was visiting with Calliope. I've never had a friend date before. It was…fun."

I leave my bike on the grass, leaning it against the porch and Kai meets me at the bottom of the stairs, wrapping me in his arms. His embrace is tight and desperate, trying to meld my front to his. He expertly maneuvers my hair to allow his face to press against my neck, inhaling deeply and pressing an open-mouthed kiss to my neck that makes my pulse flutter.

"I missed you, Blossom," he whispers into my skin, his nose nudging my earlobe.

I giggle at the overwhelming sensations he causes. "I just saw you yesterday."

"And that was too long."

Shifting from my neck to my lips he presses a desperate and seeking kiss to them. Starting hard and impatient, the kiss is beyond heart melting and turns into something soft and gentle. Feather-soft brushes of his lips against mine that create more tingling desire than the bruising kiss.

My tail curls tight around my thigh as desire and wetness grow between my legs. I was not expecting that. He's been so proper while in areas we can be seen by others. I guess now I can't argue with Calliope that he isn't my boyfriend after that little display of claiming. Because that's what it feels like to me. Kai staking his claim on me. Or is it mine on him? Could be both.

"That's better," he breathes against my lips, resting his forehead against mine while we both recover from the kiss.

Trying to regain my composure and lower my heart rate, I pull back from him enough to put an inch or two of space between our bodies. Having his naked chest pressed so close muddles my brain and makes me think of what the rest of him looks like naked.

"Where have you been all morning? Tobias said there are more cars at your place now."

"Yeah, my parents and my brother arrived. They're a handful."

"Anything I can help with?" I'm surprised by my own offer. All this socializing is making me gregarious.

Kai's brow pinches, just barely, before smoothing out.

"No Daisy, there's nothing you can do. Although another kiss would make me feel a lot better."

Another day passes with Kai showing up and following me around. He's gotten more brazen with his flirting and public displays of affection. I even had to swat him away a few times when he tried to make out with me in the middle of the greenhouse while customers were watching.

In the morning he shows up grumpy and eager to touch me, kiss me. By the afternoon he's once again his cocky teasing self, all jokes and laughter. After he stays for dinner and has to leave his mood falls again like he doesn't want to go home. Like he doesn't want to leave me.

This morning he showed up grumpy again but far less handsy. Whatever is bugging him today can't be solved with kissing and some light groping. It's been hours and he's still moping around, grumbling to himself.

"What has got your tail in such a knot today?"

The Equinox is only two days away now and I have to admit even I'm getting excited for it. Kai should be just as excited as me, right?

"Nothing. Just normal family bullshit. Don't worry about it, Blossom. Just ignore me."

"Hard to do when you're never more than four feet away from me."

He stops kicking the rocks on the ground and realizes he was pouting and trailing behind me everywhere I went. Every time I moved, he followed like a shadow, his head bent low, and hands shoved deep in his pockets.

Lifting his head, he forces his shoulders out of his ears and gives me a weak smile.

"Sorry."

"Not that I mind you being here, but every grumble you make I can hear your displeasure and frustration. I know something is bothering you and I just want to help. Frowning doesn't suit you."

He attempts to strengthen his smile and relax his frown, but it doesn't completely work. I can still see the tension in the slight pinch of his lips.

"Thank you, Daisy." Kai pulls me into a hug and nuzzles my hair, burying his face in my flowers. "You're always so sweet and kind. I don't deserve such a wonderful girl."

"Of course, you do. But I can't help make you feel better if I don't know what's causing you to be so grumpy."

Kai groans loudly and pulls away but doesn't release me, placing a kiss on the tip of my nose, but he still doesn't answer.

"Won't you please tell me, Kai?"

Closing his eyes, Kai lets out a long, controlled breath. Reaching up I wrap my arms around his neck and comb my fingers through the silky soft hair at the back of his neck. Opening his eyes, he looks down at me and I can tell I've won when his ruby eyes lighten.

"My mother is nagging me nonstop about meeting you. I told her she has to wait till the equinox but she's being an insistent pain in my ass."

His mother wants to meet me? A half human hybrid with tainted blood lines and no family name or fancy mansion? Maybe she's not as bad as I made her out to be if she wants to meet me.

"When was she wanting to meet me?"

Kai falls silent again. I can tell he doesn't want to tell me. I wait patiently for him to answer, never breaking eye contact.

"At the cocktail party tonight at the house," he finally spits out. "I told her no. That neither of us would be going. I know you don't like crowds and that crowd of people is particularly unbearable."

"You don't want to take me to your family's party?"

I know I'm not the type of female his family wants him to be with, but I thought Kai didn't care what they thought about us. That he wasn't ashamed of me, but that's exactly how I feel discovering his mother invited me specifically to attend their very exclusive equinox party and Kai doesn't want us to go. Doesn't want to be seen with me.

"No, of course I don't. Those people are poisonous vipers, and I don't want you anywhere near them."

If I were a more logical person, I would probably realize he's trying to protect me, but in the growing hurt the initial seed of doubt is growing in my chest all I hear is he doesn't want me around his family and friends.

"Are you ashamed of me?" The words slip from my lips as I pull free of Kai's embrace, putting needed space between us so I can think. Thankfully we're in the outer gardens far from prying ears.

"What?! Of course not. I'm honored you even give me the time of day. It's them I'm ashamed of. It's them I don't want around you."

He reaches for me, but I shift out of his reach. I need to think, and I can't do that if he's touching me.

"But they're your family."

"Not by choice. If it were up to me neither of us would ever have to see or speak to any of them ever again."

"But if your mother is so adamant about meeting me, maybe she's not as bad as you think. Maybe you should give her a chance to prove herself. Give me a chance to prove them wrong about hybrids, and to decide for myself."

Kai's fingers curl into fists at his side and I can sense his refusal and I'm already deflating in defeat. I don't know why all of sudden I have an urge to meet his family that I've only ever heard unpleasant things about. Maybe because my previous beliefs have recently been proven wrong on other matters, so maybe the gossip about them is all wrong too.

My eyes drop to the grass, and I focus on my toes curling into the cold blades and dirt. I'm going to have to start wearing shoes soon.

"Do you really want to meet them that badly?" Kai's voice is quiet and gentle, his fingers reaching out to lift my chin, so I have to look into his glittering eyes.

"I mean...maybe. It just doesn't seem right not to when you've met mine."

He sighs heavily and I allow him to wrap me in his warmth once more.

"If we go, I have a few requirements."

I nod, my optimism growing.

"You cannot leave my side. I must be with you at all times. If I say we have to leave, we leave. And you don't speak to anyone I say not to. Okay?"

"Seems a bit controlling to me, but I guess I can go with it. Not that I have much practice at parties anyways. You'll probably have to do all the talking."

"Fine by me."

I never thought that day would come that I would argue to attend a party rather than avoid it. Kai slips his hands under my sweater and presses a warm hand to the bare skin of my back, instantly I feel more grounded and calm.

"You've already got me wrapped around your little finger, don't you?"

I shrug. I didn't realize I did, but I'm finding I might like it. Leaning down Kai presses a kiss to my temple and presses his cheek to the side of my head. My forehead falls to his chest on instinct, and I inhale his campfire scent.

"I don't mind if you do. I'll do anything for you, Daisy."

I'm struck momentarily breathless at the bone deep certainty in his words, and I cling harder to his shirt to keep myself from falling. Although I think I've already fallen for Kai and his dirty mouth and playful teasing.

"I guess if we're going to attend the party you'll want time to get ready."

It's not even noon. How long do girls usually take to get ready?

"I think I have plenty of time. It isn't until this evening, right?"

"Well yeah, but my mom and sisters have already started getting ready back at the house. I thought it was like a thing for females to take an entire day to get ready for a party."

I laugh and the tightness in my chest unfurls.

"I don't think I've ever taken an entire day to get ready for anything, but maybe I could call Calliope and ask her to come over and help me?"

"Probably a good idea. I wouldn't be of any help. I think you look magnificent in anything."

He pinches my butt through my long wool skirt, and we spend the next half hour chasing each other through the gardens and laughing. Only stopping when we fall into a pile of freshly raked leaves that start to burn and sizzle under Kai's touch.

Chapter 15
Kai

I had very different plans for this evening. Mainly not being at my family's house and exposing Daisy to whatever my mother has planned for tonight. I still don't want to go, but I'll do anything to make Daisy happy. I'll just have to be extra vigilant. Most in attendance aren't accustomed to having a hybrid at one of their parties.

This is going to be a fucking disaster. I need to convince Daisy not to come. But then she'll just think I'm ashamed of her, when in fact it's the opposite. In the beginning I wanted others to see us together to spread gossip to my mother, now I want everyone to know she's mine for real. Just without the familial meet and greet.

Everything is a mess. I just want to spend time with Daisy and ignore my relatives. Maybe I could at least make the evening more bearable with Endo and Keiko's help. Endo's always on my side and Keiko, with her sweet nature, would help anyone.

Running through the forest between Daisy's place and mine, I use my enhanced speed to return to the house I was hoping not to see until tomorrow.

Dozens of luxury cars line the circular drive and staff in white blazers scurry around setting everything for the party. Ridiculous pomp and circumstance that they roll out at any given opportunity.

I bypass the task focused waitstaff, my nieces and nephews who run around like this is their own personal amusement park, and cousins tapping away on phones who raise a brow at my rapid pace.

I want to spend as little time away from Daisy as possible. Since Daisy doesn't require twelve hours to prepare like my mother and sister, I only left her with an hour to get ready. More than enough time, at least that's what she said. So, this trip home has to be quick; change my clothes, talk with my brother, and warn my mother to be on her best behavior. Because once again she's getting what she wants, no matter how many times I said no.

Endo is in his room getting dressed when I find him. Lots of males, and females, go topless or all natural for the equinox celebration, but for our swanky soirée clothing is not only required but usually high-end brand labeled. Thankfully it's not black tie. Endo dons a pair of dark brown slacks and an ivory dress shirt with gold buttons. Just enough flash to appease our mother.

"Hey. I thought you were gone for the night. What are you doing back here? You know if Mom sees you, she'll guilt you into staying."

"No need." Leaning against the door frame, I watch as he meticulously buttons the shirt and makes sure the collar lays flat. "I told Daisy about Mom wanting her here for the party and she said she wanted to come. So, looks like we'll be joining you tonight."

Endo stops fidgeting with his shirt and turns to face me, a frown marring his face.

"You sure that's a good idea? It's not just mom she'll have to contend with tonight."

"No, it probably isn't a good idea, but when I told her I didn't want her to come, she got upset. Thought it meant I was ashamed of her. Even trying to explain it's for her own good wouldn't appease her. She wants to meet my parents. Weird as that is, I couldn't tell her no."

Sighing, I run my hand through my tangled hair. I'll have to brush and style it before I leave to pick up Daisy. I wonder what she's going to wear tonight, if she's going to do something different with her hair. I know she likes to wear it down to cover her ears, even though I find them immensely alluring and perfect. She'll no doubt be shoeless. I never have asked her why she doesn't wear shoes. With the nights getting colder I don't want her walking here with bare feet. I'll have to drive to pick her up. When I first arrived, I rented a luxury sports car to get here. I haven't had much use for it since arriving but I'm glad I have it so I can pick up Daisy and save her feet from the cold.

"Have you told mom yet?" Endo asks concerned. He should be, I am.

"Not yet, I wanted to talk to you first. Ask you to keep an eye on her if I'm not around. Run interference if needed."

"Of course," he answers immediately. I knew I could count on him, and since he already knows Daisy, he'll be a friend for her to talk to if I get pulled away.

"Thanks. Can you mention it to Keiko too? I plan on introducing them, but I want her to know ahead of time that Daisy will be coming so she can help too."

"Sure, no problem. Have you warned her about...everyone?"

"She knows enough. She's not naïve to the type of people our family associates with. Which is why I found it even more surprising she wanted to come. Usually, she would choose staying home in her gardens over going out."

Endo smirks and hooks a gold cufflink in his cuff. "Maybe she's spending too much time with you. Your extroverted ways are rubbing off on her."

I'd like to rub something else off on her.

"Maybe you're right. I should attempt to be more antisocial so I can keep her all to myself."

Not a completely bad idea.

"Don't worry, we'll keep an eye on her, and if she gets overwhelmed, we'll sneak you out the back. I'll tell everyone you got food poisoning from the quiche." He laughs somewhat maniacally. "They'll all be so freaked out over the quiche and mom pissed at the caterer to notice two people leaving."

That would be a pretty hilarious cover up, but I don't want the caterer to take the blame for bad food when it's not. Especially knowing what someone like my mother would do to them and their credibility if they did give someone food poisoning.

"No, don't blame the caterer. No one deserves the wrath of Naomi Kingsley. Especially for something they didn't do. Just say we got tired and left. Or better yet just say we left. They don't deserve an explanation."

Endo nods, but his shoulders still shake with silent laughter. Probably imagining everyone freaking out and spitting out the quiche trying to rinse it out with champagne.

"I'm going to talk to mom and change then go pick up Daisy. The earlier we arrive the earlier we can leave."

"Got it. I'll go find Keiko and update her."

"Thanks."

I leave my brother to find our sister and head for Mom's dressing rooms. Because just having a bedroom to get dressed in isn't enough, she has to have a series of rooms set aside specifically for the laborious task of putting on clothes.

Knocking on the gilded double doors, I wait for someone to answer. No way in hell am I barging in and catching my mother half naked. One of her personal assistants, the one who does her hair and makeup I think, answers the door after a long delay. She ushers me in without a word.

I find my mother standing in front of a mirror that covers one entire wall, adjusting her various expensive earrings. She has many, many earrings to choose from, one pair in particular, handed down from my grandmother, would look especially ideal on Daisy's delicate ears. A diamond and emerald encrusted floral piece that cuffs around the helix and antihelix covering a large portion of the mid and lower ear and held in place with a piercing at the lobe. Mom barely ever wears it, calling it old fashioned and outdated, choosing more modern, geometric designs.

I wonder if I were to pilfer it and give it to Daisy if she would even notice its absence. Probably. Then she would blame the nearest staff member for stealing it and fire them and maybe even file theft charges against them. No, if I took it, I would have to make sure she knew it was me. Which doesn't deter me in the slightest.

"Kai, what a surprise. I thought you had run off for the evening to escape my horrible party," my mother says in a sardonic tone that reveals every ounce of her displeasure, not even turning away from the mirror and her primping.

"Oh, I had, but it turns out Daisy wants to come and meet you. So, here I am informing you that I'll be attending with a guest."

She finally turns to face me, far more interested in our conversation, now that she's finally getting what she wanted.

"Is that so? I'm so glad she changed your mind."

"She didn't but I'd do anything for her, even introduce her to you if she wants. But before you enact whatever the hell it is you're plotting, I have a few rules."

"Rules? Must I remind you whose house this is? I make the rules here dear," she scoffs with the arrogant huff of a queen. She is no queen, though she fancies herself one.

"Not tonight, you don't. Not when it comes to Daisy. You will abide by my rules or we're not coming." I stand firm, hands on my hips and spine straight and solid as granite. On this I will not budge.

My mother looks me up and down before her cobalt lips pull into a smirk, a devilish twinkle in her eyes.

"Very well, what are your rules?"

"Do not call her a half-breed. Do not announce her hybrid or human heritage to anyone. If you must say anything, just say she is an earth nymph. You will not ask about her parents or family. You will not make her feel uncomfortable in any way or we leave. Understood?"

Her smirk doesn't fall, and that fact worries me. As does the fact she doesn't even question Daisy being a hybrid.

"Of course, dear. Anything you say. I want her to feel welcome in our family, especially if she's this important to you. This is after all the first female you've ever deemed worthy enough to be serious about. She must be very special indeed."

She is, but I can't voice that to my mother. Pretending to be promised to another for a mate bond or in a fake relationship to get her off my ass is one thing. She would get irritated and try to talk me out of it, not really putting much effort into it.

But being in a real relationship with someone important and special? My mother will try to shred it to pieces, force us apart, because none of her children are allowed to mate for love. Leaving this family permanently is sounding more and more appealing by the day.

"Just behave Mom. Don't make me regret coming here. Tell dad he has to abide by the same rules, and my brown-nosed siblings for that matter. If anyone even breathes the word hybrid, it'll be years before you see or hear from me again."

That at least gets her attention. I'm not joking or lying. I will gladly abandon this family and their archaic beliefs for Daisy without a second thought. Inheritance be damned.

"Very well Kai. If that's what you require."

She says she'll abide by my request, but the tone of her words implies otherwise. Not necessarily malevolent but definitely callous. The glimmer of a secret flickering in her eyes as she continues to smile her plastic smile at me.

"Right. Well, I'll be picking Daisy up in an hour."

"Very good. I can't wait to meet her."

"Uh huh."

You ever have that feeling that the person you're talking to is just saying what you want to hear so you'll stop talking? That's what I'm feeling right now with my mother. Like she's hiding something and just can't wait to spring it on me and is giddy at the idea of my response.

There's no backing out now. If something goes wrong tonight, we'll just have to leave.

Chapter 16
Daisy

Calling Calliope was the right move. When Kai went home to change and inform his mother we would be attending tonight, Calliope and I headed upstairs to my room. My wardrobe mainly consists of denim shorts, denim overalls, long flowy hippie skirts and a few sun dresses, and to no one's surprise only one pair of shoes. The slip-on fur lined rubber boots Sage bought me.

"Is this event formal? Cause if so, you're going to be underdressed," Calliope calls from deep inside my closet.

"I don't think so. Kai said to wear whatever makes me feel comfortable. But maybe a dress or skirt? I don't want to show up in grass-stained jeans."

"Good idea."

Calliope digs around in my closet more while I sit on my bed, legs crossed and waiting patiently. I'll wear whatever she tells me to. I'm going to have to defer to her knowledge of party attire. I am completely out of my comfort zone here.

Calliope rambles on about choices as she goes through every piece of clothing I own, while my attention wanders to the plants in my windowsill. They're looking a little droopy and sad at the lack of warm sunshine. I stand and go to them brushing my fingertips across their petals and leaves, sending them my magic to help them grow and flourish. Infusing their roots with missing vitamins and nutrients. The green of their leaves brightens and the pink and yellow blooms perk up and stand taller. In their strange flower way they thank me.

"Ok, how about this one?"

Turning around to see Calliope's choice, she's holding up a short baby pink dress with tiny white flowers on it.

"I don't think so. It's too spring and this is fall."

"Okay there's always this one."

She produces a lacey white dress I bought for my twenty-first birthday. It's spaghetti strapped and shows too much skin and I tell her as much.

"Alright then."

With one more shuffle through my closet I hear Calliope call out in victory.

"I found it! This is the one."

"The one" is a long ankle length dress in a brown mustard, burnt orange color with puffy little cap sleeves, a drawstring at the neckline and a fitted bodice. Tiny red embroidered flowers line the hem of the ruffled skirt.

"I think you're right. That looks perfect."

"Okay now for your hair and...do you own any makeup?"

"No."

"Okay not a problem I think I have some mascara and lipstick in my purse we can work with. You don't need it anyways because you're naturally pretty."

I blush at the compliment. Outside only Kai has called me

pretty. Actually, I believe his words were 'arousingly beautiful.'

"Okay sit here and let's see what we can do with all that glorious hair of yours."

Gripping a handful of my thick chestnut hair in my hands I look down at it. I need to do something with my hair? It's long and wavy falling nearly to my tail and I've always just let it do what it wanted.

"We don't have to. I think it's fine as it is."

"Nonsense." Calliope grabs me by the shoulders and sits me in the chair at the desk I used to use when doing my homework for school. "We don't have to do much but let's start with brushing it."

She starts to part my hair and shift my flowers and then the panic hits me. She's going to see my ears, she's going to realize the flowers are growing out of my head and not just pinned to my hair.

She's so fast with her hands—and freakishly strong, must be from all the batter mixing—that I can't stop her before she pulls back one half of my hair revealing my ear, the one with Kai's golden cuff.

"I really don't need you to do that. I can manage." I rush to pull the hair back over my ear, but again she swats away my hand with unexpected strength and pulls the hair back again. My obviously pointed and non-human ear on display.

"It's okay, I don't mind."

"No really, it's okay."

"Is this because you're trying to hide your ears?"

My hands freeze midair trying to pull my hair out of her vice grip to cover the pointed evidence of my non-human heritage.

"It's okay, Daisy. I know what you are."

"I? What? I'm a horticulturist."

"Yes but...you're also part nymph. Right?"

I swivel around in my seat so fast I almost give myself whiplash.

"A what? What do you mean? I have no idea what you're talking about."

"Yes, you do, and it's okay. You don't have to lie or hide it from me."

"But...but..." I'm speechless. Not uncommon in my life but usually not because I was rendered wordless and dumbfounded by my human best friend's proclamation of knowing I'm a nymph. "How did you find out?"

"Well besides the pointed ears, tattoos that move and flowers that obviously grow from you; my great aunt left me a journal explaining the world of non-humans. Apparently, she was half human and half non-human and didn't want her descendants to forget about the non-human half of their heritage. She just never had kids of her own to pass it down to."

"So, you've known all along what I am?"

"Not the entire time. I was skeptical at first, as I expect most people would be but over time, I paid closer attention to things and started to catch sight of things I couldn't explain away. Once I read more about the different types of non-humans, I figured you had to be an earth nymph. It made the most sense."

I'm frozen in shock until a massive wave of relief washes over me and I spring to my feet and wrap Calliope in a tight hug.

"Oh, my goodness I'm so happy you know, this makes things so much easier."

Calliope squeaks and squirms in my arms. "Okay, too tight, can't breathe."

"Sorry," I release her and give her space to breathe.

I always knew her great aunt was a half-breed like me, though far-far older. Half human and half leprechaun, a very rare mix. I wonder if that means Calliope has non-human blood in her ancestry then.

"Wait. Does this mean you're also part non-human?"

Calliope shakes her head, giving me a sad smile. "Sadly no. Apparently Great Aunt Greta was more like my great, great, great, great Aunt Greta and according to her journals my side of the family was her human side that she stayed connected with through the generations. She's been Great Aunt Greta to everyone."

"Oh. Well, that's okay. As long as you're okay with me being a half-breed too. I'm also half human."

"Of course, I am. You're my friend Daisy, and your family bloodline isn't going to change that."

One more example of how wrong I've been about people's views on half-breeds.

"Can we just keep the fact that I know about non-humans between us? No one else knows that I know and I don't want to cause any issues." Calliope's lips pinch in worry as she watches me.

"Of course. Who would I tell anyways? You're my only friend."

We both laugh and Calliope's shoulders sag in relief.

"Now can I please brush your hair. It desperately needs it. And if you're going to be meeting your hot boyfriend's family it should at least be brushed. By the way, what is Kai? I haven't been able to figure him out. His glamour is too good."

I laugh because he is absurdly good with his glamour. I also like that she doesn't ask why I don't use a glamour.

"He's also a nymph but his abilities are animal and fire based."

"Okay you are so going to have to explain that and what his real body looks like. I want to know everything."

And I tell her, all while she brushes my hair and uses a few bobby pins to hold up small braids keeping the strands out of my face, forming a small circlet crown on my head, winding it around my flowers. Now daisies and hydrangeas. Happiness and optimism.

Kai returns just as I'm walking Calliope out and we both stop to watch him approach. His glamour shifted into place in a fraction of second when he saw Calliope, but I still see the real him. He added a gold band to one of his horns and put something in his hair to keep it under control and far less wind wild than it usually is. His customary earrings, necklace and rings in place along with a few bracelets.

The end of his tail swings lazily behind him as he saunters up the front drive where a sleek black sports car is parked. I guess he didn't feel like walking. He's dressed in black slacks and a deep blood red dress shirt left open at the collar, the top buttons undone to show his chest beneath. I think he has an aversion to shirts the way I do shoes.

"Does he look as hot in his true form as he does in his glamour right now?" Calliope whispers to me.

"Probably."

Kai smirks, obviously hearing us—nymph hearing and all that—because he instantly drops his glamour. I can only tell because his form shimmers for half a second.

"Wow." Calliope's mouth drops as she openly gawks at my boyfriend. That's right boyfriend. Might as well call him what he is at this point.

"Calliope. I didn't know you knew about non-humans." Kai says in greeting as he meets us halfway to the house.

"Yeah well, no one but you and Daisy knows I know. Not sure if I'm supposed to or if I'll get in trouble for knowing."

Kai mimes zipping his lips shut and winks at her.

"Yeah, okay. I'm gonna go now. You two have fun." She gives me a quick hug goodbye and gets into her car and drives off leaving hot as sin Kai staring like he wants to devour me in my driveway.

"Hello, little Blossom. You look exceptionally beautiful tonight. I like what you did with your hair. It shows off those cute ears I like so much."

He reaches out and runs a finger down the exposed cartilage and I shiver at the sensual touch. A possessive and undeniably sexual growl emanates low in Kai's chest.

"Later, Blossom." Kai taps me on the nose and grins. "Are you ready to go? If you've changed your mind I would completely understand."

"No, I haven't changed my mind. I still want to go."

"Very well. Just remember my stipulations."

"I haven't forgotten."

Kai gives me a definitive nod before leaning down to press a chaste but intense kiss on my lips, making my brain all fuzzy.

Apparently, the sports car is for my benefit because he knew I wouldn't be wearing shoes and didn't want me to hurt my feet walking over in the growing dark. I have to admit the fancy sports car is pretty cozy, and warm.

"Why don't you like to wear shoes? I don't think I've ever asked." Kai eyes my bare toes on the carpeted floor of the car.

"Why don't you like to wear shirts?" I mimic his tone and eye his revealingly unbuttoned shirt. Not meaning to linger but unable to immediately look away from his tantalizing skin.

Every day we spend together increases my desire to lick him. An unfamiliar emotion I'm still trying to come to terms with while trying not to lick him. Maybe sometime soon he'll let me. I bet if I asked he would without hesitation.

Kai clears his throat, drawing my attention and my gaze up

to his grinning face.

"I tend to get hot. Wearing no shirt or unbuttoned open collared shirts helps keep me cool. A side bonus of my fire magic." He answers my question while continuing to smirk at me then licks his lips as his eyes drift down my body. "And you? Why no shoes?"

"It's kind of for the same reason. Not that I get hot, but because of my magic. It's grounding, connecting me to the earth. I can hear and understand the plants better."

"You can hear the plants? I thought you just liked talking to them like a human talking to their pet dog. A one-sided conversation. Not that you were actually talking to them."

Most earth nymphs have a sixth sense regarding the earth and plants, an instinctual understanding. I sense them differently, more of a conversation and feelings. I can tell if the flowers are happy or sad, hungry or sick because they tell me, rather than a logical tallying of soil nutrients and moisture. Sage explains it as seeing into the chemical and biological breakdown and a knowing of what is needed and what is missing. When he connects with them to make them grow or move it's a command. An intrinsic knowledge and power over them. Whereas I speak to them, asking them to grow and coax them to do as I say through feeling. Because of that I've always felt closer to the earth through touching it.

"It's hard to explain but yes, I can talk to them in a sense. Not quite as direct as you can with Delphi, but similar. Feeling a tactile connection to the earth makes it easier."

"Thus, no shoes." Kai concludes. "I like that you don't wear shoes."

"I like that you don't wear shirts."

My confession slips free before I can think better of it. Kai's pupils expand and the heat in the car increases noticeably.

"For you, Blossom, I'll never wear a shirt again if it's what you desire."

That part of me that wants to lick Kai likes that idea a lot. I lick my lips and swallow coating my dry throat before speaking, Kai's eyes shift from the road to me, tracking the movement before returning back out the front windshield.

"Maybe I do," I admit in a smoky tone that barely sounds like my voice.

"Very well."

Kai reaches up and starts to unbutton his shirt even more. He's already gotten down to his delicious abs by the time I'm able to reach out and stop his progression.

"Maybe after the party?"

Huffing in faux irritation the corner of Kai's lips twitch in amusement. "Fine, if you insist."

He doesn't immediately re-button his shirt, needing both hands to do so and one is still firm on the steering wheel. Instead, he reaches out his free hand and twines our fingers together, resting our linked hands on my thigh after pressing a kiss to the back of my hand.

Our hands remain linked for the rest of the short drive to his house or rather mansion. I know it's not his but his parents, but it's still intimidating to drive up to with its manicured lawns, shaped hedges and dramatically up lit spot lights.

Kai parks the car and the bravery I had hours ago has dwindled to steam in my veins. I'm not sure I'm strong enough to go in now. I'm going to say something wrong. Or everyone will think my dress is ugly and cheap. Shit, they're probably all going to be wearing shoes. I should have asked to borrow some from Calliope. Just because Kai thinks my bare feet are cute doesn't mean everyone else will.

Maybe this was a bad idea. Maybe Kai was right, and we

should just turn around and go home. I'm so out of my depth. Why did I want to do this again? Oh right, I was trying to prove to myself and everyone else that I'm not a total shut-in and can participate in normal social events like everyone else. I think I might have been wrong, or at least jumped the gun on my abilities.

My grip on Kai's hand tightens to the point my knuckles go white and my markings shift restlessly on my skin.

"Daisy," Kai forces me to look at him with just my soft-spoken name. "It's okay. If you need a minute, we can wait, or we don't have to go in at all. It's all up to you."

"Okay. Just, maybe another minute?" Apparently, I'm still determined to participate. Something inside me needing to push myself out of my comfort zone, if just to learn where my limits are. Without trying, how will I ever know?

He doesn't turn the car off allowing the heat to keep pumping in so I don't get cold and I know he's doing it for me. As he said, his fire magic keeps him warm.

Peeling my eyes from the mansion, and few people I see through the windows, I look down to our intertwined fingers and focus on Kai's rings and bracelets. Most of them are gold, some with precious stones, a lot of them are red, probably rubies. One of his bracelets is a simple gold band with a single small ruby set in the gold. It looks different from the other jewelry he wears. No brand stamped on it or recognizable markings. Just smooth warm gold with a perfect drop of red. I finger it and spin it on his wrist to get a better look at the stone. It's vibrant and cut in a smooth perfect circle, inlaid in the band, literally. I can feel the bottom of it on the underside of the bracelet.

"It's pretty, isn't it? My sister Keiko gave it to me. The stone is a red beryl, one of the rarest stones in the world. She had it made for me for my birthday. Told me she had to find a stone as rare as I was."

His face softens with remembrance and affection for his sister. The one he told me is the best of all his siblings, even more than Endo.

"It's beautiful."

I rub the stone between my fingers, it's smooth to the touch, not faceted like most stones to make them reflect the light. More like a polished rock. The simplicity a perfect pair to its rarity I suppose.

"Here."

Kai unlinks our hands and slides the bangle style bracelet off his wrist. Taking my hand again he slips it onto my wrist. It's far too large for me, and way too precious to give to me.

"No Kai, I don't need it. Your sister gave it to you, you should keep it. Plus, look, it doesn't fit."

"That's not a problem."

Engulfing my wrist in both his hands he holds the gold bangle off my skin.

"Now don't move."

"Why?"

"You'll see."

The hands around my wrist begin to glow red like a hot poker and my arm begins to heat. Just when I think it's going to get too hot and burn my skin, the heat instantly dissipates.

"What did you do?"

Lifting his hands he reveals the bracelet, now much smaller and cooler, around my wrist.

"Now it's a perfect fit, and you can't give it back without ruining it or the talents of a skilled fire nymph."

The gold band isn't even warm as it rests against my skin. I slide it to the base of my wrist and realize what he's done. He's sized it perfectly to be loose around my wrist but too small to slip off over my hand. It's never coming off.

"Kai, you can't. Take it off, it was a gift from your sister, you should have it, not me. This is too much." I try to argue to no avail. He's already shaking his head and grinning at me.

"It's not enough. I want to give you more. Give you earrings and rings, diamonds, and sapphires, because you are the rarest gem in the world, Daisy. And I will gladly give you anything you ask of me. No cost is too great if I get to see you smile."

My wavering smile is accompanied by wet eyes, and I blink trying to hold the tears at bay. I can't go into his parent's party with tear tracks down my cheeks.

"Don't make me cry. Calliope put mascara on me and said it'll run if I get it wet."

Kai laughs, deep and warm. The sound bright enough to dry my tears, but he swipes a thumb under my eye anyways to make sure none escaped to ruin whatever Calliope did to them.

"You look perfect, Blossom. And now whenever you're nervous or scared, you can look down to your wrist and know I'm always there with you and I will always be there to protect you. To make you smile and laugh so hard you cry, but only when you're not wearing mascara."

The straitjacket around my heart unbuckles and the restraints loosen as Kai melts them with his words and unique charm, and I can breathe easily again.

"Thank you, Kai. I love it." *And I think I love you.*

The realization of something I sensed growing, but am too afraid to admit. This is all still new, and I don't want to be that girl that falls in love with the first guy she dates only because he was the first. But something in me knows that's not the case, that if I spoke those words, they would be true. I just don't know if Kai would feel the same. So, I keep them inside for now.

"It looks better on you than it ever did on me."

"That's because you wear so much jewelry, its simplistic beauty is lost amongst the mass."

"I suppose it was. Now it can shine on your wrist, getting the recognition it deserves."

Lifting my hand to his lips he kisses my knuckles and I realize I'm no longer panicking or white knuckling his hand.

"Are you ready to go in now?"

Looking up at the huge mansion and opulence I no longer feel overwhelmed with Kai at my side.

"Yes."

Chapter 17
Kai

When we first step through the doors to the house no one seems to notice us. Nymphs of all kinds are present, holding champagne flutes and cocktail glasses. Some nibble on tiny finger foods delivered on silver platters by white coat staff members. None of the food present is any larger than an appropriate bite size so as not to make anyone look like an uncivilized commoner. Not a burger or plate of pasta in sight.

The first to spot us is thankfully Endo, who weaves his way through the guests to meet us, his bright smile in place and directed at my blossom.

"Hi Daisy. Nice to see you again. You look lovely tonight." My brother is only being polite, and his tone only suggests friendship, but I still don't like him looking at Daisy like that.

"Thank you."

"Have you seen Keiko yet?" Endo asks, turning to face me and the possessive fire burning in my gut simmers with his eyes off Daisy.

"Not yet, we just got here. Thankfully no one seems to have noticed us yet."

"That won't last long. Mom is impatient to meet Daisy. I'm sure she'll spot you soon. Until then, why don't we get a drink and maybe even enjoy ourselves?"

I keep an arm wrapped around Daisy's waist as we make our way to the bar in the rec room, specifically built to host such parties. The ceiling is high, and the furniture is sparse. Tall tables are set up along the perimeter with a central table to break up the open space, ladened with a massive floral bouquet I don't recall making with Daisy. Mom must have gotten it after arriving from somewhere else. I have no idea where, since there's nowhere else in town to get flowers except for Daisy's Gardens. The lights of the crystal chandeliers are set low to create a soft warm glow in the room, imitating an autumn sunset.

Behind the bar, set along the far side of the room, two bartenders tend to drink orders, both female fairies. Neither that I recognize. Much like the rest of the staff they were probably brought in from out of town. The pale blue fairy takes our drink orders and quickly prepares them before efficiently moving on to the next waiting guest.

We manage to find an empty table in a quiet corner, when I spot Keiko in the crowd. Waving her over, she moves gracefully through the guests like water around stones. Her butter yellow dress trailing behind her like a wake.

Daisy is pressed close to my side sipping her drink, her eyes scanning the crowd constantly and doesn't notice my sister heading straight for us. She's obviously nervous, but I admire her strength attending an event I know she must feel out of place at.

"Keiko, there you are," Endo casually announces our

sister's arrival, as she gracefully glides up to our table.

Keiko is the one who looks most like our mother, with her pale silver-blue skin and matching hair, with the same tri-pointed fin ears and dark blue spots resembling freckles. Her eyes are a luminescent aquamarine that light up with joy at our presence. Cobalt blue lips pull into a soft smile as she greets us.

"Hello Endo, Kai, and this must be Daisy. I'm Keiko, Kai's sister and I am very happy to meet you."

Keiko extends her long delicately fingered hand to Daisy who accepts it with a gentle squeeze.

"It's nice to meet you, too. Kai has spoken very highly of you."

"Is that so?" Keiko gives me a knowing look but isn't at all displeased.

"You know you're my favorite, Keiko."

Keiko just hums and smiles with closed lips. She may be quiet and demure but she's not ignorant. She watches and listens and knows a lot more than my family gives her credit for.

"Sadly, Kai has told me very little about you, other than how wonderful you are and that you own the flower nursery in town with your brother. Did you make the arrangements for the house?"

Daisy smiles, at ease talking about flowers and arrangements.

"Some of them, yes. Not this one." She gestures to the large one in the center of the rec room that's more like a ballroom. "Although it is lovely."

We all momentarily turn our attention to the massive arrangement of autumn blooms in reds, yellows and oranges. It's nice but unless the flowers are in Daisy's hands or hair, I don't care what they are.

My sister and Daisy fall into a quiet conversation about flowers, and I watch and listen but don't interrupt, only joining in when Keiko turns the conversation from flowers to our relationship.

"How did you two meet? Kai never told us."

Daisy giggles and threads her hand through my arm, sliding down to grip my hand under the table. I reciprocate the gesture and rub my thumb across the soft skin of her hand, relishing in the small intimate act.

"Kai found me in the woods arguing with Delphi over her stolen goods."

"Who's Delphi?" Keiko asks.

"She's a nosey little sprite Daisy has befriended," I interject, recalling the sprite's fascination with me. "Cute thing, overly friendly but harmless."

"She just likes you," Daisy squeezes my hand and smiles up at me, comfortable and at ease, which alleviates the concern constricting my chest. "I was checking on her nest in the woods before winter to make sure it was sturdy, and Kai just strolls up like we're not alone in the middle of the woods and starts a conversation."

I recall when I first saw her and my fascination at her conversing with a sprite and how cute she was with her tail and ever-changing hair flowers. I still don't know what all of them mean but I have an idea about one of them. At least I hope I know what it means. I'll find out soon enough.

"Let me guess, he was shirtless and charming?" Keiko raises an eyebrow at me and smirks. She knows me all too well even if I haven't seen her in months.

"How did you know? Does he do that a lot?"

"Meet girls in the forest? Not that I know, but he does like to prance around shirtless and can talk his way out of anything."

"I do not prance," I argue, but it does no good. The two females ignore me completely and Endo muffles a laugh enjoying not being the topic of conversation. I can't wait till he finds a girl and brings her home to meet the family. We'll see who's laughing then.

"Yes, you do. Like a proud peacock."

The two girls, and my brother, break down with laughter at my expense, but I can't be mad. Not when Daisy is laughing and happy and getting along with my two most important family members.

Servers circle the space carrying trays laden with the bite size appetizers. One approaches our table and offers us a plate of tiny quiche. Endo and I snicker silently at my previous comment about poisoned quiche. It's vegetarian and Daisy plucks two off the tray and sets them on a napkin on the table. I'm going to need to make sure to find her some real food soon. Or maybe we'll go to Dottie's after we leave early. That sounds like a grand plan to me, because I know I'll be starving after this.

"That's a lovely bracelet, Daisy. It looks just like the one I gave Kai." Keiko inspects the bracelet on Daisy's wrist as she bites into a quiche.

"Oh, I tried to tell him to take it back, but he resized it and now I can't take it off. I said it was too much and I didn't want to take it, but he wouldn't take no for an answer—"

"It's okay, Daisy," Keiko interrupts Daisy's frantic apology. "I don't mind that he gave it to you. Actually, I'm happy he did."

"You are?"

"Of course. I gave it to Kai because he's important to me, and he gave it to you because you're important to him. It doesn't matter where the item originated, only why it was given."

Daisy curls her arm into her chest, cradling the bracelet

clad wrist to her heart, her fingers stroking the golden band.

"Thank you."

I can't stop myself from reaching out to comfort her, hold her. Sliding my hand across her lower back and curling around her hip, I bring our sides flush and press my nose to her hair, inhaling the perfume of her flowers and essence, and whisper in her ear.

"Told you so."

I hear Daisy let out one small chuckle and pull back to see Keiko and Endo watching our interaction, approval, and something akin to disbelief marring their faces. I don't blame them. I've never been the possessive type, or the overly sweet and affectionate type. Flirtatious, suggestive, and physical absolutely. But nothing emotional or intimate. My siblings are rightfully stunned at my behavior.

A few relatives and family friends stop by our table and offer greetings and a few words of *nice to see you again, who is your date, we'd love to see you at more events,* etcetera etcetera. Nothing meaningful or honest, simple pleasantries bred into them from birth. Not once do I detach from Daisy's side, blatantly signaling our relationship to one another.

During one similar conversation, I spot a familiar and unexpected female in the crowd. Nysa, an animal nymph from a high bred family with uncommon characteristics of a moth, including a stunning set of wings and furry antenna, her coloring pale pinks and teals, flutters about the room speaking with guests as if she's always attended our family equinox event.

I haven't seen her in almost a decade since our short, and purely sexual, relationship. As far as I knew, our families only interacted socially at large important public events, but nothing more. Not that my mother hadn't wanted a closer relationship to the family known for their impeccable breeding and high standards. I just didn't realize she'd finally established that connection. But that still doesn't explain why she's here.

I lean into Endo and whisper, trying not to be overheard by Daisy and Keiko so as not to concern them.

"Why is Nysa here? Did Mom finally convince them to be part of her inner circle?"

Endo tilts his head to better see Nysa, then shakes his head.

"I have no idea why she's here. Then again, I try to stay out of Mom's business as much as possible, so there could be a logical reason for her presence."

Whoever was talking to us politely excuses themselves with regurgitated friendly formalities, and that's when I see my mother, from all the way across the room, set her sights on me and Daisy.

Well, here we go. The moment I've been dreading the entire night. I lean in to speak directly into Daisy's ear.

"My mother is heading our way, are you ready to meet her?"

Daisy sucks in a breath and stands taller, but nods.

"Yes. I'm ready."

"Okay. Remember I'm right here with you, Blossom. If you're ever uncomfortable, just say the word and we'll leave. Your comfort is most important to me."

To punctuate my words, I give her dainty ears a nibble and kiss. Daisy's heart rate quickens but she holds her composure with only a slight shift in her flowers. That's when my mother appears at our secluded table, with Nysa right behind her. *Shit.*

Chapter 18
Kai

My mother approaches our table with a gorgeous Nysa at her side. Pink and teal moth wings are folded demurely at her back, her opalescent hands folded at her waist, while her downy antenna bob gently above her brow. Her smile is pristine and conveys easy friendliness. She looks kind enough, but I know that's a farce. She's as prickly and deadly as a machete.

"Kai, there you are. Where have you been hiding?"

"Not hiding, just not attempting to speak to every single person in attendance," I mutter but she doesn't seem to hear as she turns her attention to Daisy.

"And this must be the elusive Daisy. How nice of you to attend. I was worried that I may never meet you."

My mom extends a hand in that strange way that's more expecting a kiss on the knuckles than a shake. Daisy, to her credit, accepts it only a little awkwardly not knowing what to do with it.

"Yes, it's so nice to meet you Mrs. Kingsley."

"Oh, please call me Naomi." She looks Daisy up and down in her inquisitive and judgmental way. "You're quite pretty. Not what I expected."

I want to demand what exactly she did expect, but keep my mouth shut, not wanting to start an argument in the middle of a party and in front of Daisy.

"Um, thank you."

My mother remains silent for a long awkward moment. No one offering to fill the space and break the tension until she's done with her perusal of Daisy.

"I'd like to introduce you to a special guest of mine. This is Nysa." Nysa takes a half step forward and inclines her head in greeting, having waited dutifully for her introduction before participating in the conversation. High bred, indeed. "She's a friend of the family. I believe Kai is already acquainted with her, aren't you Kai?"

So, her play is to rub my past sexual partners in Daisy's face. Low blow even for her. I haven't concealed my past from Daisy, but I also haven't paraded it out in front of her, in public. I had hoped to keep the past in the past, but it seems my mother has made that choice for me and is strutting it out on a red carpet for all to see.

"Yes. Kai and I met nearly ten years ago. We were very close."

Nysa practically eye-fucks me and brushes her fingers along her collarbone all demure and shit. She is *not* demure. She may act like it and have all the practiced mannerisms of a socialite, but she is devious and heartless. Ten years ago, I was fucking anyone who struck my fancy and there's no denying her physical beauty. Once I discovered her inner ugly, I was out. I didn't want her then and I most definitely don't want her now.

Pocket Full of Posies

My expression remains flat and impassive, an expression I'm not used to wearing but am tired of masking and smiling and playing the part of idiotic party boy. Not that I don't still enjoy a good party—current environment excluded—and having fun, I just want to spend all that time with Daisy now.

And I'm tired of being brushed off as the dumb one. Just because I like to drink, fuck, and have a little fun doesn't mean I'm uneducated. Something most people don't know is that I have my Doctorate in Veterinary Medicine. In between traveling and ignoring my family I went to school. Sure, it started because I was bored but it led to me continuing my education. I like helping animals. I would love to work with them on a regular basis but how? Where? Who would hire me? And hire me for my skill and ability, not because of my family name. It's a pipe dream I sometimes dream about but have no idea how to manifest.

"Oh. It's very nice to meet you Nysa. I'm Daisy."

Daisy extends her hand to Nysa, who just looks down at it distastefully, not reciprocating the civility.

"Yes, Naomi has told me all about Kai's new female. I must say I'm surprised he's committed himself to only one. If memory serves, he was quite the philanderer."

"And the past has nothing to do with the present. Daisy is my girlfriend. My *only* girlfriend."

My declaration may be made a tad aggressively, but I don't give a shit. Mom may be abiding by my rules, but I won't let this slide. She can parade around females and males and flaunt my sexual proclivity and none of it matters. Daisy is my present and my future. Nysa is my past and that's where she's going to stay.

"I never thought I'd see the day when Kai Kingsley was monogamous."

"And I never thought I'd see the day when a Chambers attended a Kingsley private event. What exactly are you doing here again?"

Nysa doesn't even flinch, not even a twitch in her wings. Only a tightening of her lips indicates her displeasure.

"I'm a personal guest of your mother's. I was invited and I decided to attend, just like every other guest present."

Yeah, I don't believe that for one second. I don't know what my mom said to convince her to attend tonight, and it doesn't matter. We just need to get through this conversation, appease both Daisy and my mother then leave and get dinner at *Dottie's*.

Daisy

From the tone of the conversation, it's obvious Nysa is a past sexual partner of Kai's. It's easy to tell that Kai is irritated at her presence, and I don't even have to hear it in his words, it's written all over his face. I don't think I've ever seen him unsmiling for this long.

I want to assure Kai that I knew of his past and I accept him as he is, but now is not the time. And although it's clear where his affections lie, it's hard not to feel jealous staring at his beautiful ex-lover. Nysa is magnificent. Her coloring, wings, elegance, and beauty. She's a perfect match for Kai. Wearing a chic low-cut dress that shows off her figure and unique skin tone, she's the type of female his family would want him with, who they would approve of. That must be why his mother invited her tonight, in the hopes they would rekindle their romantic relationship.

The thought makes my heart catch in my throat and a hot chill run down my spine. That familiar panic of not fitting in and being unaccepted makes my previous state of elation vanish. The easy conversation and familiarity with his siblings is smothered under the evidence of my obvious deficiency.

My spiraling emotions are brought to an abrupt halt when I feel Kai's warm presence surround me. His strong arms holding me close while his breath heats my exposed throat, a sensation that eases my nerves and calms my doubt.

"Are you alright, Blossom? Do you need to go?" Kai's voice is a balm and I want to lather myself in it.

"I'm fine. I don't mind, really."

"Okay. If you say so."

Turning away from Kai and back to his mother and the others, I catch them all watching us very intently. It brings me up short and I trip over my thoughts trying to get our conversation back on track.

I want his family to like me for some reason. I've never had a boyfriend, and I always imagined what it would be like to meet the family of the male I'm with and be greeted with smiles and open arms. What it would feel like to be accepted and fit in for once.

"You're a local, correct?" Naomi asks conversationally. I'm thankful for the somewhat normal topic and shake off the lingering nervousness. I came here to get to know his family and that's what I'm going to do.

"Yes. I actually live on the east border of your property. We have a flower nursery there."

"Is that so? Going for convenience Kai, or lack of options? Small towns can have a diminished dating pool to pick from." Nysa's sharp words are delivered with such flatness, I would think she was being impartial except for the bitterness in her tone only a nymph could hear, and she knows it.

Kai bristles at my side as I internally wither and die. So

much for fitting in. This female doesn't even know about my human heritage and still I don't belong. I'm still the odd one out. I think I bit off more than I could chew coming here. I blame the endorphins I experienced on my outing to *Sticky Buns*. It made me feel capable and brave to the point where I ignored who would be in attendance.

Even if they don't know about my human half, I'm still considered lower than these people because of where I live, how much money I don't have, that my last name can't be tracked back dozens of generations, and that I don't have an ivy league education. No matter what, they will always find fault with me. I'll never measure up and I'll never be enough, and that thought makes me question everything Kai and I have together.

There's no way a male like him, from a world like his, would give it all up for me and my lame flower garden. Kai is an extroverted world traveler and so completely different from me, the introverted homebody. I was stupid to believe this could work.

I open my mouth to begin to give some kind of excuse to leave but Kai beats me to it.

"I'd argue the dating pool among people who isolate themselves from the rest of the world is more diminished than the low population of Snowberry. There's so much muddled blood among your circles, how can you tell if the male you're sleeping with isn't your half-brother or cousin?"

Endo bursts out laughing, not even caring about the affronted look on Nysa's face or the clenched jaw of his mother. Even Keiko covers her mouth with her hand to conceal her giggle and smile. I'm so shocked by Kai's words I can't decide what I should do. I don't think this is about me anymore, and although I'm grateful to no longer be the center of attention I don't like where this conversation is heading.

"You weren't complaining while you were in my bed," Nysa retorts, trying to regain the upper hand over Kai.

Looking up at him at my side, I want to pull on his elbow and urge him to leave. This is only making a scene and I can see his mother's patience dwindling by the second. He was right we shouldn't have come.

"That's because you were too busy staring at your own reflection in the mirror to realize I wasn't even looking at you. You could have been anyone, it didn't matter."

"Oh, and it matters now?"

"Yes! Because when I'm with Daisy I don't feel like I'm being smothered by overbearing, demanding, greedy, self-centered people who care more about what I can do for them than how I feel. She makes me smile, laugh, and feel more like myself than I have in decades. Being with her isn't a chore that eats away at my soul." Kai looks down at me and although he's speaking to Nysa, his words are meant for me. "Daisy is sweet, considerate, beautiful, and secretly funny even if she doesn't realize it. She cares about her family and friends, treating them with respect and love. Spending every day doing what makes her happy." He turns back to face his mother and Nysa not at all withering under their glares like I did. His words brand themselves onto my heart and I nearly melt into a puddle at his feet as he keeps reprimanding the two females. "I'd rather spend every day watching her tend to her flowers than spend one more minute attending pointless parties only orchestrated to fulfill your own self-importance."

Kai concludes his speech, and no one makes a sound. Endo, Keiko and I remain silent bystanders, observing and waiting. The atmosphere shifting drastically in the wake of his declaration. My own heart stutters and trips and I want to wrap my arms around Kai and kiss him. Kiss away the deep hurt in his heart and be everything he thinks I am. We may come from completely different worlds and families, but we're both misfits that don't fit quite right in the world around us. Yet we fit together.

"Come on Daisy, I think it's time to go. Endo, I'll talk to you later. Goodnight Keiko." Kai focuses on both his siblings before turning his attention back to his mother and Nysa. "Thank you for another unforgettable evening, mother. I'd almost forgotten why I avoid such gatherings. Nysa, I hope whatever she promised you was worth it."

With his strong and sure hand in mine, Kai directs us out of the house and away from his family.

Chapter 19
Daisy

"I am so sorry about all that. I had no idea she was going to do something so juvenile." Kai mutters and continuously apologizes as if what just happened was any of his fault.

"It's okay, Kai. I knew about your past already. It really doesn't bother me to know you had lovers in the past."

Kai abruptly stops and whips around to face me. We're halfway down the driveway to where he parked the sports car we arrived in, blissfully alone and far away from the muffled sounds of the party within the house.

"You knew?"

"Yes. More than one person warned me of your flirtatious and promiscuous ways."

Defeat and disbelief wash over Kai, his face and shoulders falling as he looks down at me. I reach up and cup his cheek brushing a thumb across his high cheek bone. His brow smooths out and he leans into my touch, tension leaving his taught body.

"And you still want me?" he asks in a small voice, his lips brushing the palm of my hand.

"Very much so."

"Even knowing how many others I was with before you?"

I tense thinking about him and Nysa together, the reminder almost enough to make me pull back, almost.

"As long as it was the past, I don't see how it has anything to do with the present."

In one swift motion Kai engulfs me in his arms, body and tail holding every part of me he can and pressing it tight against him. Almost as if he were to let me go I would disappear into the air. His lips follow a half second after his body, slanting over mine and sealing us together.

The kiss is desperate but tender. More about assuring him I'm still here than anything. I give into the kiss and allow him to take all that he needs. I want it too. Need it, need him. Need to know what he said wasn't just words spoken to hurt his mother.

Arms still tight around his neck Kai pulls back enough to speak against my lips, our noses brushing.

"Can we go back to your house now? I don't want to be here anymore."

I nod because I can't speak. He kissed the words from my mouth, my body shifting from frayed nerves and dazed confusion to molten heat and liquid desire. Kai's touch will do that to me. I don't care what his family thinks about me, at least not his mother, not anymore. All I care about is being with Kai and making us both forget all the unpleasantness from tonight and replacing it with something better.

The rain starts as a light drizzle as we make our way back to my house. The drops growing into small splatters on the windshield. Kai's hand is firmly in place around my thigh, ensuring the desire he stoked with his kiss only intensifies, as he parks the car in the small gravel lot in front of the gardens and greenhouse, instead of the private drive leading to my house.

For a long moment we're both quiet, sitting in the car watching the rain roll down the windows. I can sense the apology on his lips before Kai opens his mouth and I cut him off before he can start talking about things that aren't about kissing me or removing all our clothes and having him demonstrate his skills.

"You know what I like to do when it rains?"

Kai licks his lips and gives me a weak but grateful smile. "No. What do you like to do when it rains, Blossom?"

Reaching for the door handle I give him my most mischievous smile. "Follow me and find out."

Without a second thought, I thrust the door open and run out into the rain. It's cool against my heated skin but it does nothing to douse the flames in my heart and farther south. I want more with Kai and I'm tired of the flirting and teasing and promising touches that lead to nothing. I want them to lead to something. A lot of something.

I laugh and squeal when I spot Kai shirtless chasing after me. The ground is damp and soft beneath my bare feet, and I love the feeling of earth and water against my skin. Making my way to the rows of manicured shrubs and flowers, I run down one row and make a quick turn up another. The rain has completely soaked through my dress now. Strands of wet hair fall from my braided crown and stick to my cheek.

"You can't escape me Blossom," Kai calls in the distance behind me and I'm sure he's going slow on purpose.

I look back over my shoulder and see his red hair soaked and plastered to his bare shoulders, the ring of gold around his horn gleaming in the moonlight, his lickable muscles flexing as he maneuvers around a rose bush. I swear there's steam rising from his bare chest where the rain slicks his skin.

I stop on the opposite side of a row, keeping a barrier between us. Kai stops directly across from me, grinning like a predator about to catch his prey.

"I don't want to escape you," I tell him, breathing heavily and speaking over the sound of the rain.

"Then what do you want?"

"You'll have to catch me to find out."

Lifting the wet hem of my dress I pivot and dash towards the greenhouse, Kai's laughing growl following close behind.

The doors to the greenhouse are unlocked, as they always are, and I only pause for a half second to throw one door open and run inside. The raindrops tap on the glass roof creating a symphony only mother nature can create. Over the muffled sound of the rain, I can hear Kai's crunching footsteps, fast and light behind me. Before I can stop to look, red striped arms encircle my waist and lift me off the ground, halting the chase. The sound of our joined laughter mixing with the rain drops, only adds to its beauty.

Kai's hot lips press to the crook of my neck as his arms tighten around me. My head falls back onto his chest, exposing my throat to him. The soft sensation more intense than the gentle press of lips should illicit. A prickle of goosebumps and a quickening of my heart as it leaps into my throat, forces a breathy gasp from my lips. Kai growls in approval and the sound vibrates down my spine and settles between my thighs. I'm soaked from head to toe, and I can still feel my pussy growing wet and wanting.

On some instinct I didn't know I had, my back arches and my ass presses into his groin, the hard length of him firm against my backside. One hand glides down my stomach cupping me, holding my back firm against his chest, causing us both to moan at the pressure. A throb pulses in my core, and I want more, need more.

"Is this what you want, little Blossom? You want me here, between your thighs?"

Kai punctuates his words with a firm press against my clit with the heel of his hand and my nipples harden, creating sharp points through my damp dress.

"Yes. I want you, Kai. Between my thighs and hands and lips."

Tilting my head back, I pull on the back of Kai's neck, forcing his mouth to mine. Our tongues lash out and tangle, steam rising from our bodies as Kai's body and desire warms every inch of me.

"You can have me anywhere you want me, Daisy. As long as I can have you too."

Breaking free of Kai's hold, I step back so he can see me clearly. Pulling at the wet material of my dress I lift it and pull the garment over my head, stripping in what I hope is a sexy way and not a fumbling, inexperienced way. I may know about Kai's experience, but he doesn't know about my inexperience. I don't want him to suddenly turn noble and stop things before they get where I want them to go.

The dress falls to the ground with a wet plop, and I stand before Kai in nothing but a pair of very wet panties that I'm sure have become see through. My nipples pebble in the cool air and I want to feel Kai's warm hands on them. Kai stands perfectly still, only his chest rising and falling as he takes in my naked form. I try to still my tail, but it trembles and flicks back and forth with anticipation.

The red of Kai's eyes have become a deep scarlet, his claws

extending from his dripping fingers, his tail normally active is deathly still, sitting on the ground at his feet. The substantial bulge at the front of his pants nearly tents the material.

Feeling awkward under his gaze, my bravado wanes and I lift my arms to cover my chest. Kai is the first male to see me naked and I can't tell if his response is good or bad.

"No!" Kai barks and my arms still halfway raised. "I want to see all of you, Blossom."

Kai closes the distance between us and uses one gentle claw to press my arm back down to my side. That same claw brushes the curve of my hip, trailing up my side leaving goosebumps in its wake, until he reaches the swell of my breast. They're not large, but that doesn't seem to deter Kai. His hand cups the underside and covers one entire boob with the span of his hand.

"Perfect."

With the tip of a claw, Kai grazes a nipple, and I can feel the slight touch all the way to my pussy, and I let out an uncontrollable whimper.

"So sensitive. Do you want me to suck on these pretty pink buds?"

I nod instantly. I want his mouth on every part of me. Kai obliges, leaning down flicking the tip of his tongue against my nipple before he sucks the entire thing into his mouth. My hands thread through his damp hair and grip his horns holding him to me. He responds by nipping my nipple with his fangs.

"Kai," I moan his name, a plea, a protest, whatever to get him to do that again.

He does. His mouth closing over my breast and sucking hard. His hands reach down, and I feel fabric tear and fall away, leaving me completely naked. Then I feel hands on my bare backside. The combination of never before felt sensations has me panting and shaking.

Kai swiftly cups both of my ass cheeks, lifting me and setting me on the edge of a table. The same worktable we sat at the first day we met. How serendipitous.

Pressing his hips between my knees, my legs open for Kai, and he presses his hard length against my bare pussy. Fuck it feels amazing. Hard, hot, and long. I tilt my hips to rub against him seeking the friction I desperately need and Kai groans. Leaning in he captures my lips in a bruising kiss as our hands grapple for purchase on one another. Fingers tangle in wet hair and our tails twist together. My legs lock around Kai's thighs on instinct and I feel his wet pants under my calves. I want to feel skin.

Hesitation gone, I reach down and unbutton his pants, carefully unzipping them until I can reach in and grasp his cock. It's just as I imagined, warm and solid. I give it a long stroke getting a feel of it in its entirety. He's large and thick, the crown of his cock slick with his own arousal.

"Fuck Blossom. Do that again," Kai demands, so I do. He growls in satisfaction and pumps his cock through my hand.

Kai finishes removing his pants, sliding them down his tapered waist and narrow hips revealing all of him to me. He remains between my legs, hands rubbing up and down my thighs, but I can see every inch of him.

Crimson stripes circle his shaft, the color fading into a dark scarlet at his balls. Definitely lickable.

"I want to lick you. I have for a long time. I think about doing it every time I see you," I admit.

"Feel free to lick me whenever you want. Just know I plan on returning the favor. As a matter of fact, I think I'll start."

Kneeling, Kai's cock slips free of my hand, and he places his mouth directly at the apex of my legs, breathing hot air on my sensitive skin.

"May I?" he asks. I didn't expect him to ask, or to do this, but I want it. I want it all.

"Yes."

His lips press tender kisses to my inner thigh moving up until his lips caress my clit, then his tongue. Holy fucking shit, his tongue. Hot, wet and talented. It strokes the length of me, and I have to grip Kai's horns to keep from falling over. He seems to like me gripping his horns, because he hums against my pussy sending another spasm of pleasure through my body.

Kai lifts one leg over his shoulder and hooks a hand under my other knee, pressing me open further for him. His tongue and lips do things to me I've only ever dreamt about, and it doesn't take long for me to climb that hill racing towards the peak of my orgasm.

Swapping his tail for his hand holding my knee, Kai slides a finger inside my core and sucks on my clit.

"So fucking tight," he mumbles against my core, and when he curls his finger, I scream.

My orgasm explodes inside me like a bomb. Pure ecstasy causes my entire body to tingle and shake. The sound of the rain outside concealing my screams and moans. Thank goodness, because if my brother or Tobias heard us, I'd be mortified, and pissed because I still want more.

"Mmm, you taste delicious, little Blossom. Like honeysuckle."

Kai licks up my orgasm and slides that talented tongue over every inch of my pussy, almost sending me into another orgasm. I want another one, but this time on his cock. I've been dreaming about having sex with a living breathing male, and up until recently it wasn't a specific male. Kai has been taking over my fantasies as of late and I want to play all of them out with him.

I pull Kai up by his horns and he grins at me, bending over to suck a nipple on his way. His cock bobs as he stands, practically reaching for me, begging me to touch it.

"I want this now," I whisper into his lips, while reaching for his cock. "I want to feel you inside me. It's all I can think of."

"How do you want me, Daisy? Here on the table, with your legs wrapped around me? Bent over from behind? I wouldn't mind giving you a nice spanking. Or do you want to be on top? Fuck, I'd love to see you riding me."

Every option is viable, many I've seen in porn videos. I've had plenty of time to consider which I wanted most, which one I imagined doing with Kai. Okay I imagined doing all of them, but the first time I want to be on top. I want to slide him into me and watch as I take him. Watch his face contort with pleasure and agony as I force every second of bliss from him as I control the pace.

"I want to be on top," I tell him, a tad bashful but determined.

"Fuck yes."

Lifting me under my ass, I wrap my legs around his waist, trapping his length between our bodies. He circles looking for a good place to position us.

"There," I point to the mossy grass area, and he immediately obeys.

Sitting on the ground I kneel on either side of his hips. There're still a few rocks pressing through the moss, and I place a hand on the ground eagerly willing the moss to spread and grow, coating the area in thick, soft, spongy moss and grass. Kai grins up at me.

"That's useful."

"It can be."

Kai lifts me by the hips and lines the head of his cock up

with my entrance. I stop him before he can slam me down on his length. Maybe I'll be able to do that in the future but he's so large that I'll need to take it slow for my first time. To savor the feeling of a real cock inside me.

"Wait, slow down. I need, want to go slow. At least at first."

Stilling his frantic pace, Kai looks up at me and tilts his head like a curious animal. Those perceptive eyes of his catching on far too quick for my liking.

"Are you a virgin, Daisy?"

Virgin. What a stupid word. It relates to someone who's never had sexual intercourse by definition, but I've been using toys and dildos for years. I've experienced penetration, just not from a real penis. Does that mean I'm still a virgin?

"Not exactly."

"It's a yes or no question. How are you not exactly a virgin?"

Thankfully he doesn't pull away or move me off his lap, his cock is still poised at my entrance, and I tease the tip, rubbing it through my wetness. I'm trying to distract him and remind him what I want, and that my virginal status has nothing to do with it.

"I haven't had sex with another person, but I have used toys. I know what it feels like to be penetrated, just not by a real penis."

A multitude of emotions flash over Kai's face, confusion, intrigue, trepidation, delight, and finally a sort of awe. His arms wrap around my back, pulling our chests flush, trapping me to him. He looks over my face, memorizing every curve and blemish before settling on my eyes. His are filled with a calm reassurance and resolve. Having made some sort of decision.

"I'm thrilled to be your first Daisy. We can go at whatever pace you want."

Swiveling my hips I let his tip slip inside me, pressing down until more of him slides in. He doesn't try to take control or demand more, remaining still and allowing me the control I desire. His hot skin feels so much different than silicone. Still hard but somehow soft at the same time, far warmer and wetter that's for sure.

Then he does something no toy never has, he flexes his cock inside me. It thumps forward and back, and I love it. My eyes flashing wide and mouth falling open on a surprised gasp.

"You like that, Blossom?"

"Yes."

"Better than a rubber dick?"

"Far better."

I work his shaft deeper, inch by inch and when I sit flush on his lap, his balls pressing against my ass, he does that flex again. This time I can feel his entire length move inside me and I clench down in response, making Kai groan loudly.

Chapter 20
Kai

Holy fucking hell. Daisy feels amazing sitting on my cock. She's wrapped around me like a koala, and I still want to get closer. To feel every inch of her skin against mine.

She's a virgin. A *fucking* virgin. Literally. She's never fucked, but has had plenty of practice to prepare herself. She takes me so well and yet remains tight around me like a suction tube. She also likes it when I flex my cock inside her. Yeah, no silicone toy can do that.

My tail lashes out and latches on to her leg, her own little tail brushes against my inner thigh and sends prickles of pleasure straight to my balls. Cupping her ass, I slide a thumb up to wrap around the base of her tail, knowing the sensitivity there. Her skin prickles in goosebumps across her chest and the dusty rose of her nipples darkens as they become sharp points brushing against my chest.

I let her set her pace, riding my cock how she wants. Lifting up on her knees and slowly lowering herself again. It takes a massive amount of willpower to not thrust up into her or force her down by the hips. Every time she bottoms out, her pussy strangles my cock and I'm only going to last so long at this leisurely pace.

To distract myself I press my lips to Daisy's skin, peppering kisses along her collarbone and neck, up to her jaw and ears. Fuck her ears are adorable. Her hair is tangled and wet around her shoulders and down her back. The green filigree vine markings on her skin move in tandem with her bouncing, pulling in tight around her nipples and up her throat. The flowers in her hair, that were a mix of many things all throughout the night, have settled into only jasmines.

"I knew jasmines meant you were horny."

Daisy's eyes widen then return to half-mast, glittering with amusement. "Don't tell Sage. I don't want him to know how horny you make me."

I'm never telling anyone. Her jasmines are just for me and no one else.

Daisy presses down hard on her next downward thrust and circles her hips, rubbing her clit against my pelvic bone. My vision goes spotty as my eyes cross. That's it. I can't take it anymore.

Rolling us over I lay Daisy beneath me and thrust into her hard. Her pert little tits bounce at the force and her mouth falls open on a moan.

"You're such a little tease, you know that? Riding me so torturously slow my balls ache."

"What are you gonna do about it?"

I give her a few fast and hard thrusts, gripping her thigh and wrapping it around my hip. Like a needy little thing she arches her back and thrusts her tits towards me. Greedily I lick from the bottom swell of her breast over the nipple and around, relishing in her throaty, unhinged sounds. Each one telling me just how much she's enjoying every lick, bite, and thrust.

"You feel perfect around me, Blossom. I want to feel you come all over me."

My balls slap against her ass and I increase my pace. Her previous teasing making me painfully hard and halfway to orgasm.

"Keep that up and I will," Daisy pants out between stunted breaths.

Placing an elbow by her head I lean into her body, with one hand under her ass I shift her hips under me, her pupils blowing out when I press deep in the new position.

"Oh my god. Don't stop. Please, I'm so fucking close. Make me come Kai. Yes, yes."

Daisy rambles pleas and praise that only makes me fuck her harder. Our bodies coming together in a loud slapping rhythm that's hidden by the rain still falling outside. I bury my face in her neck and hair, her scent rounding out all my senses to engulf me entirely in her.

I can feel her pussy tighten around my cock and know she's about to come. I want to come with her. I want to break that crest and shatter with her, to experience her first orgasm around a real cock with her. Give her everything.

"Kai, Kai. I'm going to, oh fuck!"

"That's it, Daisy. Come for me, flower."

She does, on a shattered screaming groan, and I follow right behind her. My balls drawing up tight and my cock pulsing out my release inside her tight heat as it flutters and spasms around my shaft.

"That's it baby, keep coming for me. Fuck. That's it, Blossom. You feel fucking perfect coming on my cock."

Pressing my mouth against the soft skin below her ear, I

kiss the sensitive area keeping my cock buried deep inside her and rock just enough to milk her orgasm, and my own, until her body goes lax and soft beneath me. I can feel my cum dripping out of her.

Rolling to my side, I slip free of Daisy's tight channel and pull her with me, keeping her naked body curled up against mine. With the rain still coming down outside it's only getting colder. Now that we're not engaging in strenuous activities, Daisy's body will cool but mine won't. I can keep us both warm with my fire magic.

Daisy either catches on to my plan to keep her warm or she just wants to cuddle with me, because she curls into my side resting her head on my chest. I want to stay like this for the rest of the night but know we can only stay for so long. I won't risk Daisy's health.

The hand wearing my gold bracelet rests across my abdomen, and I lazily fiddle with the metal. It's far better suited on Daisy's wrist than mine. I'm glad I gave it to her. I knew Keiko wouldn't mind. It was my selfish way of marking her as mine. Unlike shifters who bite and scent mark, nymphs don't have a physical way of marking their mates.

Mate?

Fuck, I'm thinking of Daisy as my mate. Is that why I wanted her wearing my jewelry? I didn't have to give her my ear cuff or my bracelet, and I certainly didn't need to resize it so she couldn't remove it without significant assistance. My casual fling, intended only to dissuade my mother, has become something completely serious. At least—as far as I know—my mom hasn't announced my mating to anyone, which is good. At this point though, I could care less what she tells people. No matter what it is, it won't be happening. I'm with Daisy now, for real, and nothing my mother says can change that.

Pocket Full of Posies

Looks like I'll be staying in Snowberry longer than originally planned, and I'm fine with that. I'll need to find somewhere else to stay. I can't remain in my parents' house. Maybe there's a room or a house for rent. Until then, there's always the motel. Ideally, I'd prefer to stay with Daisy. To stay close to her and spend every day with her. Until her brother accepts the fact that I won't be going anywhere, and that I'm unequivocally dedicated and in love with Daisy, I don't want to push myself into their home. I want to be accepted and welcomed. Because once I'm in Daisy's bed, I'm never leaving.

I've become addicted to her smiles and trying to decipher the changing flowers in her hair. And now I've become addicted to her body, her touch, her kiss. The way her tail rests lazily entwined with mine. The satisfied smirk on her lips and softness of her skin. No one I've ever been with can compare to the way Daisy makes me feel and no one will ever come after her. She's it for me. And by the end of the equinox, I'm going to convince her that I can be it for her.

Her hair is almost dry now, strewn in slightly frizzy tangles across her back and my arm wrapped around her. The scent of wet earth and sex lingers in the air. I wonder if others will be able to scent it tomorrow or if the rain will wash it away. Shifters will no doubt scent it, even with the rain. Their noses are like our ears, their most advanced sense. I hope others can still smell us tomorrow. Just one more way to claim Daisy as mine.

"So, what do daisies in your hair mean? Sexually satisfied? And is that a gardenia? Haven't seen that one before. You're just full of surprises tonight, aren't you?" I finger the delicate petals of the flowers and Daisy's cheeks pinken.

"Daisies mean happiness."

"So, I make you happy?"

"Very much."

"Good."

Daisy nuzzles into my chest and wiggles against me. I should be concerned that we're in a building made of glass, with unlocked doors, lying on the ground completely naked, but I'm not. I'm exactly where I want to be.

"Would you like to stay the night tonight?" Daisy asks in a quiet voice, and I can hear her nervousness in her soft tone.

"I would love to. But...I think it would be better if I waited." I can physically feel Daisy drooping in dejection, and quickly add, "At least until your brother doesn't hate me anymore. I don't want him to wake up to see me in the morning and make all kinds of assumptions and then I lose all the progress I've made with him. I want your family to like me. Unlike mine, yours is important."

"Your family is important too," she argues...weakly.

"Maybe Endo and Keiko, but the rest of them can go to hell."

"Surely there's others..."

"Nope."

We lay in silence again, the only sound that of the rain on the greenhouse. Daisy's idea of family is far different from mine and now that she's met my mother, and the people she associates herself with, she has a better idea of why I want nothing to do with them.

"My family is not a family," I begin, trying to put into words what it is to be a Kingsley. "It's more like a business. There's the CEO's and CFO's, HR department, PR managers, personal assistants, assets, and minions. There's very little love or emotions between most of them. I mean nothing more to my parents than an asset they can manipulate to grow their portfolio and better their public image.

Pocket Full of Posies

"I wish they behaved more like nymphs than socialites, but I fear they've spent too much time in the human world and have lost touch with their heritage. Their *true* bloodlines. I'll admit I haven't been the best either, but that's because I didn't know there was anything better out there for me. I thought all I had was their money and partying. Now I know different. Now I have you."

Daisy looks up at me through thick lashes, with her glowing golden eyes and I can hear her wonderment in her slight intake of breath.

"And I have you?" A question not a statement.

"Yes, you most definitely have me, Blossom."

"So, when can you spend the night?"

I chuckle at her ability to take such a heavy discussion and shift it towards something easy and comfortable.

"Maybe after the equinox? I'd like to at least speak with Sage first. How does that sound?"

"Do I still get to spend the equinox with you?"

"Of course. I wouldn't have it any other way. You'll stay with me, in our tent, for the equinox and after that we'll see how it goes. But that in no way means I'm going anywhere. I'll sleep here in the greenhouse if I need to."

Daisy giggles and the sound holds joy and amusement. I think I'll make her giggle every day because I want to hear that sound and those emotions from her every day we're together.

"Come on Daisy, Let's get you dressed and in bed where it's warm and dry."

"I'm warm and dry right where I am."

"That may be so, but I don't want to fall asleep and wake up to your brother staring at my cock and your naked backside. He'd definitely never want me to come around again if that happened."

Daisy groans the most adorable grumble, pushing herself onto her elbow. Strands of chestnut hair fall across her forehead and in the dim light her features are cast in shadows. I reach up and brush the hair from her face so I can better see her.

"Will you come back tomorrow?"

"I'll come back every day until you tell me to stop."

"You might be here for a very long time then."

"That's the idea."

After Daisy is back in her damp dress, and me in my pants, I escort her to the front door of her house. The rain is still falling but has lightened up. By the time we make it to the porch both of our feet are coated in a layer of mud and grass. The sensation is gratifying. Perhaps I'll have to go shirtless and shoeless.

With one more long, lingering, erection inducing kiss, I manage to say goodnight and Daisy goes inside. Instead of returning to my parents' house, where the party is still going on, I drive to the motel. Thankfully not as many out of towners come in for the equinox as shifters do for the blood moon, and I'm able to get a room. So, I don't have to deal with any of my family or the party guests, who have no doubt become house guests staying in the many empty guest rooms my mother insists on having.

Chapter 21
Daisy

It's been two days since the night I spent with Kai in the greenhouse and had sex for the first time. It was amazing, more than I ever expected it to be. I didn't realize how having such an intimate connection with a person while being sexual, would enhance everything so much. Since then, there has been a lot of making out and groping, but no sex. Not for lack of wanting, though I'm optimistic about the equinox tonight.

We decided Kai would meet us at the house, then all four of us would make our way to the equinox celebration, in the forest on Hunter's land, together. Since that land connects to ours, we'll be walking there.

Last night I packed a small overnight bag, just a change of clothes, a toothbrush, and a hairbrush. I don't need anything else. Food will be provided, and Kai has assured me we will have a tent fully stocked with bedding and a small wood burning stove for heat, even though he can provide all the heat I need. His words, not mine.

Kai arrives before sunrise and quickly scoops up my bag and places a chaste kiss on my lips.

"Good morning, Blossom. Are you ready for your first equinox celebration?"

"She better be, because I'm not letting her back out now," Sage answers Kai's question before I can, as he exits the house locking the door behind him. "I've been trying to get her to attend since she was sixteen and I'm not letting her miss out on another one. If she tries to run you make sure to grab her, you hear me, Kai? Tobias won't force her, but I know the only reason she's going is because of you. So, you're the final line of defense if she tries to run. She's done it before."

Kai cocks his head at me and licks the tip of a fang with his tongue, a move he knows draws attention to his mouth and makes me want to kiss him.

"Is that so? You a runner, Blossom? Am I going to need to tie you up and carry you there?"

I smack him on the arm, a bare arm because ever since I told him I like him shirtless he has remained shirtless. "No, you do not need to tie me up. I'm going on my own. I want to go, I'm excited."

"Good. I'm happy you're finally joining us." Tobias wraps an arm around my shoulders and gives me a squeeze, his own bag slung over his shoulder.

"Alright all, let's get going!" Sage leads the way down the deck and towards the back of the house.

We all follow, Kai placing himself at my side and threading my fingers through his. His skin is warm and burns away any chill from the early morning hour. My feet are covered with fur lined rubber boots today. I would be fine without them. I've gone barefoot longer into winter than this. The morning may be cool, and the temperature may be lowering, but it's still nice enough out to wear shorts. However, Kai was insistent that I do. I only wear them to appease him, because he threatened to carry me the entire time if I didn't.

Ten feet from the wood line, Delphi's furry blue and white body scurries the short distance to us and bounds into my arms. She's chattering away nonstop, obviously excited I'm going to the equinox.

"Hi Delphi. I'm happy to see you too. Are you ready for the celebration?"

Delphi chirps and chitters, pawing at my hair and flowers. Daisies, geraniums and an iris today. I'm excited to be going but also nervous. What if people stare? What if they try to talk to me and all I can say is the life cycle of an annual bloom?

It's okay, even if I do Kai, Sage, and Tobias will be there with me. Oh, and Delphi. She curls around my neck and purrs, rubbing her soft body against me. I expect her to settle in for the walk but before she can, she spots Kai, and a high-pitched excited chirp comes from her mere moments before she leaps to his shoulders. She settles around his neck and Kai chuckles, scratching her behind her ear.

It takes about thirty minutes of walking before we reach the designated celebration area. The fairies have cloaked it in a shield, concealing everything inside from prying eyes. The veil has a slight shimmer that only a non-human can spot, a rainbow of colors flickering in the early morning sunlight over a dome, just as thin and flexible as a soap bubble.

All of us approach the barrier and without hesitation Sage and Tobias waltz through, disappearing to the other side. Delphi leaps from Kai's shoulders and bounces through the air passing through the barrier as well. When it's my turn, I pause at its boundary and try to see beyond the magic. I can't. There are no sounds beyond the breeze through the trees and the chirping morning birds. I can't see anything in the distance or right in front of me other than trees and grass.

"Are you okay, Daisy?"

Kai's hand presses warm and firm against my lower back, a strong reassuring presence.

"Yeah, I just needed a second."

"Don't worry. Whatever's kept you from attending in the past, I promise there's nothing over there to be afraid of. If you ever feel uncomfortable or awkward, we'll just go back to the tent, okay?" Kai pulls me by the elbow, turning me into him and wraps me in his arms. I feel instantly safe and calm. "We can lay naked in a bed of silk and pillows, staring up at the stars through the top of the tent. And if you're really upset, I can console you with my body."

With a wicked grin, Kai leans down and licks the tip of my nose. No longer am I worried about people staring at me, instead I'm thinking about all the things we are going to be doing in our tent later.

"See. All you have to do is think about me naked and everything is better."

A smile stretches across my lips, and I look up at Kai through my lashes.

"And if I'm not upset? Will you still console me with your body?"

"I planned on it either way, Blossom. There's no escaping me."

I want to take Kai back to the tent right now and skip the rest of the celebration. Food, music, and dancing have nothing on naked Kai in silk sheets under the stars.

"Come on. We'll be late."

With one hand in mine, Kai pulls me through the bubble and unveils a world of magic. Floating lights like twinkling stars hover in the branches of the trees, illuminating the waning shadows of pre-dawn. Streamers of flowers stretch from branch to branch, tables are filled with a variety of food and sweets. Blankets are laid out for picnics with games and even a space for a band to play. There's no music playing yet as things are still being arranged and people are arriving and settling in. In a matter of hours though, I imagine the scene will become far more animated.

Delphi has disappeared to who knows where. Sage and Tobias are in the distance heading towards a line of canvas tents. They're round, made of ivory canvas and wood posts with an inward slanted roof to a center peek. People come early to pick the perfect spot for their tent. The dedicated ones always come the day prior to get the best locations. I think Sage and Kai came yesterday to claim our spots. Some tents are decorated with drawings and paintings, others have flower or seashell garlands draped around the door flaps. They don't seem particularly secure or soundproof. Am I going to hear other people having sex? Are people going to hear me having sex? Our tent better be far away from Sage's.

"Where is our tent at? Is it close to Sage's?"

"It's over here." Kai points in the opposite direction of Sage's tent, thank goodness. An area off the main path and set back away from the crowds. Our own little secluded haven.

Kai must see the clear relief on my face because he chuckles.

"What? Did you think I would put us right next to your brother? The tents are sprinkled with fairy dust to keep sound out and in, so there's no chance of them hearing me make you scream with pleasure, but I still didn't want to risk it."

"Much appreciated." I give his hand a squeeze and let him lead me to our tent. There aren't any decorations or adornments beyond a small posy of daisies tied to the string closure of the flaps. I look to Kai for confirmation this is indeed our tent.

"I didn't know what kind of decorations you would like. I thought maybe you could use your earth magic and spruce it up a bit?"

He gives me a hopeful look and I return it with a wide smile.

"I suppose I could give it a little sprucing up."

Kneeling on the ground I press my fingers into the soil and take a long deep breath. The earth below responds, and I can hear and feel the plants and trees around us. This deep in the forest there aren't many varieties of flowers, mainly shrubbery and green leafy things. I pluck one of the daisies from the posy and stick its stem into the ground next to my hand. Immediately I reach out and connect to the flower. It was freshly cut yesterday and is still vibrant, easy to control.

With less conscious thought and more will, I force the flower to root and grow, sprouting more and more blooms as the vines grow up the side of the canvas and cling to every available protrusion. Within minutes there's a cacophony of daisies framing the exterior entrance of our tent.

"It's perfect."

Kai's whispered words pull my attention back to him. He's looking at me with unconcealed craving.

"Why don't we take a look at the inside? Maybe test out the bed and sheets?" he suggests not so innocently.

Although I would very much like to snuggle into whatever bed is inside the tent, I am way too nervous for naked time just yet. So, I ignore his offer to test out the bed but do open the flaps and step inside.

The interior is far more festive and colorful than the exterior. Lush, patterned carpets line the entire space, overlapping in some areas to completely cover any dirt or grass. Personally, I would like grass in my tent but it's probably more for keeping the space clean and to not track dirt into the bed. I like dirt but even I like to sleep in a dirt-free bed.

Speaking of the bed, it's not so much a bed as a giant floor pillow. Like a huge cushion large enough for two people to sleep on comfortably, covered with multicolored pillows and blankets thick enough to cocoon in. A small wood burning stove sits dead center with a tube chimney stretching towards the hole at the center of the tent roof, a pile of precisely cut wood laid to one side of the space. There's even a low table with floor cushions for eating at.

The entire interior reminds me of the inside of a genie's bottle, and I kind of like it. I really have been missing out all these years. Even if all I did for the entire event was curl up in the pillow bed with a few good books, a bag of trail mix, and a crackling fire, it would have been worth attending.

"Wow. This is amazing. You set all this up?"

Behind me I find Kai watching as I turn in a circle inspecting all the items, just now noticing the hanging lanterns with colorful glass that I imagine will reflect at night, creating a kaleidoscope of colors and patterns on the canvas walls.

"I did. Do you like it?"

"I love it. Can we just hang out in here the whole time?"

"I like that idea."

Sounds come from behind Kai and he looks out the open entry. Beyond I spot Endo and Keiko in the distance. Their tents are at least fifty yards away, through a few spread-out trees and bushes offering some separation from his family. Endo and Keiko are great but my interaction with his mother wasn't the introduction I had hoped for. I should have listened to Kai and just not gone to the party. At least then I could have continued to lie to myself that the rest of his family is more like Kai than the rumors and gossip make them out to be.

"I need to go talk to Endo. Will you be okay by yourself for a few minutes?"

Kai sets our bags at the edge of the genie bed and brings my hand to his lips, pressing a soft kiss to my knuckles.

"I think I'll be fine, just don't leave me alone for too long. If anyone shows up and tries to talk to me, I can't promise what I'll end up saying."

"I'm sure it'll be something charming and educational. Don't worry Blossom, I just need a few minutes. Then I plan on being attached to your tail the entire equinox."

His tail reaches up and curls around mine peeking out from under my shorts. In the time we've spent together I've grown less concerned with hiding it, at least from other non-humans. I still have to hide it from humans, of course, since they don't have tails. But I'm less embarrassed by it. Kai likes it, a lot if how he likes to play with it is any indication, and that's enough for me.

Chapter 22
Kai

Leaving Daisy alone only minutes after arriving at the festival was not my plan, but when I spotted Endo with only Keiko around, I knew it was my best opportunity to talk with Endo. With everything going on and my desire to remain as far from my parents and their guests as possible, I haven't been able to talk with him about me and Daisy.

"Kai," Endo calls as I hustle over to the area he's claimed for himself, thankfully the rest of the family is farther away. "You and Daisy made it. I wasn't sure you would."

"Yeah, her brother wasn't going to let her back out of coming this year and as much as I don't want to see Mom or Nysa, I wasn't going to let her miss it either. It is her first after all."

"No shit? Well, I hope she enjoys it. Are you still planning on breaking it off after?"

"Shhh," I shush my brother's big mouth and look around to make sure no one heard him. Pulling him to the side of his tent

I lower my voice. "No, I don't okay."

"But I thought she was just a temporary fix to get Mom off your back? I know you've gotten kind of smitten with her, but I thought the plan was the same," Endo thankfully whispers in a lower tone than his previous loud-mouthed statement.

"It's different now. It's real. She's mine now and I don't plan on letting her go."

"So, you're going to stay in Snowberry? That is very unlike you."

"If that's what she wants, yes. I'd do anything for her."

"That's a long way from a short fling and having a little fun."

Endo looks at me, like really looks at me. Eyes narrowed and lips pursed reading every minute expression on my face. I hope it says how much I care for Daisy, how much she means to me.

"Do you love her?" he asks, in a non-sarcastic way. The answer comes immediately.

"Yes."

"Then I'm in full support of you."

"Good because I may need you to run interference between us and the family. I'd rather not have a repeat of the party. I want her first equinox to be memorable in a good way." I beg my brother with my eyes, being far more serious than I've ever been.

"Of course. You know, I think Daisy is good for you. I've never seen you this way, all sincere and mature. I like party Kai, but I think I like in love Kai even better."

"Me too."

"Aw look at you all red and blushing."

"I'm always red you ass."

We shove at each other in that way only brothers can,

laughing and goading. I spend a few minutes speaking with him and Keiko, before making my way back to the tent where I find Daisy sitting at the low table nibbling on an apricot from the bowl of fruit, I set out for her. We didn't need to bring any food, but I wanted to make sure she had something in the tent if she got hungry.

"How's Endo?" She smiles up at me from her crossed legged position on the blue floor cushion, barefoot. Her lined rubber boots sitting neatly by the tent entrance.

"Great. I'm sure we'll see him again later. But I'm warning you now, I'm going to be greedy and keep you all to myself as much as possible."

"That's fine with me. So, what is the plan?"

I sit next to Daisy and grab an apple from the bowl, biting into it and chewing.

"Whatever we want. There'll be dancing and food, games and I think there are fairies offering fairy dusting to make you fly for a few minutes if you're interested."

The flowers in her hair curl and bloom with the shake of her head. "No, I'm plenty happy with my feet on the ground thank you very much."

We hang out in the tent for a while longer, waiting for more to arrive and to hear the music begin. Once we do I have to practically drag Daisy outside.

For the entire day I pull Daisy around, forcing her to dance with me, then to play a game of hide and seek with a group of children, and to eat every single sweet treat I spot.

The day is filled with laughter and joy, lighthearted conversation and absolutely no mention of hybrids and half-breeds or my family. I may have steered us in the opposite direction if I spotted one of my siblings or parents. We did cross paths with a few of my cousins, they don't care about my personal life choices as much as my immediate family and were even pleasant and cordial with Daisy.

Eventually Delphi finds us and mostly just rides around on my shoulder playing with my hair and holding one horn chattering away about all the fun things she's done since arriving. There are a handful of other sprites running around and Delphi has been playing with them.

As the sun is beginning to set, we come upon the band area while one group is leaving and new people are setting up, this one including the mayor's new mate. The not human, human Lottie, also known as Alexandria the famous pop star. I knew her as soon as I saw her because unlike the luddites of Snowberry I live out in the real world. I even saw her perform once in Paris. It appears I'm going to get to see her perform again.

Lottie is strapping on a very fancy acoustic guitar, while a young male shifter sits at the drum set and Becca flits over—for once not on roller skates, probably all the grass and dirt—carrying a pink tambourine and giddy as a kid on a candy high.

I pull Daisy to sit on one of the many communal blankets laid out in front of the band stand. She doesn't argue and sits next to me, scooting close and resting her head on my shoulder. Instinctually, my tail reaches out in search of hers and doesn't still until it's wrapped around it. I'm the most comfortable I've ever been, legs stretched out in front of me, leaning back on the heels of my hands with my girl tucked against my side. Perfection.

Lottie settles in and starts with a slow but sweet ballad, then a more upbeat tune. On her third song she picks up the tempo and a little girl, another earth nymph with moss green skin and sparkling gold eyes, maybe about eight years old, pulls Daisy up forcing her to dance.

Pocket Full of Posies

I sit and watch reveling in the joy radiating from Daisy's smile and laughter. Her chestnut brown hair fanning around her as she spins the flowers and vines like a crown on her head, the green markings on her skin perfectly still and content to remain so.

If I had to spend the rest of my life reliving one moment in time, it would be this one.

"Come make a necklace with me," the little girl says tugging on Daisy's hand. She's pointing towards a table set up not too far from the band stand where non-humans of all ages sit and thread beads on string making necklaces and bracelets.

"Oh, um, okay sure."

Daisy follows helplessly behind the girl as she's pulled to the table and promptly told to sit. I join them watching over Daisy's shoulder. The little girl pulls a bowl of beads in front Daisy and begins rambling about picking the best beads. I pick one up, inspecting the small item. They appear to be made from glass and stone. Probably made by an earth nymph or fairy.

"So, I'll make you one and you make me one," the little girl says.

"Alright," Daisy agrees, her smile never wavering.

The little girl picks a variety of beads both in color, pattern and material having no obvious relevancy or design in the choice and strings together a long strand easy to slip over Daisy's head.

"Okay, close your eyes, it's a surprise. No, don't look. Lean down and I'll put it on you."

Daisy does as instructed and dutifully waits until the little girl instructs her to open her eyes.

"Oh, my goodness, it's beautiful," Daisy swoons as she inspects the necklace that makes no sense. "I love your choice in beads, very eclectic."

"What's calectic mean?"

"Eclectic. It means having a broad and diverse range of style. It's a good thing. Non eclectic people are boring."

The little girl giggles and almost falls out of her wooden chair holding her stomach.

"You're funny."

Daisy blushes and tries to conceal her face from the girl. Lifting her chin with a finger I force her not to hide and she looks up at me. I give her a reassuring smile which she reciprocates.

"My turn, my turn. What did you make for me?"

Daisy holds up a shorter strand of precisely matched beads in an ombre of greens, slowly shifting from dark to light and back again.

"It's so pretty and eclectic." The little girl uses her new vocabulary and is quite proud of it.

"Yes, very eclectic."

"Thank you." The little girl wraps her arms around Daisy's waist and gives her a tight hug, right before bouncing up to her feet and running off yelling, to her parents I'd guess, about her new eclectic necklace.

Daisy and I relinquish the seat at the crafts table for the next person and make our way back to our tent. While Daisy was dancing with the little girl I secretly asked Tobias to deliver some food to our tent for dinner so we could eat alone. Although I love watching Daisy's social abilities blossom, I would really love to spend the rest of the evening with her alone.

"That's a very nice necklace you have there," I compliment Daisy's new accessory as we walk back to the tent. "It suits you."

"What? Random and nonsensical?"

"That and it's colorful and unique. One of a kind."

Her blush returns, this time running all the way down her

neck to her chest, and I want to strip her shirt from her body and trail that blush with my tongue. As a matter of fact, I'm going to do just that. The day has been long and we both need to relax. I know the perfect place.

Directing Daisy by the small of her back, I guide us in the direction of my secret place. A place I've only gone to alone, to unwind and decompress after too much time spent with my family during the festivities I was forced into in the past.

"Where are we going?" Daisy asks but follows my direction.

"It's a surprise, you'll just have to be patient and find out."

Her instant trust in me has my heart skipping a beat or four. Everyone usually dismisses me and my input. Labeling me the foolhardy party boy with nothing of substance to say. The fact that Daisy doesn't look at me like an empty-headed sex addict, only solidifies my love for her. She sees past the surface level to the me underneath all the gold and flirting.

It takes us a few minutes to leave the bustling celebration and festival areas, entering a quieter, less populated area of the forest. Following the stream, I know in another handful of minutes we'll find what I'm looking for.

An incline in the terrain creates a small waterfall and pool in the stream. I don't know what causes it but the water of the pool at the base of the small falls is heated like a natural hot spring. I plan on stripping Daisy down and getting her naked in that water. Maybe massage every inch of her tempting flesh.

"This is beautiful. You knew this was here?"

"Of course. It's why I brought you here. The water is heated, like a jacuzzi or hot relaxing bath."

I'm already unbuttoning my pants, more than ready to get in that water and let it soothe my anxiety I've had all day making sure my mother didn't come anywhere near Daisy. Endo must have been trailing her like a hound because I didn't see her once.

"Oh, we're getting in?" Daisy sounds surprised but also hopeful.

"Oh yeah. I didn't drag you out to the middle of the forest to show you a hot spring just to look at it. I will always want to get you naked Daisy. Every opportunity I get."

I drop trou and stride butt naked over to Daisy. She watches my cock the entire time, causing it to swell and harden. Not that I wasn't already half hard, but her eyes on me quicken the process.

"Now you, Blossom."

She bites her lip and a flush colors her cheeks and chest. Perfection. When she doesn't begin to undress herself, I take that as an invitation to do it for her.

First her loose plain green t-shirt, pulling it from the hem and over her head, revealing gorgeous caramel skin inch by glorious inch. Green swirling marks accentuating her small breasts and long neck. Definitely going to be tasting those. I love that she hates bras as much as she hates shoes. Makes for easy access for me.

Next is her jean shorts. I hook my fingers in her underwear and remove both at the same time. Kneeling I kiss a path down her stomach, to her hip bone and lower, stopping right above the patch of dark curls above her pussy. My tail twitches with the restraint to not take it farther. *Patience Kai, there is plenty of time to take it slow and tease a little.*

Finally, Daisy stands before me naked wearing only her new necklace, and the gold bracelet and ear cuff I gave her. I wrap her in my arms and squeeze her to my chest, pressing every inch of skin together. I can feel the slight chill in her subsiding as the heat of my body warms hers. She doesn't flinch or shy away from my touch, instead embracing me as tightly as I do her. Wrapping her arms tight around my neck and standing on her toes, she brings her mouth to mine.

I could drown in her kiss, but we're still naked in the woods. Lifting Daisy to my chest I walk to the water's edge and step in. Steam billows off the surface and Daisy gasps when her bare ass breaches the water.

"Wow. That is a lot warmer than I expected. How is it so hot?"

"No idea. But I like to come here when I visit for the equinox to escape my family."

"I like it."

"Good. I'll bring you here whenever you want, Blossom."

I release my hold on Daisy, and she floats away sinking into the water until it reaches her chin. She tilts her head back and submerges her hair and flowers. When she lifts her head, the flowers are gone, floating in the stream, and her hair is slick and dark, plastered to her neck and shoulders.

"I don't think I've ever seen you without your flowers."

"Do I look different? Is it good or bad?"

She's so cute when she's unsure. She nibbles on her lower lip and to ease her worries I wade over to her and suck her lip from between her teeth and nip at it.

"You look beautiful no matter what, Daisy. Flowers or no flowers."

The tension evaporates from her expression, and I press another kiss to the tip of her nose. I want to kiss every part of her, the curve of her neck, the point of her ear, the tip of her breast. In time. Since most of her is currently under water—and I can't hold my breath for that long—I'll have to wait till we get back to the tent.

There's a ledge under the water, and I pull Daisy over to it. Sitting I prop her on my lap, a knee on either side of my hips.

Her bare pussy presses against my cock and it throbs at the pressure, and I moan.

"Keep that up Blossom and I'm going to have to bend you over the edge of the pool and punish you."

Her expression becomes wicked, and she grinds into my cock harder. My eyes roll back into my head and every thought vacates my brain.

"Promise?" Daisy whispers against my lips.

This woman is insatiable. I must have altered her brain chemistry the first time we had sex because she seems to be addicted to me now.

My arms wrap around her and hold her still, stopping her from torturing me anymore.

"How about you just sit still for a few minutes and relax with me?"

Dexterous fingers slide through my hair and trail the length of my horns, sending tingles down my spine, even submerged in the hot water. It's soothing, yet pleasurable, making my body—all but my cock—go limp.

"I needed this. Dealing with my family is always exhausting."

Daisy kisses my cheek, jaw, and neck. Light delicate kisses conveying affection and tenderness. Just like her. Delicate, tender, affectionate. Better than me in every way. I'm not worthy of her, but that isn't going to stop me from accepting what she gives.

Satisfied that I'm thoroughly destressed, Daisy settles against my chest, her cheek on my shoulder and nose pressed into my throat. I think I could die happy right now. Daisy naked and cradled in my arms, her bare pussy snug against my cock, not another soul in sight, surrounded by peace and quiet. I wonder how long we can remain before someone, or something ruins it all.

A loud squeal and chirp come from the branches overhanging the pool, followed closely by the fluffy body of Delphi the ever-intruding sprite.

So that was what? A whole two minutes? At least it's only Delphi. She bounds through the air and no lie, belly flops into the hot spring. Apparently, I'm not the only one who knows about this secret place. Good thing Delphi only talks to Daisy and me, she can't tell anyone how to find the hot spring.

Daisy sits up and giggles watching Delphi do rather impressive strokes through the water. She looks a little bit like a wet racoon, but in a cute way.

"Did you follow us out here, Delphi?" Daisy asks, while, sadly, slipping off my lap to join Delphi in her swimming.

"No. Delphi find hot water on her own. You follow me. It's okay, I'll allow it."

A bark of laughter bursts from me and echoes through the empty forest. If Daisy only knew the similarities between her and Delphi. If I didn't know they couldn't understand each other, I would think their personalities had rubbed off on each other. They're both adorable, funnier than they think, loyal and vegetarians.

I let Daisy swim around and play with Delphi, watching from my spot on the underwater bench. Marveling in the perfection that is Daisy's backside, as well as her gently pointed ears still wearing the gold cuff I placed there, and the gold bracelet on her wrist. A primal sensation washes over me seeing her in my gold.

We wade around the water for at least another half hour. Delphi demonstrating her masterful water abilities and then spraying us when she shakes off like a dog.

Daisy and I stand naked at the water's edge as we dry. My

internal heat warming our bones and drying us from within. I may take small advantage of the situation and steal a few rated R kisses before redressing and returning to the festival.

Chapter 23
Daisy

Kai may not have taken me over the edge of the pool like he threatened but whatever restraint he possessed at the hot spring evaporates when we return to our tent. The moment we step through the canvas doors, and he ties them shut, his hands manically roam my body.

"You've teased me enough Daisy. Now it's time to make up for it," Kai breathes into my lips between kisses, nips, and licks.

"Finally. I thought I would have to tie you down."

He chuckles against my throat sucking gently then harder, probably leaving a mark. I want his mark on me. I want him all over me.

"You still can if you like. I'm not opposed to it. To anything. You can do anything you want to me Daisy, and I would relish it."

"Maybe another time. There's nothing to tie you to in here." I really hadn't considered tying him down, but I too am not opposed to it. *When we're somewhere with real walls and supports.*

"So practical," he murmurs, walking me backwards to the low bed and cushions.

We stop just shy of tripping onto the cloud of pillows. Kai steps back and for the second time today, reaches to unbutton his jeans and slide them down his thighs. Exposing his hardening cock and leanly muscled body.

Before I lose my nerve, I lean into him, starting at his throat and lick. Lick him like I've been wanting to for days. The tip of my tongue tracing his red stripes over his pecs, down the valley between his abs, across the peaks of his hips and then to the warm heat of his cock. Starting at the base and slowly drawing the flat of my tongue up the underside and wrapping my lips around the dripping crown. Tasting him for the first time. Salty and smokey. I want more.

My mouth circles his tip and I slide him inside me to the sound of his growing moan. A hand slips into my hair but doesn't do more than caress and twine my long strands around fingers. His thumb slides under my chin when I manage to get a good seventy-five percent of him in my mouth. With both hands I glide up his inner thigh and revel in the shake it causes and slight buck of his hips when one cups his balls and I squeeze just so.

"Fuck Daisy. I thought you said you were a virgin. You sure as hell don't suck dick like one."

I hollow my cheeks and suck-swallow while sliding up his length until only the tip remains and swirl my tongue around the head. Kai swears again and groans like a wild animal, his tail lashing wildly behind him.

"Shit, do that again," he commands.

His hand is on the back of my head and he could force me, but he doesn't. I do it again, and again, and again. Until Kai is a whimpering practically incoherent mess. Nearly unable to stand. Then I make him fold over me by swallowing as much of his cock as I can without choking, my hand covering his balls and fingers latching onto the base of his shaft. Kai's hand does push me closer to him then, but only a little.

"Fuck Blossom. I am going to need you to do that every day until I die. I don't know where you learned that, but I may be the luckiest male on the planet."

I pull off his cock with a wet pop and let him pull me to my feet. I let Kai remove my shirt and shorts and underwear, but once naked I move away. He promised to take me from behind and I want him to fulfill that promise.

Walking backwards I wait till my heel hits the bedding, all while keeping eye contact with Kai. Lowering myself and twisting to crawl over the mattress, presenting him with my backside. Once I find a suitable position in the center of the bed, I turn to look over my shoulder. Kai hasn't moved, his gaze predatory and watching. Muscles flexing and cock glistening with my spit and his own arousal.

He moves forward, prowling and circling. Stalking me as I wait on my hands and knees throbbing with need for him. My pussy drips with anticipation and I widen my knees ever so slightly, lifting my tail out of the way for him to get a better view.

Kai growls deep in his chest and falls to his knees behind me, crawling the rest of the way to me. His lips make contact with me first. Kissing and biting on the round globe of my ass.

"You're perfect Daisy. So, fucking perfect."

His tongue darts out and licks from my hip to the base of my tail and I can feel the touch all the way up my spine and around to my clit.

"You don't even know how beautiful you are. How good and right you are."

His hands join his kisses cupping each cheek and groping greedily. Moving up my back he continues his praise both verbal and physical.

"Smart and sexy as fuck. I've traveled the entire world and never met anyone like you Daisy, and I never will. You're one of a kind, and not because you're a hybrid." His lips reach the back of my neck, and he brushes my hair to one side revealing my neck and ear. I tilt open for him. "But because you're you. You're my blossom. My pure, wholesome, naughty flower."

Warm wetness trails the shell of my ear as he licks from lobe to tip and nips at the point.

"Even your ears are unparalleled. None like them in the world."

"Kai…"

I want to respond, say words of affection and praise but I can't speak. No one has ever said such beautiful things to me. my heart swelling and pressing against my ribs with each word spoken.

Kai presses his body flush to mine, his chest to my back, his hips cradling mine, the hard length of him sliding between my slick thighs and settling against my core. The next words whispered directly against my ear.

"I know Daisy. I love you too, Blossom. I may be crazy for it, but I don't care. They can lock me up in an asylum because I'm crazy about you."

The breath catches in my lungs and tears sting the corners of my eyes. That's not what I was expecting him to say, at all. More compliments and seduction but not love. Not real emotion.

"Kai…I…you…?" I try to form words, a sentence, something to convey what I feel for him but everything inside me is jumbled.

Pocket Full of Posies

"Shh Blossom. You don't have to say anything, as long as you feel it. Feel me."

He rocks his hips, sliding his hard length through the center of me teasing my entrance before sliding back up and teasing my clit.

"Can you feel me, Blossom?"

I nod eagerly. "Yes. I feel you, Kai."

"Good."

I can feel Kai repositioning his knees, readying himself. Fuck I want him to sink inside me. The words, the blow job, his lips on me, I am so ready for him. His heat disappears from my back and his hands grip my hips.

My mind is so fuzzy I don't even try to think, I do what he suggested and just feel. The slight prick of his claws against the soft skin of my waist, the press of his hips and stomach to my ass, his velvety tail caressing my thigh, and of course his thick cock rubbing back and forth down my center and through my wetness, coating himself in my need for him.

With every rock of his hips his cock bumps my entrance then my clit, and on one more slide he expertly lines himself up and instead of sliding against me he thrusts inside me. In one smooth movement he goes from being outside me to inside me and I moan at the fullness. The stretch of him inside my tightness, the heat of him warming me from the inside out.

He presses deep and holds there, our moaning and sounds of pleasure mixing as we both revel in satisfaction. Kai's hands hold me stable as he sets a rhythm. Hips smacking ass, balls slapping my clit. All of it sending my brain into shut down mode. No more thinking, only feeling.

My nipples harden with each deep thrust and my breath quickens as Kai does.

"Damn it Blossom, you make me so god damned hard I

want you constantly. Once isn't going to be enough, I'm going to take you all night long, in every fucking position. I want to come in you, on you, in your mouth. Fuck that mouth, I want to fuck it and feed you my cock."

"Yes, yes. I want it all. Give it all to me."

"Oh, I plan to."

Kai's hand reaches around and cups my pussy, his fingers playing with my clit and opening to hold me and his cock where it moves in and out of me. I revel in his touch, and he seems to like it as well, his speed increasing and his moans growing louder. More words of praise and approval falling from his lips. All of which only make me wetter for him.

"That's it Blossom, you're right there I can feel it. You want to come for me?"

"Yes. It feels so fucking good. I want more, more. Harder."

He complies and pounds into me hard, his fingers sliding to my clit and pinching it.

"Do that again," I echo his words from earlier and again he complies. Pinching then, holy shit, lightly smacking my swollen bud.

He must realize what that does to me because he does it again.

"You like that? Like it when I smack your sweet little bud?"

"Mmhmm."

My elbows buckle and my face falls into a pillow, which does something to the angle of Kai thrusting behind me. Pressing against new nerves that make me clench down on his cock. He does that wonderful flex and I groan into the pillow.

Kai's hand leaves my clit and presses between my shoulder blades, forcing my chest farther down and my ass higher.

"That's it Blossom, right fucking there. That's it, that's it. Fuck I'm gonna come soon baby. Come inside this tight pussy, fill it with my cum, watch it drip from your pussy."

Shit the words Kai uses make me want anything he would offer. But I also want to make him feel as brain dumb as I do. There's something I thought of before and wondered how well it would work. Knowing Kai is open to anything I want, I decide to try it.

With great mental strain, I focus on my tail and slip it around my waist and between my thighs from the front until I can feel Kai's length and balls as he feeds his cock into me. His movement stutters when he feels my tail caress him, but if the guttural groan is any indication he's enjoying it, I don't stop. Wrapping the tip of my tail around his balls and base forming a makeshift cock and ball ring. When in position I tighten my tail until I have a snug hold on him.

"Holy fucking Christ. What the hell are you doing to me? Because I love it. Squeeze tighter," he grinds out between clenched teeth.

When I do his hips fly forward and he plunges inside me with so much force my knees skid forward.

"Don't fucking let go Daisy."

"I wouldn't think of it. You like my tail grabbing your balls?"

"Fuck yes I do."

I hold on tight to him as he vigorously pounds his hips against my ass. Every thrust, slide, and slap building my orgasm, forcing it higher and higher, till I sit on a razor's edge, my channel baring down on Kai's cock.

"Oh my god, right there. I'm gonna come Kai."

"Yeah, you are and I'm gonna fill this cunt."

He does this amazing swivel dip thing and tops it with a loud and hard slap to my ass forcing my orgasm to crest and shatter. My body shakes so violently Kai has to hold me up by the hips as I ride out the most intense orgasm of my life. Waves of pulsing pleasure swallow me in a tsunami as I feel Kai thrust fast then hold still deep inside me. His release pumping inside me causes aftershock orgasms to spasm through me.

Kai's guttural growl behind me is possibly the most erotic thing I've ever heard, including all the dirty talk he spoke tonight.

He holds still as his cock pulses inside me, his hot seed warm and dripping down my thigh, just like he promised.

We lay together in the bed designed for genie bottles, sticky with sweat and breathless. Kai curls around me pulling me into his embrace, my face burying in his chest. He smells of sweat and campfires, burning embers and sweet candy.

"You're a dream come true. You know that, Daisy?"

"No. We just...have good chemistry."

"There's definite chemistry, but also more—"

"Love. You told me." I pause, gaining the courage to verbalize my emotions as he has. It's difficult since I've never experienced anything like this with another before. But if he's not afraid to be open and vulnerable then neither am I. "I love you too Kai. But..."

"But? But what?"

Kai pulls away to look me in the eye, tilting my chin up with a finger and brushing a thumb along my bottom lip.

"Are you still planning on leaving after the equinox is over?"

The words are a whispered confession and plea. We haven't talked about what was to come after the equinox. He's claimed, in not so many words, that he would be sticking around for a long time. But he's never said it, never confirmed he wouldn't be leaving again. I don't think my heart could handle him leaving after falling in love with him.

"Of course not. I'm never leaving again unless it's with you by my side and we're going on some grand adventure." Kai presses a kiss to my nose and a smile brighter than the sun beams down at me.

"Good, because I think my brother might actually kill you if you did."

"I wouldn't doubt it. And he would be right to if I did. I would be a fool to leave a female as sweet and perfect as you. I give you and Sage full permission to cut off my tail if I am ever stupid enough to give up the best thing that's ever happened to me. And just to be clear, that's you Daisy."

Heat infuses my cheeks, and Kai seems proud of himself for making me blush. So much so, I can feel his length hardening against my stomach. I give him an incredulous look.

"Again? Already?"

"What can I say? I like it when you turn red."

Lifting my leg, he wraps it around his hip and situates himself comfortably between my legs. The flesh there is tender and sensitive, but he doesn't take me like he did before. He's gentle and slow. Rubbing his length against me leisurely. Pressing kisses to my cheek, jaw, and lips. Cupping the back of my head and running his fingers through my hair. Our love making is unhurried and delicate. Exploratory and passionate. And when he slips his cock inside me our bodies rock together in a natural rhythm that takes nearly twice as long to bring me to orgasm. Slowly coercing it from my body rather than ringing it out.

After our second round of drawn-out sex, we fall asleep staring up at the star-filled sky through the open center of the tent roof, a tangle of limbs and tails. The scent of plumerias lingering like a strong perfume in the tent.

Chapter 24
Kai

Sharp rays of sunlight streaming in through the tent's venting hole in the ceiling, wake me far earlier than I want. But the view of Daisy sleeping naked and halfway on top of me is worth it. I'd wake up at dawn every day if this is the view I get to wake up to.

Her dark hair is strewn across my red and pale skin, a contradiction in tone but fitting perfectly somehow. Pulling the blanket up to cover her bare backside I linger at her shoulders. Running feather light fingers over her tan skin and green filigree markings. In her sleep they're still and motionless.

Daisy is the most divine creature I've ever encountered and when I told her I was never leaving I wasn't lying. Until the day she forces me to leave or leaves with me, I'm not going anywhere.

I wonder what kind of ring she would like if I were to propose to her like the humans do? Because I'm going to need to bond with her as soon as she's willing. I'm not letting her go and I'm definitely not going to let some other male steal her from me. From the outside it may not seem like it, but I think Daisy and I were made for each other. Two different pieces of a puzzle that when put together make a perfect picture.

A cool breeze drifts in from the open venting hole and goosebumps prickle on Daisy's skin. I pull the blanket higher and increase my body temperature to warm her. Spotting the bathtub in the corner I think Daisy might like to bathe after yesterday and last night. I myself wouldn't mind freshening up.

As delicately as possible I slip free from under Daisy and slip on a pair of pants before setting off to obtain what I require. It takes me less than five minutes to return with a tray of food and drinks that I set on the low table before walking over to the water filled tub. The water has been there since yesterday and is now cold. I dip a hand into the chilled water and heat it to the perfect temperature before waking Daisy.

She's the cutest thing first thing in the morning. She's normally a morning person but apparently, I exhausted her last night because she's all sleepy eyed and yawning as I carry her to the tub. I use my tail to pull my pants off and step into the tub with Daisy still cradled in my arms, settling her between my legs and against my chest in the warm water.

The tub is plenty large enough for two and we fit comfortably. I languidly wash Daisy until she's completely awake then assist in detangling her hair and washing it. She then insists on washing mine, which I admit is wonderful.

"Do we have any plans for today? The celebration doesn't officially end till sunset, right?" she asks once we're both washed and relaxing back in the soapy water.

"That's right. I hadn't planned anything other than spending all day with you. Most of it I'd be happy remaining right here in this tub. I can keep the water warm indefinitely, so we'd never get cold or need to leave."

"What about food? We need to eat."

I smirk because she thinks I didn't already consider that. Gesturing a hand towards the low table I draw her attention to the tray laden with food she hadn't noticed.

"Already taken care of. We have plenty of food and drink for the day. I can hand feed you and we never have to put clothes on."

Daisy laughs and turns her head up, sparkling emerald eyes smiling up at me. So many moments in the past I felt life was all it was going to be, that the hidden hole inside me would remain so until the end of time. Looking into Daisy's bottomless green eyes I can feel that hole filling in sealing over. I'm finally where I'm supposed to be. Finally, I've found my place in this world and it's not what I expected, but everything I ever wanted.

Stealing a kiss from the love of my life, I take Daisy by surprise, but she soon melts against my mouth accepting all that I give and giving all that I need.

Everything is perfect inside our secluded tent, away from the rest of the world. Away from our families and nosey neighbors. Here it's just us, and that's all that matters. That's all I need.

If I would have let him, Kai would have kept me in that bathtub indefinitely. Thankfully I was able to convince him we needed to get out after two hours because my skin was pruning and the flowers in my hair were wilting from the steam and over watering. He tried to argue that you couldn't over water a flower, which he quickly learned was very possible. As soon as the first plumeria fell from my hair, wilty and sad, he conceded to exiting the tub.

It took even more convincing to get him to put on pants and leave the tent. To my great surprise, I was the one who wanted to get out and socialize. Finding my brother and Tobias, playing with Delphi and her new sprite friends she brought along. Returning the scarf she stole from someone's tent.

The day was going well. It isn't until midafternoon that Kai's family sends Keiko to retrieve him to speak with his parents. We have successfully avoided them until this point. Only speaking briefly with Keiko or Endo. Apparently, his mother has grown tired of waiting. She requested both me and Kai, but he wouldn't allow it, and honestly, I am fine not going. I tried to befriend her at the party and learned quickly that would never be happening.

While Kai follows Keiko toward his parent's tent and private garden area, I go in the opposite direction and find a quiet place by the stream to sit and wait. I've barely been here a few minutes when a body appears at my side, looming over me.

"Where's Kai? I assumed you would have kept him hidden away in your tent."

Great, just who I wanted to see. Nysa, Kai's ex-lover and his mother's favorite—apparently—stands over me. She doesn't sit. I think she likes looking down on me. Wouldn't be the first time a full-blooded snob thought she was better than me.

In the past it would have bothered me. Her status and confidence would have made me retreat into myself and let her say whatever she wanted, which usually only made me feel worse. Now though, something in me has changed. I don't feel as threatened as I once would have, I don't feel the need to hide or apologize for nothing. Her pure blood and higher stance don't concern me anymore.

"Kai's with his parents. And, not that it's your business, but he was the one who wanted to stay naked in bed in our tent today. I was the one who convinced him to leave. For a little while anyways."

I guess I'm a tad sassy now too. Rubbing it in that I got the guy, and she didn't, is a little petty but I just couldn't help myself. Kai must be rubbing off on me.

"I suppose you can have your fun. It won't last long."

Nysa's flippant, and far too confident, statement has me faltering. Mainly because of the certainty in her tone. I look up to her, wanting to gage her expression. She looks smug. As if she knows something I don't. Which makes no sense. I just asked Kai about him leaving last night and he said he wasn't going anywhere. He was speaking the truth, I could hear it in his voice. I would know if he were lying.

Wanting to get somewhat closer to her level for this conversation, I stand, although still not eye to eye with her.

"What do you mean? How would you know anything about us?"

The corner of her mouth pulls into a cruel expression I don't like.

"You may think everything is perfect and you and Kai will be together and live happily ever after. But the truth is, you're just a pit stop on his journey. Someone like Kai wouldn't bond with someone like you. He's only using you for a little fun. A plaything to work out his fantasies before settling with someone proper for his station."

Nysa's words are sharp and dry, grinding against my skin like sandpaper until it wears down my flesh to bone. I want to argue, to call her a liar and prove that Kai's past is just that. That now he wants to be with me and only me. Forever. But I can't. She's not lying. My tongue sticks to the roof of my mouth and my protests sink to the pit of my stomach.

"He was never going to stay with you. He never even wanted you to begin with. He was only using you to stop his mother from announcing *our* bonding. You are just a passing fling to work out his wanderlust. Eventually he will tire of you and move on like he always has.

"If he decides he wants to keep you as a mistress, I have no objections to it. Many mated males have side pieces. I can't be expected to entertain all his sexual desires. All I require is the appropriate number of heirs and the status of being a Kingsley. What he does in his spare time is his problem."

Nysa flits her hand at me like a servant while my brain spins trying to keep up with all her allegations. Most of it just sounds preposterous. Kai would never do such a thing to me. Then again, I've known from the beginning he was not the settling down type, was even warned numerous times about him and his "ways." But I ignored them. I wanted to learn for myself what kind of male he was without judging him based on gossip. Turns out I should have paid more attention. Nysa's allegations ring true. Her words hold no deceit. A lot of bitterness and cruelty but no lies. She believes what she's saying.

"What do you mean he never wanted me? He was just using me?"

"Oh honey, you don't think he really chose you, do you? He found out about his mother arranging our bonding and panicked. He isn't ready yet and needed a naïve little girl to use as a fake mate to try and delay our bonding. He was never intending to stay with you. It was always temporary. If you don't believe me, ask his brother. He knew all about it."

Wait, what? Endo knew about this? But he's my friend, he

Pocket Full of Posies

acted like he was happy for us. This is all so confusing.

"Oh, look there's Endo now. Go ahead, ask him. You'll see."

With a flare of her wings and swing of her hair, Nysa spins and walks away leaving me open mouthed and heart lodged between my ribs. She has to be wrong, must have heard something and misinterpreted. She, like Kai's mother, doesn't approve of us and wants to get rid of me and place herself in their family. It's just more games high society people like her like to play. Right?

I'll ask Endo and he'll put her right. He'll tell me she's mistaken and nothing she said was accurate and Kai would never bond with her.

I turn in the direction she indicated and indeed find Endo stalking towards me, frowning at Nysa's receding back. His expression of derision and disapproval at Nysa is reassuring. He'll tell me the truth, and everything will be fine. Everything will go back to what it was, and me and Kai will enjoy the rest of the festival as we planned.

"What was *she* doing here?" Endo asks when he reaches me, still standing rooted in place by the stream's bank.

The relaxing sound of water bubbling over stones and down inclines does nothing to soothe my nerves. Not until I hear him negate her claims.

"She told me Kai is only with me to use me as a shield from his mother's plans for him to bond with her. That he never truly intended to be with me. That it was all fake."

Where I expect Endo to adamantly deny her outrageous allegations, I'm only greeted with silence. His mouth dropping open and snapping shut, copper brow pinching with indecision. Like he isn't sure what he should say. His eyes shift between mine and away then back. The longer he remains silent the more I realize it's because she wasn't wrong. He doesn't want to confirm, but he also can't deny her words.

Kai didn't want me. At least not me specifically, he just needed a female, any female, to fulfill his scheme. And my heart shrivels and bursts simultaneously.

"She's right, isn't she?" I ask in a soft whisper.

"Not completely. But it's not how she makes it out to be. In the beginning maybe, yes, he was just looking for a female for not so honorable reasons. But you're different Daisy. Things changed. He really does love you, I swear. Whatever else she told you is false. You can't listen to her poison. Females like her and my mother thrive on hurting others to get what they want. Don't let her manipulate you."

Endo is reaching for my arm and trying to plead with me. I want to believe him, but I don't know what's true anymore. Even being able to hear lies in someone's words there are ways around it. Nymph's have learned ways to word things to keep from outright lying but still skirting the truth. I thought Kai wanted me from the beginning. How much of it was fake? How much of it was for show? Do I even really know him? He said he loved me. He wasn't lying about that, which only makes this more confusing.

"Let me get Kai and you two can talk. Okay? You'll see, just stay here, and don't move. I'm going to get Kai and we'll straighten this all out."

Endo jogs away and as soon as he has his back turned to me, I know I can't stay. I need to leave. Return to my safe space at home in my gardens. The only place I was ever happy. My refuge. Refuge that has now been tainted by Kai. It's where we've spent most of our time together and it's all so fresh and raw. I can't be there, no matter how much I want to.

If I stay it'll cause a scene. People will talk, they'll stare and put blame on me, the *half-breed*. No. I don't want that. So,

Pocket full of Posies

I leave. Running in the opposite direction of everyone. Away from the music and laughter of the festival, toward the quiet empty forest. Just for a little while. Until I can think straight, until I can figure out what's real, if anything was real.

Maybe this will be what finally gets me to leave town. If I go somewhere with more humans than non-humans, perhaps I can finally have a normal life.

The grass and leaves crunch beneath my bare feet as I run through the trees, seeking a new refuge and new place to hide where nothing and no one can find me.

Chapter 25
Kai

My oh so wonderful conversation with my mother is interrupted by Endo bursting in through the flap of their massively opulent tent. The fur around his neck is standing on end and his ears twitch in agitation. Whatever the reason for the interruption, it is not good.

"Kai, you're needed. *Outside.*" He tilts his head sharply at the exit, eyes wide and pleading for me not to argue. Like I would. I'd take any excuse to leave.

"What is this about Endo?" my mother demands. Luckily neither of us care about her demands and both ignore her.

"Gotta go. Let's not do this again soon." I turn on a heel and head for the door, sounds of my mothers' complaints and guffaws behind me.

I could care less if I offended her or am acting improperly for a male of my position. I've never behaved properly before and I'm not going to start now.

Outside our parents tent I follow Endo as he strides quickly in the direction of the stream.

"What's going on Endo? Not that I don't appreciate the assist, but your pace is concerning."

"It's Daisy. I found her talking to that snake Nysa, who somehow knew about your stupid ass plan to use Daisy as a shield from mom to avoid being bonded to Nysa." The constant heat in my vein's chills to a temperature I've never experienced before at his words. "Nysa told Daisy and now she's upset, and I told her it wasn't true, at least not completely—"

"What do you mean *not completely?* What did you tell her?" My voice comes out in a near growl and my tail whips angrily back and forth. I love my brother, but I will disown him if he costs me the love of my life.

"I couldn't lie to her. But I told her she was different, and you really do love her, and Nysa was spewing deception—" Endo's ramblings cut off as he abruptly stops at the edge of the stream and spins in a circle.

"I swear she was right here. I left her right here."

I don't doubt he did, but if Daisy was hurting, she probably didn't want to stick around for more. I have to find her. She couldn't have gotten far. I have to explain and make sure I haven't lost her forever. If Nysa fucked this up for me, I'm going to do the same for her life. After I'm done with her, no respectable high society anything will accept her. She'll be a social pariah, unwelcome wherever she goes in every country.

I may have spent my life flitting about from party to party but being the immensely attractive and friendly social butterfly that I am, I've made a lot of friends, who would gladly snub anyone I asked them to. Even if everything works out between Daisy and me, I might do it anyway. Just to teach her a little modesty.

"Where would she have gone?"

Pocket Full of Posies

Endo rubs at the back of his neck and grimaces. I can tell he feels bad, but I know it's not his fault. He didn't open his mouth and tell the girl I love that I was only using her. No, that was all Nysa, and my temper flares once more wanting to find my ex and put her in her place. But finding Daisy and fixing us first is more important.

"Maybe back to the tent?" Endo mutters, trying to answer his own question.

"No. Too many people around. She doesn't like crowds or people in general, they make her nervous. She'd want to be alone, somewhere quiet. Her greenhouse. She loves it there, says it's her safe space."

"You think she went all the way back home?"

"Maybe."

I stand still and try to hear Daisy. Her sweet voice and light breathing. I hear plenty of voices and breathing, way too much actually. So many different voices and noises it creates a blanket of sounds I can't filter through to find her. I'll have to rely on my lesser senses, which are still ten times better than any human.

Sniffing the air I try to catch her scent, the one that's filled my nose and coated my skin. Having spent a lot of time skin-to-skin with her over the past twelve hours, has engrained it in my mind. A sweet floral musk that makes my mouth water. Like rain-soaked honeysuckle.

I catch her alluring scent heading in the direction of the forest. I don't know where she's heading but I'm going wherever she is.

"She headed this way."

"How do you know?" Endo asks skeptically.

"When you spend as much time licking her skin as I have, you remember the way she smells."

Endo raises a brow at me, eyes sparkling, a tiny smirk playing at the corner of his mouth. He's trying not to smile. I smack him in the back of the head. Playfully of course, he is my little brother after all.

"I'll go back to your tent in case she comes back," he offers, rubbing the spot I just smacked.

"Thanks bro. If all goes well, we might not be back though."

"Not a problem. I'll just enjoy your tent for myself then," he grins at me now. It won't be there for long.

"You know we had sex all over that tent, right?"

His smile drops and he sneers. "Gross."

I try to give my brother a reassuring smile, but I know it doesn't reach my eyes. I'm not in the smiling mood. Not until I find my Blossom.

Leaving him to deal with our family, I follow the scent of Daisy away from the festival and into the quiet forest.

Chapter 26
Daisy

I can't hear the sounds of the festival anymore. I've gotten far enough away that I'm practically alone in the woods. Well, almost. Delphi trotted after me as I made my escape. Even distracted as she was with her sprite friends and the children playing, she sensed my distress and followed after me. If Kai were here to translate, I'm sure she'd be saying things like *What's wrong? Where are we going? Who hurt you so I can gouge out their eyes and feed them to the squirrels?*

Okay so she might not ask that last one, but I'm sure she would do it if I asked her too. Delphi sits on my shoulders now, quiet since I wasn't answering any of her chitters. The tiny, clawed hand she brushes through my hair is oddly comforting.

I pick out another black dahlia from my hair and toss it to the ground, stomping on it as I walk. Black dahlias represent pain, suffering, heartache. *Why must my flowers show exactly how I'm feeling?*

My body lags as I walk, I ran for a while to get away from

everyone. I don't need witnesses to my embarrassment and stupidity. I fell for the bad boy and his sweet-talking dirty mouth. Stupidly I thought I was special. That I meant more to him than some fling or hook up. Turns out I was wrong. I mean even less than that. Because at least he was honest with them about their relationship. I'm not worth honesty.

A heaviness slows my pace, and I plop down on a dead tree stump. Normally I would encourage the tree to resprout and grow anew. Right now, all I can do is water it with my tears.

Delphi climbs off me and sits at my feet, petting my knee. Watching her only makes me feel worse about myself. I love Delphi, but I have to be really unwanted if the only person to care about my feelings is a sprite. Sure, Sage and Tobias care but family is supposed to, they're obligated to.

"It's okay, Delphi. I just need a few minutes to get it all out," I tell my furry friend. "I just don't know what to believe anymore. I thought he was being honest. I thought he was different. But now I don't know if I can believe his words."

Delphi purrs and coos, almost like a cat would, rubbing her chubby little body against my leg and wrapping her tiny little hands around my calf. Her warmth on my feet is nice, I ran off without my boots and my feet are actually getting cold. I think this deep in the woods winter has settled in faster.

I wrap my arms around myself and rub my bare skin to create friction and heat, having forgotten a sweater as well, I'm only partially paying attention to the dropping temperature. Thoughts of Kai and his smiling teasing face distract me and send my emotions down a spiral of confusion and heartbreak.

The bracelet Kai gave me heats my skin where it rubs. I don't know how he did it, but the damn thing always seems warm to the touch. Plus, I can't take it off. Which I didn't mind at first, now it irritates me. I want to rip it off and throw it at a tree. Pulling at the gold band I try to do just that. Like I knew it wouldn't, the bracelet doesn't budge, remaining snuggly on my wrist. I'll probably have to cut it off.

My hand falls to my lap, and I sigh out a watery groan. I'll never be able to leave my house again. People are going to laugh at me for being so blind and ignoring everyone's warnings not to get involved with Kai. I thought I was better than all of them, accepting Kai for who he is and not judging him for his salacious past. Looks like I should have paid a little more attention to his track record. A guy that can't commit to anyone or place for longer than a few months should have been a major red flag.

I have no idea how long I sit here and feel sorry for myself, but it starts to get darker. The sun falling below the canopy of the trees. I should probably head home. There are creatures in the woods that even non-humans don't mess with. Wraiths and banshees' dwell in the darkness of the world. We don't encounter them often, but they are out there, and I most certainly do not want to meet my first any time soon.

Scooping up Delphi I cradle her in my arms and start walking. I got a little turned around while running away but if I go southeast, I should find my way back to a populated area. I hope.

Less than a minute into my walk of shame—hopefully towards home—I hear a sound. A rustling in the bushes and snapping of twigs. I spin towards the sound, stupidly hoping to see Kai bursting through the trees to apologize and beg my forgiveness. There's nobody there. Just darkening shadows and an eerie cold breeze.

"Perhaps we should walk a little faster," I say out loud to Delphi, hoping the sound of my voice will calm me. It doesn't. I think it makes it worse, because there's no echo and it only amplifies the silence around us.

That's when I notice the lack of natural noises the forest usually produces. No birds, no bugs, no small animals. Yet there is evidence of a presence. That's not good.

My feet begin to move faster, not full out running yet, just moving faster. My sadness over Kai and his omissions falling away to be replaced with a fear of the unknown, or rather fear of the known but unseen.

Wraiths are ghostly spirits that can suck the life right out of you, filled with darkness and sorrow born from horrendous acts in the world and fueled by fear. To be caught by one is to be absorbed into its endless void, and I'd rather not learn firsthand what one looks like.

My pace increases, but amidst the dimming sunlight, my panic and having to veer off course to avoid thick underbrush and fallen trees, I fear I've gotten turned around again.

"Shit, shit, shit. Which way do we go, Delphi?"

The sprite leaps from my arms and lands on a shimmering disc of magic midair, her cute little nose twitching as she sniffs the air and looks around trying to distinguish our location. When her fluffy ears perk up, I know she's discovered our way home.

Following Delphi's guide, we make a sharp right and take off. Roots and vines tangle with overgrown underbrush and I have to look down frequently to keep from tripping. I look up when I should have looked down and my bare foot catches on something and I trip, falling body first and barely catching myself with my hands, before my face makes contact with a thorny bush.

Rolling over I push myself up onto my elbows before I look up to spot a cloud of black hovering over me. It's like staring into the center of a black hole. No light or life stirs inside it.

Pocket Full of Posies

Two glowing yellow orbs stare down at me. Those must be its eyes.

I scream on instinct crawling backwards trying to put distance between myself and the wraith that I've just discovered. The black mass shifts and grows arms and hands tipped in claws that reach out for me. Before its dripping claws make contact with my face, my sweet cuddly sprite pounces. Snapping her tiny fangs at the black spindly hand in an oddly successful attempt to ward off the wraith. That is until the wraith reaches for Delphi with its other hand, slashing at her small body until she unhinges from it and falls to the ground. Red blood streaks her blue and white fur but she's still moving.

"Delphi!"

My self-preservation instinct disintegrates at the sight of my best friend injured. I lunge for Delphi barely getting to my knees before scooping her little body into my arms and holding her close. Curling my body around her smaller one, I just hope that the wraith kills me quickly and spares poor Delphi.

Eyes squeezing shut, I brace myself for the inevitable pain. It never comes. The silence of the wraith filled forest is shattered by a growling shout. The sound made by someone other than the wraith or myself. Made by a male I know too well.

Kai stands over my huddled body, his spine curved, and claws extended, fire practically bursting from his body. Flames and heat extend from his hands like whips striking out at the wraith, forcing it back. The dark shadows shrink away from the fire and light.

Kai roars at the wraith, a sound purely animalistic and feral. A beast protecting its own, thoughtless of his own safety. There are twin lines of red marring his shirt where the wraith's claws made contact. He ignores them and focuses solely on forcing the wraith back, away from me and Delphi.

He doesn't stop his advance and fire whips until the wraith grows wary and disappears into the night, his yellow eyes vanishing. Kai doesn't back down until he's sure the wraith is gone. The fire streaming from him recedes back into his body, which continues to radiate heat that I can feel even from a distance. It warms my pebbling skin as he stalks closer to me still clutching Delphi to my chest.

"Blossom." The endearment falls from his lips on a broken sob as he falls to his knees in front of me.

Chapter 27
Kai

I nearly lost it when I saw the wraith hovering over Daisy's curled up body, protecting Delphi. There's red blood smeared all over her shirt and I have no idea if it belongs to her or Delphi. Either way, something inside me snapped. A fierce fiery need to protect what's mine, my Blossom, my love, my mate.

I placed myself between the wraith and my future on instinct. My inner fire becoming my outer fire. I've never fought a wraith, but it only made sense that a being made of shadows, darkness and iciness wouldn't like fire. It's its polar opposite. I didn't think, I just acted. Thankfully it was the right thing to do, and the wraith didn't absorb and kill all of us. If it had, I would have died willingly, knowing I did everything to protect Daisy.

"Where are you hurt?" I ask, kneeling in front of Daisy and running my hands over every inch of her looking for an injury.

"It's not mine, it's from Delphi." She lifts Delphi so I can see the poor injured sprite cradled in her arms. "She protected me from the wraith."

Tears pour down my blossom's beautiful face and I brush them away. I may not know how to heal the hurt I have created, but I can heal Delphi's wounds.

"Come on, Blossom. Let's get her back to your house. I can help her there."

"What? What do you mean? We have to get her to a doctor or a vet…fairy…someone…" Her words trail off as I help her stand, and she carefully shifts the sprite in her arms.

"There are a few things you still don't know about me. One of them is, I just so happen to be a vet."

Large glassy green eyes stare up at me in confusion.

"It's a long story but trust me, I know what I'm doing. I can help her. I promise."

She doesn't look like she wants to believe me, and I don't blame her. With no other options and Delphi bleeding in her arms, she concedes. Nodding once and sniffling.

She doesn't argue or pull away when I hold her under my arm and close to my side. Her shoulders rise and fall with each heart wrenching sob, and I feel like an even bigger asshole. If it weren't for me, she wouldn't have been out here and neither of them would have been in danger.

My heart nearly ripped out of my chest when I thought I might have lost Daisy and only with her tightly in my hold does it settle into a steady rapid beat.

When I realized she wasn't in the woods surrounding the festival and had wandered deeper into the forest, I connected with any animal in range searching for her. I'm only happy I found her when I did.

Daisy follows my lead as we enter familiar land and finally make it back to her property. Her house sits dark and empty, Sage and Tobias still at the festival, no doubt on their way home soon. The festival ends at sunset. In the next hour everyone will be making their way back home for the night to sleep off the revelry.

"Do you have a sewing kit, Daisy?"

"Um, I think so."

"Where is it?"

Daisy shakes her head trying to focus on my question. I'll need a needle and thread to stitch up Delphi's cuts, and Daisy needs something to focus on other than Delphi.

We make it into the kitchen, and I send Daisy off to find the sewing kit while I clean Delphi's wounds. Thankfully they're just deep cuts with no internal damage. I make quick work of everything. Once the wounds are stitched, Delphi's sprite healing will kick in and finish the job. It's stopping the bleeding that's important, to allow for her magic to replenish.

Sprites are one of the most magical creatures in our world, but even they can't survive bleeding out. I look down at the sprite that most likely saved Daisy and stroke her blood-stained fur. I owe her for that. I'll give her every trinket she will ever want. I'll even build her a larger nest so she can fit everything.

"Will she be, okay?" Daisy asks softly. She clings to my arm, needing something to hold on to as she watches Delphi sleeping in the nest of towels and blankets I made for her in the kitchen sink.

"She'll be fine Blossom. Now that she's stitched up her healing magic will finish the job."

I press a soft kiss to her hair covered in lilies and one black dahlia. I've never seen that flower in her hair before and I know it has something to do with me and not Delphi.

"Come on Blossom, you need rest too. It's been a long day."

She nods and allows me to guide her to the couch in the

living room, still within line of sight of Delphi in the kitchen. I sit and pull her down with me and she curls into my side. Even while angry at me she reaches for me for comfort. Presses against me for warmth and reassurance.

When she's settled our tails naturally twine together. The action comforts me just as much as her. Daisy's petite body curls into a ball, her knees pulled up to her chest and her head tucked under my chin. I pull the blanket off the back of the couch and wrap it around us both.

"I'm sorry, Blossom."

Her eyes turn up to look at me and she frowns, a cute wrinkle forming between her eyes. "It wasn't your fault; she tried to protect me from the wraith."

"Not about that."

Her expression drops and understanding flashes in her eyes. For a moment I expect her to pull away. To call me names, vow to never speak to me again, claim she doesn't love me. She doesn't do any of that. She does turn her face down. Hiding her eyes and expression from me.

"Endo told me what Nysa said. And I'm sorry I didn't tell you first. When I first found you in the woods, I wasn't out there intentionally to deceive you. I was trying to clear my head and figure out a way to avoid my mother's meddling. I just happened to stumble upon you. I thought you had been delivered to answer my prayers. And in a way you had. I just didn't realize which one at the time.

"I thought we could have a little fun, I could deter my mother, and no one would get hurt. But the more time I spent with you the more I wanted to be with you. The more I was drawn to you. You became far more than just a fling for the equinox."

I take a breath, pausing to allow her to scold me or perhaps forgive me. She doesn't do either.

"Anyway, I'm sorry that you had to hear it from Nysa. She shouldn't have opened her mouth. All she wants is to make other people's lives miserable. Whatever she said, just know none of it's true. Yes, my initial intentions were indecent—sometimes they still are."

Daisy's head jerks up to glare at me but there's humor swimming in her emerald gaze. I grin back.

"What can I say? You make me want to do indecent things."

Her cheeks pinken and she presses her face into my torn shirt. The scratches the wraith caused have already healed, leaving only a little dried blood on my ruined shirt. I should probably remove it but I'm comfortable right where I am. Once Daisy is ready for bed I'll strip for her.

"Thank you, for what you did for Delphi."

"Of course. I'd do anything for you, and her. She's important to you and you're important to me. I'll always be here for you both. No matter what."

Daisy toys with the frayed edges of my shirt where the wraiths claw cut through it. Her long delicate fingers just barely make contact with my skin beneath. It was just this morning when I had her naked in a bathtub and moaning, and I already want her again.

"How did you know how to take care of Delphi? You said you're a vet?"

"Yeah," I chuckle. "I got bored one year and went perusing online for something to entertain me. Stumbled upon online courses for veterinary school. I took classes online and even attended some in person. I've always loved animals and when I started classes it just seemed logical. Haven't done much with my credentials yet but I think I'd like to change that. Do you think Snowberry could use a vet?"

Her pretty pink lips purse in that adorable way when she's trying not to smile.

"Maybe. Do you plan on staying long enough to open a clinic?"

"I plan on staying forever. Think that's long enough?"

She blinks rapidly, mouth dropping open slightly. I want to kiss her. Suck on those pouty pink lips. I take her mouth in mine before she can argue. Relishing in the way she melts against me the longer we kiss. I suck gently on her bottom lip before releasing it and brushing my nose against hers.

"Yeah, I think forever will work," she breathes the confession against my lips.

"Any chance you have room for me here? I don't think I want to stay at my parent's place anymore and living at the motel doesn't sound enticing."

"I don't know. You'll have to convince Sage to let you stay too."

"Do you think he accepts bribes?"

Daisy giggles and the sound lightens the ten-ton load on my heart. I never want to see her cry again. Nothing has ever ripped me apart like knowing I hurt her. If she'll have me, I'll strive to make her smile each and every day.

"That depends. Can you cook?"

"Not even a little."

"How about we just tell him about your heroic rescue of me and Delphi from the wraith?"

My smile falls. Although the story itself would be a great tale of heroics, her reason for being in a situation to be attacked by a wraith in the first place was all my fault.

"How about we tell him how many times I made you orgasm at the festival?"

"Kai!" Daisy squeaks and slaps at my chest playfully, the

pink in her cheeks darkening to red. "Don't you dare."

"Why don't I just tell him how much I love his little sister? And that I'll sacrifice my life to save hers. That I'll do everything in my power to make her smile and laugh every day. That having her as mine and my future, makes life worth living."

Stretching up, Daisy presses a soft kiss to my lips, pulling away before I can deepen it.

"I think that might work," she whispers against my lips.

"How long do you think we have before they get home?"

She shrugs, grinning at me. "How long do you need?"

"To make you come? Five minutes. To love you? Forever."

"Well then, we should get started."

In a sweep of my arms, I scoop up Daisy and settle her legs around my hips. My tail circling her waist and holding on tight, as I walk us to the stairs leading to her bedroom. The one place I haven't had her yet that I've dreamt of taking her. But, like we've already established, I'll need to be quick. Sage and Tobias could be home at any minute.

Daisy directs me to the door of her room, and I kick it open then shut behind us. Tossing her on the bed, she bounces and laughs, but immediately begins stripping her clothes.

I do the same, pulling the destroyed shirt over my head and shoving my jeans off. Leaving me naked and erect overlooking my Blossom blooming for me, nude on her bed.

Crawling over her body I'm sliding inside her in seconds, filling her with my cock and my love. Stroking it deep inside her in smooth hard thrusts. Her body arching and opening to me, begging me for more, that I promptly oblige.

Just as I promised, I have her coming around my cock in less than five minutes and follow immediately behind her with my own release, panting into her flower strewn hair and sucking on the soft salty flesh of her neck.

"I love you, Blossom. No matter what anyone says to you, never doubt that." I breathe the confession into her ear and love the way her body shivers underneath me.

"I love you too Kai."

Epilogue
Daisy

3 years later

Kai finally did it. He finally convinced me to leave Snowberry and go on a European vacation with him. His veterinary clinic has been open for two years now, but I didn't think his new vet tech was ready to handle it all on his own. Kai reassured me Endo is more than capable of handling everything for a few weeks. He hasn't completed his schooling yet, but he's a quick learner. Plus, he was already training to work in the medical field, so it wasn't a big shift to move to veterinary.

"What do you think, Blossom? Is it everything you expected it to be?" Kai asks from the seat next to me on the gondola he insisted we ride.

I'm not complaining. Venice is beautiful and I'm excited to be here. I thought I would be anxious, traveling to a place full of humans, cameras, and tourists. I didn't need to be. There are so many people so focused on their own experiences that they barely notice a girl with shifting vine tattoos, slightly pointed ears, and too many flowers in her hair. Wearing long skirts and dresses conceals my tail and the remainder of my anxiety is washed away by Kai's reassuring hand laced in mine and the kisses he constantly presses to my temple and cheek.

"It's more than I imagined. Better even."

"If you'd let me, I'd take you everywhere in the world and show you my favorite places."

"Maybe not everywhere, but I wouldn't mind visiting Norway."

"Anywhere you want Blossom."

Kai pulls me close, his invisible to humans tail wrapping around my ankle. I like that they can't see his true self through his glamour. With the majority of those around being human it's kind of like our little secret.

We circle through the canals of Venice and return to our hotel on the Grand Canal; Hotel Danieli. I know it costs a small fortune to stay here but Kai insisted for my first international trip we go first class. First class flights, private car service to the station where we had another private boat to deliver us to our five-star hotel. I'm going to have more say in planning our next trip. But the hotel is really nice.

We don't go into the hotel though, instead we go on foot, walking down one of the thousands of alleys that make up Venice. We don't go towards the famous Piazza San Marco, but down a quieter, less populated alley. The buildings are tall and the path narrow, but every step is more beautiful than the next. Flowers fill window boxes and crawl over gates. Kai leads me to one gate with purple and white flowers decorating its bars.

"Where are we going?"

"You'll see."

He opens the gate and ushers me into a secluded and breathtakingly gorgeous garden. White orchids, violets, orange marigolds, pink oleanders, and every color of daisy cover every spare inch of space. There's almost as many flowers in this small bricked-in garden as in my greenhouse.

"It's beautiful, Kai. How did you know this was here?"

"I have my ways."

He winks at me and pinches my ass. Our laughter fills the garden, and we make our way to the small metal filigree bench practically being swallowed by blooms. Kai sits, pulling me into his lap when I try to sit next to him. His arms bracing around me. My tail twitches beneath the maxi dress I'm wearing wanting to reach out and hold him.

"I think it's time Daisy."

"Time for what?" I ask, pecking a kiss to his nose. His fangs graze my lips when he nips at my mouth.

"Time to bond with my mate of course."

My playful mood stills and my heart races. Forming a mate bond with another non-human is like a human marriage but far more permanent and important. I knew Kai wanted to bond with me, he's playfully mentioned it over the past few years but never seriously. He is definitely serious about it now.

"Right now?"

"Yes. I want to bond myself to you forever, Blossom. I want the rest of our lives to be as bonded mates. I want to make a family with you and travel the world with you. I want to curl up on the couch with you and pick flowers in your garden with you. I want everything with you, and no one will ever change my mind about that. Will you bond with me, Blossom? And then we can celebrate for the rest of our vacation in our five-star hotel suite."

Even when being amazingly sweet and loving he remains the same horny male he's always been.

"Yes. I'll bond with you. And celebrate after. I may not want to wait to get back to our room though."

Kai is rubbing off on me too much, but he loves it if his impish grin is any indication.

"Works for me." Kai clears his throat and looks me directly in the eye. "I, Kai Kingsley, bond myself to you, Daisy Rosenfeld, for the rest of my life. I promise to always love you, protect you, and pleasure you. To never intentionally hurt you or lie to you. To be true and faithful to you, always. I promise to make you smile and laugh as much as possible and give you everything you want that I have the power to give. For always and ever I promise all this and more to you my bonded mate."

The truth in his words rings through his voice and settles deep in my bones, the magic of a nymph's mate bond promise knitting our souls together, waiting for my words to finalize the bond.

I take in a deep breath and say the words that I've been running through my mind waiting for this day.

"I, Daisy Rosenfeld, bond myself to you, Kai Kingsley, for the rest of my life. I promise to always love you and put up with your perverseness. To indulge in your desires. To be faithful and devoted only to you. I promise to trust you and support you. For always and ever I promise all this and more to you my bonded mate."

The magic that took hold when Kai began speaking snaps into place inside me. Binding my soul to Kai's. A warmth reminiscent of Kai's fire magic settles in my chest and instills a comforting calm inside me.

Kai smiles up at me, feeling every sensation mimicked in his own chest. The truth and honesty of our words strengthening our bond to near unbreakable. Not that any bond can be broken once made, just circumvented if the vow is vague. Ours were not.

Pocket Full of Posies

"What does this flower mean? I've never seen it before." Kai fingers a flower behind my ear that I can't see.

"What flower? I can't see it." I was pretty sure by now he'd seen all my flowers.

"I think it's a daisy but it's red. Your daisies are usually white."

"Really? I've never had a red one before."

I reach up and pull the flower from my hair where he's still stroking. In my fingers I hold a fire engine red daisy, just like he said. I turn it over in my hand twirling the red petals in a pin wheel.

"I have no idea what it means."

"I think I do." Kai plucks the red daisy from my hand and holds it up to his nose inhaling deeply. "It means that you're mine. It smells like us."

"It must have something to do with our mate bond," I suggest.

"Probably," he agrees. "I like them."

"Me too."

I take the flower and tuck it behind Kai's ear, it almost blends in with his red hair. I smirk once it's in place. Sliding one leg over Kai's lap I straddle his waist, hiking my loose dress up around my hips. Kai groans and grips my ass, kneading my flesh, encouraging me. No encouragement is needed but it's appreciated. A needy throb strums between my splayed thighs. My attraction to Kai hasn't dwindled over the past three years, he's proven his stamina and imagination.

The bulge beneath his jeans thickens and I grind against it, just to tease him. He likes it when I tease him. He also likes it when I'm on top.

I work myself over his erection, enjoying the friction and lust on Kai's face. He reaches up for a kiss and I pull back, denying him. He grins, enjoying our game. But we are in a public place and don't have forever to play.

Reaching between us I unzip his pants and reach in, clasping my hand around his hot hard length. He groans, biting his lip and bucking up into my hand.

"Sit on it Blossom, use me."

"You want to pleasure me, mate?"

A shaky breath tumbles from Kai's parted lips, his eyes glazing over at my words.

"I will always want to pleasure you, mate."

Positioning his cock, I raise up on my knees. Kai pulls my panties to the side and slides a finger through my wet slit.

"Fuck Blossom, so wet for me. You're such a naughty flower."

The brush of his knuckles across my clit makes my core clench on nothing. I want his thickness filling me. I love the stretch and fullness of his cock inside me.

I replace his fingers with the head of his erection. It slips inside with ease. I'm embarrassingly wet for him. We both stifle groans as he slides all the way in, bottoming out until I can feel the press of his pelvis against me. I don't wait or tease, we don't have time for that. I rock and grind against him, rolling my hips in that way I know drives him to the edge.

Kai holds on to my hips and helps guide my movements, making sure his cock hits the perfect spot inside me. My fingers spear through his silky red hair, running along the base of his horns.

"That's it, Blossom. You've already got me so close." Kai forces my movements, increasing my pace.

I bite back my breathy moans, riding his generous cock in the middle of a garden in Venice where anyone could walk in and find us at any minute. The thrill of being in public and the possibility of being watched only increases my desire, spurring me on.

"God damn it Daisy, you're beautiful taking my cock."

"Make me come Kai, I wanna come."

"Oh, I will."

His hips thrust up as he presses me down, setting a punishing rhythm that sends tingles up my spine.

"That's it baby, come on my cock."

Kai presses kisses to my exposed throat and when he sucks on the tender flesh I come on a silent scream. Pressing down hard on Kai's length, my pussy clenches around him as he spills and comes hard inside me. Ropes of his hot cum coating my insides.

I remain seated on his lap, cock still inside me, while we both catch our breath. I think this is the most public place we've ever had sex.

"That was amazing Blossom, but I'm not done with you yet. Would you mind putting my cock back in my pants so we can go back to the hotel, and I can worship your body properly?"

"With pleasure."

Letting his half hard length slip free I gently tuck him back in his jeans and zip up his fly. He presses a lovingly, languid kiss to my lips that almost lasts as long as the sex did, before letting me stand and straighten my skirt.

"Come on mate. We have the rest of our vacation to enjoy." Kai stretches out a hand and I place mine in his.

Hand in hand, and his cum dripping down my leg, we walk back to our hotel room, and he does worship my body, for hours.

Acknowledgments

To my BETA's for always giving me their honest opinions. Without you I would second guess everything. Thank you for keeping it real with me. And for giving Kai the label "The man, the nymph, the legend."

To all my readers and followers for supporting my shift in genre writing and loving it just as much as the others.

Also by Rebecca Rennick

Books in the Snowberry Novel Series
Sing Sweet Nightingale
Pocket Full of Posies

Gummy Bear Orgy Series
Pinky Promise
Her Favorite Jack-O-Lantern
Just My Luck
Tied Up In Knots

About the Author

Rebecca spends her days daydreaming about love stories and witty banter, and how to avoid sweating in the Florida heat. When she's not writing, she's thinking about writing, visiting Florida's amusement parks, or watching horror movies and documentaries.

Born in California she's now a happy transplant in Florida, where she lives with her husband and fur babies.

www.RebeccaRennickAuthor.com
Instagram: @RebeccaRennickAuthor
TikTok: @RebeccaRennick.Author

www.ingramcontent.com/pod-product-compliance
Ingram Content Group UK Ltd.
Pitfield, Milton Keynes, MK11 3LW, UK
UKHW042003230426
12048UKWH00009B/519